By the same author:

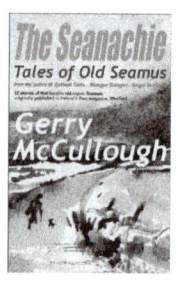  

Cover design: *Raymond McCullough*
Cover photo: © *Jaroslaw Grudzinski* | Dreamstime.com

Dreams, Visions, Nightmares

A collection of eight literary and
award-winning Irish short stories
(newly expanded and edited)

Gerry McCullough

Published by

www.preciousoil.com/publications

ISBN 13: 978-0 9929432 5 7

ISBN 10: 09929432 5 6

First published **2016**

www.preciousoil.com/publications

**10a Listooder Road, Crossgar,
Downpatrick, Northern Ireland BT30 9JE**

Contents

Acknowledgements

The stories in this collection have all been extended from the original versions on the advice of Patrick Ramsay of *Lagan Press*. I am very grateful to Pat for his advice and support.

The extended versions here published have been professionally edited by Hazel Orme, to whom I am also very grateful.

The *Arts Council of Northern Ireland* made it possible for me to pay a professional editor by awarding me a grant under their *Support for Individual Artists Scheme*. Thank you, *Arts Council, NI*.

The original short versions of these stories were published in various literary magazines and anthologies as follows:

Magazines: *Verbal; Ulla's Nib; Luciole Press; Brazen City* and *West 47*.

Anthologies: *The Cúirt Annual* (published by *Galway Arts Centre*); *Sharp Sticks Driven Nails* (published by *The Stinging Fly Press*, Dublin); and *Crime After Crime* (published by *Bridge House*, England).

Primroses was the winner of the *Cúirt Award for New International Writing*, Galway, in 2005.

Stevie's Luck was shortlisted in the *Brian Moore Short Story Award*, Belfast, 2008.

Slipping won the Star Prize for short stories in *Ulla's Nib* Spring Issue, Belfast, 2009.

Giving Up was commended in the *Sean O'Faolain Short Story Competition*, Cork, in 2009.

I would also like to thank my publishers, *Precious Oil Publications*, Downpatrick; and especially my husband, Raymond, for his continual support and encouragement, and for designing the cover.

1 – Primroses

Winner of the *Cúirt International Literary Award* for New Writing, Galway, Ireland 2005, published in the 2005 *Cúirt Annual* and in *West 47* magazine

After Annie died, Clare asked me – well, told me – I'd to move down near her and her man, Billy. It seemed a good idea, I thought. It would be nice to live a bit closer to my daughter and her family.

'You'd need to be a lot more handy, Da,' Clare said, giving me a straight look, 'if you're expecting me to be running in and out, keeping an eye on ye, all the time.'

That's Clare. Speaks her mind. Always has. Well, Annie used to say she got it from me. 'I don't expect you to do anything of the sort, girl,' I told her. 'I can look after myself.'

But I let her talk me into moving, all the same. It was lonely, living in the house on my own, now Annie was gone. Thirty-nine years we'd been there. Came there straight after we were wed.

So, about six months after the funeral, I mentioned to my landlord, Jimmy Murphy – I'd known him since we went to school together – that I was planning to move soon, and I went to the Housing Executive, and put in my application to be rehoused, on family grounds. After another six months, they gave me an old people's bungalow. Okay, yes, I suppose I'm an old fella. Sixty-seven. I don't feel all that old though, just yet.

It was funny, moving. Only fifteen miles, when all was said and done, away from the wee village, Kildun, where Annie and I had grown up. To the edge of Ballykillen, the town where Clare and Billy lived. It seemed a lot more.

Mind you, as for Clare running in and out, keeping an eye on me, it was little enough I saw of her. Maybe every two or three weeks at first, if I was lucky. And then less and less. And, d'ye know, at the end of the day, she wasn't all that near to me after all? A good bus ride away, as it turned out, right the other side of the town.

1

I suppose she'd enough on her mind just then, without having to be thinking of me into the bargain. It wasn't long after I moved down, that Billy up and left her. I never knew whose fault it was, and I didn't ask. Billy was a nice enough big lad when she married him, with plenty to say for himself, and a good enough tempered fella. But the last few times I saw him he seemed very quiet and grouchy.

And before I moved, I heard tell from my mate, Barney O'Hagan, that he was spending most of his nights in the King's Head, his local, getting on rightly with the barmaid, or so Barney said he'd been told by his son Johnny, who lived near Clare and Billy. It didn't sound much like Billy, the sort of him when I first knew him.

Whether he left because he got fed up with Clare bossing him about, or whether there was more to it than that, and maybe he'd been and taken up with another woman, maybe this barmaid, I never heard for definite. I was out of touch with Barney by then, and I wasn't that great with my new neighbours for any of them to tell me. And I wouldn't have asked Clare.

It was a quare thing what a difference the fifteen mile made. I just didn't seem to run into any of my old friends, the way I used to, and so far I hadn't made any new ones. The houses round me belonged to young couples, mostly, with weans and jobs and suchlike. Busy, all of them, and with not that much in common to talk about, if we happened to meet in the street.

I'm not a great one for getting on with new folks. I was taught to keep myself to myself. It takes me a while to get on real close friendly terms with someone. It doesn't come natural, to be chatting away with someone I hardly know, d'ye see?

After quite a gap, a brave few weeks, Clare came down to see me, and she had the youngster with her. She stood just inside the doorway, with her hands on her hips, giving the place a good look round. I watched her making her examination. A good-looking girl still, nice curly dark hair and all, but an expression on her face, sorta hard, that near enough spoiled her. Then she nodded in a satisfied way.

'Well for some,' she said, coming on into the front room, where the child had run in ahead of her. 'Now, Clint, get down off that table and leave your Granda's books alone. Watch, now, you'll have the photo cowped if you take a holt of the shelf like that!'

I made a grab at the table, not so much to keep my library books and the photo of Annie from sliding off the shelf above it, as to make sure wee Clint didn't end up hurting his-self.

'Sure the child's doing no harm, Clare,' I said.

1 – Primroses

She paid me no heed, just frowned, and said to the wean, 'Away you go outside and play, and give my head peace.'

The child ran outside. I looked after him as he went out the door. It would have been nice to have him stay in for a while at least, maybe have a bit of a chat with him, give him more of a chance to get to know his Granda.

I'd thought, when he was born, I'd be able to take him off Clare's hands now and then, let him have a bit of fun growing things in the garden with me, take him to the swings, things like that. Even go out fishing, the two of us, in my mate Barney O'Hagan's wee rowing-boat, if Barney woulda give me the lend of it.

The sorta things I'd always wanted to do with my own two, Clare and wee Desi, but somehow or other never found the time for it. And then before I knew it they were fully up, and had their own lives to get on with.

Now there was Clint, my first, and so far only, grandson, and I'd thought I'd get a chance to do some of the things with him I hadn't managed with Clare and Desi.

But there, somehow or other, it never seemed to happen. Clare had turned me down, every time I offered. 'Sure, Da, you'd need to stay home and keep an eye on Mammy, you know fine she's not that good. She needs you with her, Da.'

So she did, then, poor Annie. Clare was right there. The cancer was eating into her in a bad way, so that she didn't look like herself, or act like the Annie I knew, any more. And like Clare said, she needed me to be there, to help her with her medication for coping with the pain. As well as for the company, I suppose.

So one way and another, I'd seen little enough of the child, the first few years, and nowadays Clare never seemed to expect that I might want to get to know him. Sometimes she didn't even bring him with her, and when she did, like now, it was always, 'Away you go out and play, Clint.'

She sat down carefully on the sofa, pulling up the rug where it had slipped down and straightening the crocheted cushions first, looking as if she expected to find dust and cobwebs all over. Then she gave me a look to match. 'Well, Da, it's a great wee set-up you have here, and no mistake.'

'Is that a fact?'

'It is, aye. You should count your blessings, Da. There's many a one would think theirselves lucky to have a nice house like this. Sure wasn't it a great idea of mine, to have you move down here?'

'I like it fine, Clare,' I said, 'but the thing is I don't know my neighbours.'

It was the truth, though maybe it was mostly my own fault. Back in Kildun, I'd known most of the people round about since my school-days, or before. There was Barney O'Hagan, who I mentioned. Barney used to call round for a yarn with me every Thursday, after the kids were grown up and away off, and when his wife Maggie and my Annie were out at their women's meetings.

We'd sit, one on each side of the fire, and smoke our pipes, and swop a bit of banter and crack, and catch up on the news. I could picture Barney now, his bald head, with the few wee wisps of hair straggling across it, gleaming in the firelight, his cheeks seamed and wrinkled with age, cracking a joke as he tried to keep his pipe going – he was never that good with thon pipe of his. He was grand company, Barney.

Then there was wee Geordie Thompson next door, a small slip of a man, but bright and chatty enough, who used to borrow my gardening tools and give me a cutting or two from his own plants to make it up. He'd lean over the hedge most days and talk, maybe about the new type of roses that were coming out that year, or maybe about what thon people on the television said you should do with your tomatoes and your early lettuces. He was a great man for the tomatoes, wee Geordie.

And there were all the people I met at the mobile library van, Lizzie McCormick the school teacher, and Kevin McNamara who used to run the grocer's until he passed it on to his son Johnny, and a wheen of others, ones that knew me well and would usually stop and lean up against the outside of the van for a wee natter when they saw me, for I went along every week or so to change my books.

Any time I went out for a dander, I could be sure of running into one or another of my old pals, and they would all take the time to stop and speak.

People who knew me, who knew all about me.

Here in Ballykillen, I might have been a creature dropped in from another planet.

Well, maybe I'd get to know some of them in time. I supposed I'd have to make an effort, now Clare'd got me moved here.

She was still giving the new place a good look over.

1 – Primroses

'Aye, ye've fallen on yer feet all right, Da,' she said, after a moment or two. 'Thon other old dump was falling down round you. I never knew how you could stick it as long as you did. You didn't even own it.'

I said nothing. No point in starting an argument with her.

But I'd put in a lot of work on that house. Sure, it didn't belong to me, right enough, but it felt as if it did. Clare knew rightly that Annie and me'd lived there since we'd got wed, more years ago than I liked to think. I'd had a dacent enough job, in the mill at Ardmore, away the other side of Kildun.

It meant a bus journey there and back every day, but sure when jobs were hard to come by, and harder to hold on to, I was ready enough to do it. The pay wasn't great, unless you took the overtime, but there was plenty of that on offer as a rule. Enough coming in to let me spend a bit on the house from time to time.

Many's the weekend I'd put in, when I wasn't working overtime at the mill, painting and papering the place, fixing up the kitchen, putting up shelves in the front room, digging in the garden and planting flowers and vegetables. Our own potatoes, we had. Not many could say that, these days.

It was a bad feeling, to think that it all seemed to have gone for nothing, as far as Clare was concerned.

Clare didn't seem to notice that she'd said anything out of place. Just went on talking about how well off I was now, with this new place. 'The Executive's done well by you, for sure, Da.'

I got up and went and looked out of the window. 'The youngster's gone out of the garden onto the street, Clare. Is he all right, d'you think?'

'Ach, you and that child, you never stop worrying about him any time you see him. He's fine! Now, I'll make you a wee cuppa tea. I'll have to be looking out for my bus, in half an hour or so.'

It was quiet after she'd gone. The child was looking as fit as a fiddle, every time I saw him it was hard to believe the size of him, he was growing that fast. He had the same black hair Annie had, and for the matter of that, Clare, too. And a real look of Annie when he smiled. Something about the way his lips curved up into his cheeks and made dimples in them. Whenever I saw him, it made me think of her.

I went and stood at the window for a bit. It was still light, but the sky was getting some pink in it. I could see the sun lying down behind the round hills over the valley, trying to hide. At least, that was what

Clare said about it one time, when she was still just learning to talk. I concentrated on trying to feel pleased about the nice view out. And the garden.

I'd a good enough wee garden in this new place. I'd made sure I planted bulbs in the autumn, nearly broke myself paying for them, and they were coming up now a treat. Daffs, mainly, but there'd been all the crocuses before, and even a few snowdrops back in February. They'd be over, soon, even the daffs, and I'd need to be thinking of what I wanted next. Primroses would be the thing. If I could get hold of them, that was. I'd need the plants – it was too late now to think of seeds. Mind you, I didn't think I could afford plants from a garden centre. Have to wait another year, likely.

I looked out beyond the low stone wall, and watched the light begin to fade over the hills across the valley. I was glad the new house was out at the edge of the built-up area. It was one thing I'd not been happy about, where I used to live in Kildun, the number of houses growing up, new building in all directions, hemming me in.

When you're young, there seems like there's broad open spaces all round you, everything opening up, all sorts of things still ahead, and possible. I don't just mean in the place where you live. More in your head, I suppose I mean. So many ideas and plans. So much to look forward to.

Then it all starts crowding in round you, and there doesn't seem to be the same amount of chances there used to be. You feel as if you're shut in, in prison, sort of. Not much you can do any more. Just got to stick it out with the way life's ended you up. And for me, anyway, it got to be true about the place I lived in, as well as about my life. A metaphor, is that the word? I'm a reading man, I can remember reading something about that sort of thing once.

Back in Kildun, looking out, it had got so you could only see houses instead of flowers. The open spaces built over. The space you looked out at where you were living, and the space you felt you used to have inside your head. Here, in this new house, the green fields and the trees were round me on three sides.

There was a crowd of weans playing about, just outside my garden wall, doing a fair bit of laughing and carrying on. One of them was about four or five, and something the cut of our Clint, the dark hair and all, forby it was a girl.

I was still standing there, thinking about things, when a great fierce Alsatian type of a dog came round the corner skidding fast on its heels, its red tongue hanging out and the slabbers dripping from its jowls. It scared the life out of them. There was a squeaking and a squealing, and then they were all pushing at each other and running all directions.

Well, they all got away okay, nearly. All but this wee girl who had the look of our Clint. And what way she managed it I didn't see, but she tripped herself up someway, and came a clatter down on the pavers, and from the howls and bawls of her, it might have been sore.

And there was thon big brute of a dog all set for lepping on her.

I've always been one for keeping myself to myself and not interfering, but I lifted up my blackthorn stick and took off and outa that door like the devil was after me, and I had the old brute chased away down the street before he knew what hit him.

The wean was still bawling her head off, but when I got her up, and had a look at her, sure it was nothing but a scraped knee.

There was some sweeties in my pocket that I'd been hoping to slip to wee Clint, but Clare had been watching me too close. When she saw them, the youngster perked up rightly.

'Now, away you home to your mammy, and get her to put a bit of plaster on that terrible injury, and it'll be as right as rain come the morning.'

And so off she goes full of beans, and I thought that would be the end of it.

Howandsoever, the next day she was round knocking on the door. 'My name's Jacqueline McKinley, I'm from up the back there.' She gave me a bashful sort of a look. 'Mammy says to say thanks.'

'Sure that's all right.'

She was twisting and turning and acting shy, so I reckoned it was up to me to help her out. 'I'm just away out here to sort out my garden. Are you any good at the gardening at all?'

'Yes I am.'

'Well, there's nothing like a bit of confidence. Come on, then – you'd be quare and good at the heavy digging, I'd think.'

After that she used to come round most days, and think she was helping – dear knows, she did more messing than helping, but sure she seemed to enjoy it.

It annoyed me, I have to say, when a woman I'd seen about the place stopped at the garden wall one day and said, kinda sharp, 'Jacqueline McKinley, it's after half four, shouldn't you be away off home for your tea by now?'

She was middle-aged, I suppose you'd say, thick-set and with gingery hair, mostly grey, and a scarf tied over it, and she had a sharp, disagreeable sort of a face. The type of old biddy that liked poking her nose into other folk's business, though when I say old, I have to admit she'd likely have been a quare bit younger than me. But the sort of her that would put years on you, with her way of glaring as if you'd done something wrong on her, when all you were doing was quietly minding your own business. I can't say I took to her.

Jacqueline spoke back to the woman, sounding a bit rude, but sure, I thought the old bat more than deserved it. 'Mammy doesn't make the tea till six o'clock, Mrs McCarten. I'll be going in plenty of time, so you don't need to be bothering about it.'

'Aye. We'll see what yer mammy has to say about that, next time I have a word with her, Jacqueline McKinley.'

And with a grump and a shake of her head, and a fearsome glare at me into the bargain for free, as if I'd done anything, off this Mrs McCarten stumped.

'Who was thon, Jacqueline?' I asked the wean, and she told me, 'Ach, that's only ould Maggie McCarten, she's a pal of my granny's, Mammy says she can't stand her – interfering ould witch, Mammy calls her.' She laughed, and pushed her hair back off her forehead with one dirty wee hand, leaving a right trail of muck, and went on digging with the small size of a trowel I'd been letting her use for a spade.

'I'm surprised at you, Jacqueline McKinley,' I said, thinking I'd need to act a bit strict with her. 'You've no call to be speaking like that about your elders and betters. Maybe you'd best be off home to your mammy for your tea, like Mrs McCarten's telling you.'

'Ach, no, Tommy!' she wailed. 'She's just an old spoilsport, that one, honest, Mammy told me not to come back until nearly six, honest she did, Tommy!'

I could see she was thinking of crying, which is a thing I've never liked to see in any of the weans, and I thought to myself she was likely right, and this McCarten woman was just an interfering old besom. She'd a sour enough face on her, I'd have to admit. So I said, 'Well, never mind, Jacqueline, you can stay for another half-hour, I reckon,' and she brightened up rightly.

I let her plant some nasturtium seeds, which is easy to grow, and she was that pleased when the leaves started to come up a week or two later, and I told her how in another few weeks there'd be all the different bright shades of red and yellow and orange flowers peeping out among the green of the big leaves.

1 – Primroses

'Tommy, can I plant some more?' was the cry after that. For some reason, maybe I'd got to talking about it for, as you know, the idea was in my own mind, she'd taken the notion into her head that she would like to plant some primroses. Now, I can manage fine on the pension, but I'm telling you it doesn't go too far when it comes to the extras. I hadn't reckoned I could stretch to buying plants right now. And it were plants or nothing, far too late now for the seeds.

Still, the wean had her heart that set on it – it were a pity if nothing could be done.

I kept my tongue in my teeth, but come the next Sunday, when she was away off visiting with her mammy, I got myself on to the bus. Heading away from the town, back in the direction of Kildun.

The bus was a blue single decker, like they all were now, and the driver, Stevie O'Neill, was sort of a mate of mine, not my best pal or anything, like, but I knew him and he knew me.

'Heading back to Kildun, Tommy?'

'Nah. Bradford's Lane. Ye'll be passing it?'

'Ach, aye, we'll be passing it. I'll give ye a shout.'

I went on down the bus and got a seat by myself at the back. I could have sat up front and chatted to him whiles he was driving, but maybe I'd got out of the way of talking to folks, these days, for I didn't much feel like making the effort.

It was a while since I'd been out this way, but when Annie and me was courting, we used to go for walks most Sundays, and as often as not we'd end up down Bradford's Lane – Lovers' Lane it used to get called. It came to me that I should have been back long before, while Annie was still there to go with me. What with working the bit of over-time whenever it was going, just to have what we needed to keep on paying the bills, and taking every spare moment to fix the house up nice, and then later on with Annie not always feeling the best, the years had fairly gone in, but it was late in the day now to be regretting it.

Stevie O'Neill gave me a shout, like he'd said he would, when we were getting near the stop. And, mind you, it was well he did, for I could easy have missed it. I was looking for open fields, with the cows out grazing, and a turn-off between the hedges but, dear save us, it were all built up with dinky wee new bungalows like Clare's always saying she'd love, every one the image of the next, and to tell you the truth it fair sickened me to see it. Still, the folks has got to live somewhere when all's said and done.

I got off the bus and looked around me but, heaven knows, I couldn't have told you what I was planning on doing next. It was looking like I'd wasted my time coming.

There were no fields, nor no banks with hedges, and none of the wild flowers growing over them, anywhere to be seen. None of the things there used to be. Just the road and footpaths and the bungalows. Where was I going to get primroses here? It seemed there was no reason to hang about, and I might as well get the next bus back.

But there'd be no bus for another hour, and after standing round on the road at the bus stop for a while, I thought it would do no harm to have a dander round, to put in the time while I was waiting.

I set off up the road past the neat wee gardens. Most of them had a few daffodils, and a stretch of grass, cut tidy enough. Not a lot of variety. After a bit, there was what I suppose you'd call a bit of a park, with wooden seats and benches painted green, and them still not too badly scratched, and a bush or two with not much size to it yet. So you could tell the place was new.

I sat down on one of the seats, enjoying the sun. There was a border, with a few flowers in it, beside me – wallflowers, and some daffodils on their last legs, and a few primroses.

I had brought a Tesco's bag folded up in my pocket, to carry the primroses back in, and my wee trowel to dig up the plants. Piles of them, there used to be, down Bradford's Lane, and Annie would lie back against the bank and laugh, and the scent of them got into her dark hair when I leaned over to kiss her.

'You'll ruin me dress, Tommy!'

'I'll do more than ruin your dress, girl.'

Long, slow hours, in sun, or wind, or rain. All the time in the world, and nothing to stop us.

Where had it gone?

Well, waste not, want not, and I didn't like to see the Tesco's bag going to loss. There were these scaldy wee primrose plants, growing just beside the bench I was sitting on. There was nobody about to notice anything, and I was soon away back on the bus again.

When I got home, I set the plants in the cool near the back door, until we could get putting them in the next day.

Clare came down that same afternoon. She hemmed and she hahed, and then out with it.

1 – Primroses

'You'd need to be careful, Da. People gets ideas into their heads. Peggy Allen, that lives up the back there, gave me a word of warning to pass on to you. She used to go to school with me, remember.'

'I mind her fine.' A mean, nasty type of a girl, I always thought. She bullied our Clare, or so Annie used to think, but we could never get Clare to tell us if that was the right of it.

She came home one time, I mind it well, with a great bruise on her cheek and mud up to the oxters, and crying fit to bust, but as for telling us what had happened, all we could get out of her was, 'I'm finished with that Peggy Allen! Her and me's broke up – don't be having her round here again, Mammy! I don't know why you'd want to be forever asking her!'

Not that'd we'd had her round except once for Clare's birthday, but Annie, who had a lot of wisdom in her own way, said after that Clare needed to blame somebody else, and it so happened we were the only ones available.

I was for going to the school and putting in a complaint, but in the end we let it lie, and sure, a week later, Clare and Peggy Allen were the best of friends again, from what we could see.

Annie said that was what the weans were like and, dear knows, it wasn't as if I'd had the time to look into it any more than I did, with the hours I was working right then. It was only now I wished I'd maybe taken the time, somehow or other.

'Aye, I mind the girl,' I said. 'What's she up to now?'

'It's not what Peggy's up to, Da. It's what she tells me the people round here are saying about you.'

I gaped at her. I'd no thought of what was coming.

'These days, you hear all these things on the television – people get suspicious easy. Peggy tells me the wee girl's round here all the time. It doesn't take much to start the talk. You were giving her sweeties, I hear. Ach, Da, do you not know that's one of the things they warn kids about in the programmes?'

I don't mind saying I was angry. Clare's the only one I've got left, now our Desi's away in Canada, Clare and the wee one, but I was as near as that to having a row with her.

I caught myself on in time. 'I reckon I know the sort of talk people get up to, Clare,' was all I said. 'The wean's never been over my threshold, much as I'd have liked to ask her in – and it's people's tongues that's the reason.'

I didn't think she looked too convinced, but it was time for her bus.

She went out the door. Just before she shut it after her, she threw a word or two at me over her shoulder.

'Sure, never worry, Da, I know it's all rubbish, myself. Never knew you to take much interest in kids, Da, even your own! Never could be bothered, could ye?'

I stared after her for a bit.

Then I went and looked at the primroses in the Tesco's bag. I was in two minds about throwing them in the bin.

I sat up late that night, reading my library books. It's one of the things I like about having so much time to myself these days, being able to walk down to the library whenever I feel like it. Kildun just had the mobile van, but in Ballykillen we have a good branch library with a wheen more books and more choice – and with plenty of time, as well, to read the books when I've got them. But somehow tonight I couldn't bring myself to concentrate. The lines ran into each other and started to blur, and I found I was reading the same bit over and over again without taking in a word of it.

By the time I went up to bed and turned the light off, it was near day-light.

I thought maybe I'd go round and have a yarn with Jacqueline's mammy the next day – just so they could get to know me and not be worrying. That would be the sensible thing to do.

Or there, maybe I'd just tell Jacqueline when she came round that I was too busy, and not to come bothering at me any more. Somebody else could teach her how to plant flowers in some other garden.

It came home to me then, with a fierce shock, that when I moved house I'd done more than leave my old friends behind, and the neighbourliness of their company. I'd cut myself off from being a familiar figure about the place. Someone who was known to be trustworthy. From the boys and girls who'd been to school with me, the men and women who'd seen me married and my weans growing up.

When I moved to the new house I'd left not just my friends but my roots and security behind. Myself, in a strange sort of a way. Now I was a stranger.

Maybe I hadn't valued people, friends and family, enough, when I had them. Maybe I should have put more into people, and less into working? I'd always been taught that it was important to work hard and earn a good living. That was what everybody I knew thought, from my own Da downwards.

'Never owe nobody nothing, Tommy,' he used to say. 'Keep your own business to yourself and do a good day's work for a good day's pay and you'll be all right and nobody can say anything against ye.'

I'd believed him, I suppose. It sounded right.

Nobody'd ever said anything about knowing how important people were in your life. It was only now I was starting to think about it. What was it Clare said? 'Never knew you to take an interest in kids, Da, even your own! Never could be bothered, could ye?'

I found myself wondering if that was why she'd never let me look after Clint. Punishing me, in a sort of way, maybe without even realising it, for not bothering more with her when she was that age.

There's an old photo album Annie used to keep up to date, still kicking round in the bedroom. I was getting into bed, knowing rightly I wasn't for sleeping that night, when it caught my eye and I picked it up.

First page I opened it, there was Annie, looking like I remembered her – well, maybe younger. Dark and slim, and without the wrinkles that came later and the lines of illness pulling down her mouth.

The prettiest girl I'd ever seen, I'd thought, when I saw her at the dance in the church hall all those years ago. Mind you, we'd been going to school together for years, so it wasn't the first time I'd seen her by a long chalk. But somehow I'd never taken that much notice of her until that night.

I wasn't much of a one for the girls when I was younger. My mates used to giggle and talk about this one or that one, and there was a couple of them used to claim they had girlfriends, though whether it went beyond the odd kiss or so I had my doubts. But when I saw Annie standing there, smiling to herself, on the other side of the room, and the music playing all romantic and slow, I was off over to her and asking her to dance without a second's thought.

It wasn't just straight away that we were able to get married. We'd to save up for a quare few years before we could afford the furniture and that. But we managed it between us, in the end. And we'd been happy enough, I suppose. Never that well off, but we'd had enough to get by.

I looked hard at the photograph, and I found I could remember the day it was taken. She was standing in the garden at our house, wearing a summer dress. A white dress with red and yellow flowers all over, as I remembered it – couldn't tell if I was remembering right, with the photo being an old black and white one. She'd pulled off her apron in a hurry, for the snap, and it was lying, kicked away, nearly out of sight, at her feet, half spread out over a bed of pansies and marigolds. She had her hands folded across her chest, and she was smiling the way people do for the camera – not quite real looking.

I turned over the page, and there was Clare with her face covered in muck, not much older than Clint now.

I remembered Annie yelling at me not to take the child with her face in that state, and me saying at least she looked like a human being. I couldn't remember at first what she'd been doing to get into the mess. Then it came to me: that was the day we'd been picking out the bit for her to have for her own wee garden.

I minded well sitting on my hunkers beside her and showing her how to turn over the earth with the trowel, and the job she had getting a hold of it, with the size of it and the size of her hand, and I minded going for the camera to get a snap, she looked that pleased with herself. She looked a bit like wee Jacqueline did, now I came to think of it.

We'd been going to do great things with that garden – but though I thought long, I was hard pushed to remember anything much else that we'd done. A few seeds had got planted but, sure, she'd had to do that herself, for what with the overtime and the house needing work I'd never had a spare minute in them days.

I could remember one night at least, and I thought maybe there'd been a lot more of them, when I was lying back in my chair after work on a summer evening, trying to relax, and Clare came up to me and tugged at my arm.

'Can we go out and dig the garden, Da?' I remember her saying. 'Can we plant those seeds we bought last weekend? Please, Da?'

I'd had a long hard day at work, and the last thing I felt up to was working some more, in the garden or anywhere else.

'Away and give my head peace, Clare,' I said crossly. 'Annie, is it not time this wean was in her bed?'

I had another wee look at the picture, and I thought, if it wasn't that I knew it was Clare, I wasn't sure that I'd have recognised her, she'd changed that much.

Sharper in the face, she was now, able to look out for herself. Not expecting much from anyone, maybe. What had life done to her? Or maybe I should be thinking, instead, what had I done to her? How many times had I disappointed her, let her down? I'd meant to be a good father to her, goodness knows. So how was it that I felt now as if she'd

1 – Primroses

grown up on the other side of the world, far away from me? And as if I hardly knew her?

I fell asleep still holding the album, and I dreamed I was back years ago, walking up Bradford's Lane with Annie and Clare. The sun was shining down on us, and the clumps of primroses were growing wild in all directions, pale yellow petals showing among the green of leaves and grass. Delicate, easy to damage. That nice to see growing there.

I was holding hands with Annie and Clare, one on either side of me. I should have been happy. I didn't know why it didn't feel like that. But there was something, some sort of a dark shadow, chasing along the lane after us. A heavy cloud, was it? I couldn't seem to see. I began to walk faster and faster, but where I was trying to get to I couldn't have told you, and I had a nagging sort of a pain, telling me all the time that I was missing something that mattered, something I ought not to miss.

I could feel Clare tugging at my arm, trying to slow me down, and she was crying and wanting to pick the flowers while they were still there, but I wouldn't stop to let her.

'There's no time,' I was saying to her. 'There's no time. They've done away with all the time, and all the primroses, and there's none left, and it's too late to change things now.'

And I could see the dirty streaks on her face, where the tears had run down over her cheeks.

But when I woke up, my face felt wet, and it was me that had been crying.

When Jacqueline came to the door in the morning, I came out, and we planted the primroses together.

2 – Pink Silk

published in *Verbal* magazine, Derry, 2009

I had come to visit my great-uncle Jimmy Heaney in the retirement home where he was living out his last days in that mixture of boredom, loneliness and the itching progression of many small ailments, which makes up the pattern of old age.

The home, *Birchlands*, was a big box-like place – 1960s concrete, three storeys, flat roof. The grounds were spacious enough, with wide lawns where the grass was cut short regularly to prevent the growth of daisies, a considerable number of shrubs and bushes in shades of green, and a few winding tarmac paths where wheelchairs could roll safely, and people dependent on walkers or sticks were in less danger of tripping than on gravel paths. I don't know why the place exuded such an atmosphere of dullness – perhaps because there were never any blossoms on the bushes, and the flowerbeds were few and far between.

It was a bright, sunny day, but I saw only two of the inmates strolling about as I drove up to the reception area and parked my second-hand Volvo.

I like to get in to see Jimmy from time to time, although I don't come as often as I should. When I was a child, Uncle Jimmy Heaney was a great man in my life. He wasn't big, although he seemed big from my low-down perspective, but his personality was huge.

He used to descend on our house, roaring loudly and laughing at jokes I couldn't understand, turning my serious-minded father into a lively copy of himself for the brief time of his visit, and more often than not carrying me off to buy ice cream, play footie in the park, or even, on one never-to-be-forgotten occasion, to go to the circus. Sometimes he brought his wife, my great-aunt Sarah, with him, but more often he came alone: Sarah was a busy woman.

His round red face was always, in my memory, creased with smiles, and in those days he still had a vast mop of curly grey hair, forever falling into his eyes no matter how many times he pushed it up with an impatient hand. He wasn't what I would call fat, but sturdy, well built, far from slim. He told us often that Sarah and his doctor wanted him to lose weight, to take more exercise – 'But sure, I get all the exercise I need keeping up with this youngster, so I do!' he would roar, before taking me off, football tucked under my arm, to run round the grassy park, showing me how to dribble and do headers, as if he were still a child himself.

Strangely enough, it was Sarah, that thin, wiry, energetic woman, tough, you would have thought, as overdone steak, who died first, leaving Jimmy to the joys of life as a widower in *Birchlands Retirement Home*, where the doctors and social workers moved him five years after her funeral.

He had meant so much to me when I was a child that I often wondered why I didn't manage to give him more of my time now, when it was the least I could do for him. But it was hard to look at the withered old man he had become, and remember him as he used to be.

He was always a fund of information and stories, and even then they were mostly about when he was a young man. He never failed to intrigue me with his tales of a long distant past, when things seemed to have been so much simpler.

On this occasion when I called in, his mind was running, as usual, on the old days. He still spun me many a yarn, not always happy ones, on my irregular visits, and I always looked forward to hearing what he had to say.

On this particular night, he had been reading his newspaper when I arrived, and something in it had put it into his head to tell me the story of wee Lizzie White, a former neighbour of his, in the days when he was a young married man, living in a little whitewashed country cottage whose blooming garden was overgrown with flowers of all scents and colours. As a child I'd visited it once or twice while he still lived there, many years ago now, and I hadn't forgotten the strong impression of beauty and freedom it had made on me then.

'Lizzie White was a quare nice wee girl,' said my great-uncle Jimmy. 'She was only a couple of years married to big Robbie White, at the time I'm speaking of. She looked that pretty in her pale silky wedding dress, like a fragile sort of a flower, maybe, and as for Robbie, I've never seen him look better. Big and strong and handsome, with a beam of pride all over his face every time he looked at wee Lizzie. She was a slim little lass, bright and happy, with a saucy way about her, and a sweet, mischievous face a bit like a kitten, with a dab of a nose and enormous grey eyes. She was always smiling – in a cheeky way that brought out her dimples.

Folks came from all around to the wedding party after the church service. Lizzie's da, big Sammy Beckett, had booked the room where they held the Saturday-night dances, a big spacious affair with a polished wooden floor. It had a high ceiling with dark beams across it, and the walls were painted a dark green – which I'd always thought ugly enough, but it had room for the six big tables where the food was laid out, and benches alongside the tables for people to sit and eat at their ease.

The white cloths made the room look special, brighter than usual and full of life and light, and every table had a bunch of flowers in a big glass vase, yellow roses, same as Lizzie had in her bouquet. When it was time for the speeches, and one after another people were saying how great things were going to be for Robbie and Lizzie, it would have been hard not to believe them.

But even on that happy day, there were hints that big Robbie wasn't going to be the easiest of husbands. Sammy had hired a fiddler to give us a bit of music, and soon the youngsters and most of the older ones, too, were up jigging away. Old Martha Riley grabbed Barney O'Hanlon – he ran the village shop, a man half her age – and got busy twirling him round the room, Sammy himself seized his wife Mary Ann and galloped off with her, and there was laughing and carrying-on in all directions.

'Come on, Robbie, get your new wife up!' Martha called, trying to encourage him. But Robbie just sat there, going red in the face. 'I'm no dancer, Martha,' he muttered. Lizzie looked disappointed. Sure, she'd expected to be leading off the dancing at her own wedding party. She sat there looking pretty well let down while all round her folks were having the time of their lives. When Peter Devlin, a nice looking young fella, asked her up to dance her wee face lit up, and she was off with him without a second's thought.

Robbie got to his feet and stood with his arms folded, leaning against the wall, with a terrible scowl on his face. He followed every movement as Lizzie and Peter cavorted round the room. In the end he went bursting over to them, pushed Peter to one side, and made a grab for Lizzie. 'I didn't marry ye to have ye dancing with all and sundry, girl!' he shouted. 'If ye want to dance, ye'll dance with me!' And he began to steer Lizzie round the room.

Lizzie didn't mind – in fact she seemed quite pleased. Perhaps she liked him being masterful, and took it as a sign of how daft he was about her, which was no more than the truth. She blushed and giggled and snuggled up to him, looking right and happy.

But it made me wonder, myself.

I knew Robbie White, and knew a lot about him, although I wouldn't say he was my best mate or anything like that. I went to school with big Robbie, in the village, a long time ago now, but I can mind it clearer than some things that've happened since. I knew Robbie from our first day there when we weren't more than five or so, and though I can't say I liked him all that much, there were times when I couldn't help but feel sorry for the poor craytur.

Robbie wasn't too bright. I don't mean he was daft. But he didn't do too well with the schooling.

Ould Geordie Finnegan, the school master, was a right hellion. Didn't care what he said to anyone, or how he made them feel. And he was in his element, taking the piss out of big Robbie. Finnegan loved to make a fool of people, and Robbie was one he could go his limit on. Robbie didn't know his tables, and never managed to get his sums right, and as for his spelling, he was worst of all at that.

Finnegan would call him up to the front of the class, make him read out what he'd written by way of an essay, or get him to chalk up his sum and the answer he'd got on the blackboard. 'I'm amazed how quickly you worked that out, White,' he'd say. 'And how did you manage to get it wrong in so many places? It's a mystery to me how you did it!' Or else he'd make Robbie read aloud, and mimic him when he pronounced the words badly. 'I can see you're finding this too com-plic-a-tated for you, White.'

Mind you, he had a wicked sense of humour, ould Finnegan, and you'd be hard put to it not to laugh when he cracked his jokes. When I think of it now, we were a heartless, cruel bunch, not caring how poor Robbie felt as long as we weren't the ones getting the slagging. We let Finnegan use us as a built-in audience, and encouraged him, more often than not.

But one day he went too far.

He'd got us all roaring laughing with the remarks he was making, and Robbie was standing there looking red and upset at the front of the classroom.

All of a sudden, Robbie turned round, facing up to Geordie Finnegan and looking right at him. He was a well-grown lad, by now, and he towered over Finnegan, a wee, skinny runt of a man, to tell the truth. He was going bald on top, with wisps of grey hair and a mean, freckly face that came to a point in a receding chin. His teeth stuck out, and he looked more like a rat than anything else on God's earth. His strength was in his brains and in his clever tongue.

Robbie stood there and stared at him, and I believe ould Geordie quaked for the first time when he saw Robbie's look. 'You may be better at sums than me, Mr Finnegan,' Robbie said slowly. 'But I can take that cane off ye, no bother, if it comes to that.'

Finnegan, who'd been swishing his cane about, maybe planning to give Robbie a stroke or two when he'd finished making him a laughing stock, couldn't believe what he'd heard. 'How dare ye talk to your teacher that way, Robbie White!' he stuttered out.

But big Robbie took no notice of him. He leaned over, casually, and put out his hand. A minute later he'd wrenched the cane from Finnegan's grasp and was waving it in the air.

The roars of laughter from the class were louder than ever.

Whether that encouraged Robbie, I don't know. But whatever made him do it, next thing he was cracking the cane over Geordie Finnegan's shoulders, and as Finnegan rushed out of the room, Robbie got in two or three good whacks on his backside.

Finnegan was through the door like a buck rabbit running from the gun whiles the rest of the class went on laughing their lugs off.

Robbie seemed a bit dazed, as if he'd hardly known till then what was happening. Then he took the cane in both hands, broke it across his knee, and was away off out of the school nearly as fast as Geordie Finnegan. From that day on, he never showed his face in the schoolroom again. The truant-catcher did his best, but as far as Robbie was concerned, he had left school. And as he wasn't that far off the school leaving age, which was fourteen in them days, he was let away with it, in the end.

It was little enough I saw of Robbie for the next few years, but I was there when something else happened which I would guess had a big effect on how he turned out in later life. It was the day of the annual Sunday School outing to the seaside. The whole countryside was there, as was normal then. Robbie White and myself were long past the age for Sunday School, but it made no difference. We wouldn't have missed it, any of us.

Robbie, I was interested to see, had a wee girl in tow, Kathleen Carson, and he seemed real taken up with her. I wasn't paying all that much attention, being more interested in getting off with one or other of the rest of the girls myself, if the truth be told. It was a lot later in the afternoon, and we'd all had our sandwiches and buns and minerals, when I took note of Robbie again. He was mooching along by the edge of the sea, with a look on his face that made me feel upset, just to see it. Near desperate, he was.

It was a clear, fresh day, not brilliant sunshine but bright enough, with just a bit of a breeze from the north to put a chill in the air. The sky was a pale blue grey, with a fair number of darker grey clouds mixed in with the fluffy ones, all of them scudding across the sky at a fair speed, and with the odd blink of sunshine peeping through from time to time.

No sign of rain, but the sort of a day you couldn't trust for long. The sea was pounding against the rocks at the far end of the beach, throwing up strong white gusts of spray, and the waves were splashing up round Robbie's feet as he went.

I was just wondering what was the matter with him, when I heard giggling from behind one of the sand dunes just beside me. When I looked round, there was young Kathleen Carson, lying back on the sand in a wee hollow with Robbie's cousin, a fella called Brendan MacFaddan, holding her in his arms. They were kissing and hugging each other and carrying on rightly, and every now and then Brendan would give her a bit of a tickle and Kathleen would squeal, so no one could avoid noticing them for miles around. I saw Robbie's head jerk every time he heard the noise, and I knew then the reason for the look on his face.

This fella Brendan was generally accounted a good-looking lad – all the girls seemed to think so, anyway – and I suppose you might say he was used to getting his own way with them. He wasn't that big, but he'd a way with him, and when he smiled and scrunched up his blue eyes, and shook back his dark hair, there weren't many could resist him. I suppose he'd been used to pushing Robbie around since they were kids, showing off to him and stealing any toys big Robbie might have. Robbie used to think the world of him, and let him have whatever he wanted.

'Gimme thon ball, Robbie!' I heard Brendan demand once. 'I'll show you how to kick it right!'

Robbie handed it over. A minute later, Brendan was away over the field with it, kicking and boosting it far ahead. Robbie saw no more of his ball for the rest of the afternoon.

So, seeing Robbie with as pretty a girl as Kathleen must have roused all Brendan's worst instincts.

I was looking back at Robbie with a pity when I saw his face change. He veered away from the sea, and made for the dunes.

I went on sort of looking, knowing something was up, but still I was taken by surprise when he reached where Brendan and Kathleen were lying and began kicking out at Brendan's legs.

'Get up on your feet, man!' he was roaring, and the language he began using would have frightened ye. He grabbed Brendan by his jacket collar and tried to haul him up but Brendan, showing some sense, stayed down and tried to roll behind Kathleen.

Robbie, however, being considerably bigger, soon had him out of that, and started in flailing at him with one fist, holding him with the other hand – and he needed to, for Brendan would have taken to his heels long since if Robbie hadn't had a hold of him. I was getting nervous for poor old Brendan, much as he deserved it, for he didn't seem able to defend himself.

But that was as far as it went. Right then Mr Marshall the Sunday School supervisor and two or three of the parents – who were still fit and healthy young men – came bounding up. They soon put a stop to it, grabbing the lads and hauling them apart.

They gave Robbie and Brendan a clout or so and warned them to keep away from each other for the rest of the day if they didn't want more. Kathleen was told to get up on her feet and stop carrying on like a scarlet woman. A right good telling-off she got, indeed, before Mr Marshall had finished with her.

I saw her afterwards hobbling along, leaning on her friend Eileen Kirkpatrick's arm, for Robbie hadn't worried too much about where his feet went – he'd got in a good few kicks on Kathleen's legs as well as Brendan's.

So that was the end of that – until a couple of nights later. Somebody lay in wait for Brendan MacFaddan as he was coming home from his work in the linen factory, and gave him a serious going over. No one knew who it was, for Brendan's story was that he hadn't been able to see the boyo, it being dark. He was shaking and shivering so much as he stuck to his story that nobody liked to press him. He wasn't sent home from the hospital for two weeks, I heard.

So you'll understand that when I saw Robbie fly off the handle just because Lizzie and Peter Devlin were dancing together, I couldn't help wondering how the marriage would end up.

I used to hear about Lizzie and Robbie from Sarah and it seemed that everything was going along as fine as could be, for all that Robbie was a man with a fierce temper and a wide streak of jealousy in him.

He had got himself a job as a farm labourer, being a strong, tough boyo. He didn't earn much, but Lizzie, as was the normal way of it then, gave up her job in a drapery shop, and kept house for Robbie instead. A right nice wee cottage they had, just up the lane a piece from where Sarah and me lived. It belonged to old MacLoughlin, the farmer Robbie was working to, and was the mirror image of our own place. It was washed freshly in white, with green paint on the doors and windows, for MacLoughlin was decent enough to get it done up for the newly wed couple, and it had a big lilac tree in the front garden where Lizzie was all pleased to find swallows nesting. There was a white climbing rose up the side by the front door, two up and two down by way of rooms, so they'd have an extra bedroom for the childer when they came along.

The upstairs rooms were directly under the rafters and low enough, but Robbie could stand upright without bumping his head, which was all that mattered. The inside was a bit dark, furnished with big wooden chairs and a farmhouse table, but Lizzie soon got her mammy to help her run up some bright new curtains, and she brought in flowers to lighten the front room. There was a wee patch of garden at the back, foreby, where Robbie planted potatoes and runner beans, and altogether they were well set up and as snug as a bug in a rug.

There was no bathroom, but sure that wasn't unusual back then, and they had a fine outdoors privy, which Robbie emptied regularly, and wee Lizzie kept quare and clean, with even an old jam jar full of flowers at one end of the long wooden seat to give it a nice smell. She'd got Robbie to plant a bush of honeysuckle beside it, and was wanting to train it up round the door when it grew a bit. Altogether, though I couldn't help laughing when I thought about it, the place was a pleasure to visit, unlike most.

They hadn't been married long before Lizzie began to miss being out working and seeing people during the day, when Robbie was off at MacLoughlin's. Well, she'd plenty of friends, my Sarah included, so she took to heading out to meet and keep up with them. She had to make sure of being home to make Robbie his tea, and at first she always managed it. But there was one time when Lizzie came home late from visiting a friend that lived a bit away. She and Maggie Brennan'd been talking nineteen to the dozen and having a good laugh, and Lizzie hadn't noticed the time until Maggie began peeling the spuds for her own man's meal. Up jumps Lizzie with a start and off she rushes.

She walked for some time, going as fast as she could, knowing Robbie'd be waiting for her. She'd got as far as the lane off the main road, with its banks of white clover and purple vetch, the wild roses just starting to come out, the scent of the honeysuckle filling the air, and she was as happy as any newly married young woman heading towards her man. Still, she didn't want to be late making Robbie's tea, so she was pretty well delighted when Kenny McGill came jogging along the lane behind her with his horse and cart, and offered her a lift.

Kenny was big and fair-haired with a tanned face and red cheeks. He'd grey-blue eyes, too, with a bit of a twinkle in them that all the girls seemed to take to. He was doing well, with a farm of his own since his da had died of a heart attack, and he was on his way home from town where he'd been buying a spare part for his tractor.

'Hop up, Lizzie,' he said, pulling up the chestnut horse beside her, and giving her a nice, friendly smile, 'and save yourself the rest of the walk. Can't have a pretty wee girl like you getting your shoes all dusty when you could be up here riding in style.' And up Lizzie hopped. She sat up beside Kenny at the front of the cart, for the back of it was mucky enough in spite of the new blue and yellow paint Kenny'd treated it to a few weeks before.

She and Kenny laughed and chatted for the next mile, and I'm not saying Lizzie didn't flirt with him a bit, for she was taken with his bright face and the twinkle in his eye, but it was harmless enough. Kenny pulled up with a flourish of the whip just outside Lizzie's house. Robbie was leaning over the green half-door beside the white climbing rose bush with a scowl on his face.

Well, whether Kenny caught the look Robbie was giving him I couldn't say, but he didn't hang around for long.

Lizzie came skipping up the path past the lilac tree to Robbie, and turned round to wave to Kenny as he, the chestnut horse and the blue and yellow cart moved off, disappearing round the bend in the road. Then she squealed as Robbie's hand came down heavy on her shoulder, grasping her hard and sore. 'In!'

Lizzie didn't understand why he was so angry, but Robbie didn't leave her long in doubt.

'Out with that hellion Kenny McGill, were ye? Sitting up close beside him at the front of the cart! Keeping me standing here like a fool, waiting for my tea, whiles yer gallivanting over the country with all the scaff and raff of the day, ye wee slut!' And with that he clenched his big beefy right hand into a fist and gave Lizzie a thump over her left ear.

Lizzie gaped at him. Then she burst into tears. 'All I did was get a lift back with him halfway from Maggie Brennan's, Robbie White! Just so's I wouldn't keep you waiting so long! You've a quare nerve, treating me like that, so you have! Just don't you dare come near me again!' She pushed her way past him and up to the bedroom, where she flung herself down on the bed under the low rafters, which were ash trees cut down with the bark still on them, to make the support for the thatched roof. She lay there on her front with her head on her arms and howled and bawled her fill. It wasn't just the pain of the blow, you understand, but the anger and humiliation, and the idea that Robbie didn't love her any more, if he could do such a thing.

After a while Robbie came creeping upstairs and sat on the bed beside her. 'Ach, Lizzie, don't be carrying on like that, now! There, I'm sorry. I took you up wrong. Will that do ye?'

Lizzie peered at him sideways through her arms. He was near enough bursting into tears himself and she suddenly felt right and sorry for big Robbie. She'd never seen a grown man cry before. She sat up and threw her arms round him. 'It's all right, Robbie. I know you didn't mean it.' And they had a good kiss and cuddle until Lizzie felt quite happy. She was sure Robbie would never raise his fist to her again.

But there was a wheen of other times when Robbie lost his head for what seemed to Lizzie to be no good reason, and every time he got harsher and rougher in the way he treated her. Lizzie began to move round him carefully, trying to make sure she did nothing to start any trouble. For a while, as she said to Sarah, things went fine.

Up until the day when Lizzie took a notion to buy a pair of pink silk knickers from the traveller at the door. Why she should have wanted them, I don't rightly know, but there – women take these silly notions into their heads.

One bright afternoon in early spring, this travelling salesman with a catalogue and a suitcase of goods for sale came to the door, when Robbie was out at his work at MacLoughlin's farm, and Lizzie was at home by herself. He was a bit of a live wire, this salesman, from all accounts, not too old, a bit full of himself, but with a way about him and a bright blue eye, and he didn't find it hard to talk wee Lizzie into treating herself. It was a while since she'd bought anything in the way of clothes, not since she'd shopped for her honeymoon.

He showed her the knickers, along with some other stuff, and gave her a line about how her man would be bowled over when he saw her in them. Lizzie did some more blushing and giggling, and thought maybe the knickers would stir Robbie up a bit – what with him coming home tired out and falling asleep in front of the fire after his tea, it was a while since he'd shown a lot of interest in her. Lizzie wouldn't have minded a wean or two running about, to keep her busy and give her a bit of company. And, as she said to herself sensibly, you can't have weans if you don't make no attempt to get them.

Well, she invited the fella in for a wee cup of something, and after he'd had it, she stood chatting so long to the salesman on the doorstep that she got the fright of her life when Robbie loomed up out of nowhere, being finished with his day's work and home for his tea. He gave the salesman a look, and the man closed up his case in a great hurry and made off right and quick.

'What were ye doing wasting time talking to that rascal, Lizzie White?' Robbie demanded. 'I hope you weren't fool enough to buy anything from him?'

'Ach, no, Robbie, he's only just come. All I was doing was chasing him off!' Lizzie protested. She was frightened enough of Robbie's temper by then, and not above a bit of a lie if it would soothe him down. Lucky enough she'd taken the knickers upstairs to the bedroom as soon as she'd paid for them, and Robbie's tea was all ready to put out, so she got away with it for the time being.

At first she kept the knickers hidden in her bottom drawer, for fear Robbie would see them and wonder where she'd got them, or say she'd been extravagant, for he was a quare mean one, was Robbie.

She thought she would maybe tell him they were passed on to her by her sister, and she was waiting for the right moment, when Robbie was in a good mood to bring it up.

But the luck wasn't with Lizzie. On the very day when she couldn't hold back any longer from trying the knickers on, dear save us, that very evening nothing would do Robbie but that they should have a go at it again. Even though he hadn't been next or nigh her for weeks past. (Or so the story went that Lizzie told Sarah, and Sarah told me.) Get the notion out of his head Lizzie could not, once it was in.

So there was wee Lizzie, trying to slip the knickers off quietly, under her nightie, and hide them under her dress on the chair.

But just before he was putting the light off, didn't Robbie catch sight of them sliding off the chair from under the dress, them being so smooth and silky.

With that he let out a howl. 'What's that whore's garment doing in my house?' roared Robbie. 'No decent honest woman would own such a thing! Where did you get it, woman? Is it your fancy man bought it for you?'

Nothing would move him from it but that she must be doing a line with someone.

He even had it worked out that they must have come from the commercial traveller he'd seen at the door that time, who went around selling them, for nobody else would be able to come by a present like that. He had a point there, for none of the boyos round our way would have been seen dead in a ditch going into a shop that sold women's under-wear, let alone buying it.

Well, Sarah told me that Lizzie said he near had her killed, going round and round the bed trying to get at her with his old blackthorn stick, and landing in a good few wallops that she said near broke her back before she was able to get away out the bedroom door and down the stairs.

Lizzie was very frightened. Although Robbie had been angry with her before this, mostly over nothing at all as far as Lizzie could see, he'd always been so sorry afterwards, when he got his temper back, that Lizzie'd let him away with it. She was convinced, when he kissed her and swore he'd never hurt her again, that he really meant it. But she'd been in considerable pain many a time, and this time it looked like being worse than ever. It was the first time she'd seen him lift his stick to her. She was terrified as to what he'd end up doing in his temper. Her only thought was to get away from him.

She flew out the back door, across to the privy, and she locked herself in, thanking heaven that it was a good stout door with a lock as well as a bolt.

And there she stayed the night. It was freezing cold and the wind was whistling in through the cracks in the wood. Lizzie shivered and shook all night. But come out and get a hammering she had no intention of doing, and all the more so when she had done nothing to earn it.

The next morning, Robbie had cooled down a bit, what with having nobody to get him his fry. He went and knocked on the door and told her he might be willing to hear what she had to say for herself if she would have the decency to come out and make her man a bit of breakfast.

So Lizzie believed him, mainly because she wanted to, and out she came.

But, sure and all, it turned out she'd let herself in for it.

For Robbie had no sooner got his fry in him than he started on her again, and this time Lizzie took to her heels and away across the fields to her ma's.

The sun was out, shining on the hills in the distance and lighting up the green fields at Lizzie's feet, and as she ran she felt free for the first time since she'd married Robbie. She was sure she had escaped.

But old Mary Ann Beckett, Lizzie's ma, was a God-fearing woman. I mind her well telling me off for taking a sup of beer at the Harvest Fair one year, and me a young fellow looking to get off with a girl and needing a bit of courage to help me. (That was before I met Sarah, mind! Sarah, if you remember, boy, had enough confidence to do for the both of us.) But Mary Ann didn't see it that way. To her, booze was the devil's weapon, and she wasn't slow to let you know it. She had a tongue on her would bring up the blisters, and I can tell you she had me so scared of what she'd say next that I didn't drink another drop that evening. Not when she was looking, that is.

But that was Mary Ann Beckett for ye. She had fixed opinions on everything. And fixed opinions on the subject of marriage most of all. Opinions and attitudes that had grown up with deep roots over many a long year. So when wee Lizzie came rushing in, crying and carrying on and swearing she was never going back next or near that brute, what did Mary Ann tell her? That it was her duty to go back, and go back she would have to.

Howandsoever, she wasn't just so hard as all that: she set Lizzie down and made her a cup of tea, and listened while Lizzie told her the worst. Then she said she'd see to it that Lizzie's da had a wee word with Robbie before Lizzie had to go near him again.

Well, Lizzie told her ma that, with there being no childer yet, she didn't see any good reason for staying with Robbie. 'He's for ever punching at me, Mammy,' she said. 'It's not like this is the first.'

But Mary Ann wouldn't have it. 'Your husband's your husband, child dear,' she said. 'You can't just up and leave him. Lord save us, where would we be if everybody that didn't get on with their man was to do that? Marriage is for sticking at, Lizzie. You'll feel better about it in another year or two when the weans come along. And sure, what would the minister say if you were to do a thing like that?' She stopped for a moment and gave a wee shudder. 'And as for your aunt Aggie Henderson' – Mary Ann could hardly bear to think of it – 'I'd never be able to look her in the face again.'

So the end of it was that Lizzie went back, and her da with her to speak firm to Robbie not to treat his wee girl that way, or he'd be hearing about it.

Big Sammy was a quare size of a boyo – he even loomed over Robbie – and for a while it looked as if Robbie was for taking him serious, and letting bygones be bygones. In fact, Sarah told me Lizzie said she was glad she'd gone back, for it was just like when they were on their honeymoon, and things were great. She was in great hopes that it wouldn't be long now before there'd be signs that the first wean was on the way.

Come Christmas time, Lizzie bought Robbie a wee treat. It wasn't much, for there wasn't the cash in them days that all you young ones seem to have now, but she thought it would maybe please him. It was a fancy lighter for his fags, for Robbie was like the rest of us and liked a bit of a smoke. That was the time when the doctors still hadn't managed to knock another bit of fun out of life, finding out that the fags would kill you, the way they done afterwards.

My great uncle had been a heavy smoker in his time and was now forbidden his old pipe on doctor's orders. 'There's times,' he said, 'when I near enough think there's so little pleasure left in life that there's not much use wanting to keep going, boy.'

'Ach, now, Uncle Jimmy!' I protested. But I thought he had a point. I hoped I'd never come to a life like Jimmy's. I hurried to say something to distract him from such thoughts.

'And so, was Robbie pleased with his present?' I asked.

Come Christmas Eve, Robbie went up to the bedroom for something. I don't rightly mind what Sarah said it was, if she ever knew herself. Maybe it was a safety-pin for his trousers, for he went rooting in Lizzie's top drawer, unbeknownst to her. The first thing Lizzie knew about it was when she heard him letting out a gulder you could have heard away up in Belfast.

Then he comes pelting down the stairs like he was fit for Purdysburn. 'What's this doing in your drawer, woman?'

He no more waited for an answer than Daisy Bell's heifer with the bull after it.

'I know fine you didn't buy yourself that out of the housekeeping!' he roars at poor Lizzie. 'It was bad enough them pink silk knickers, but when it comes to your fancy man buying you stuff like this that costs a mint, you needn't tell me he's not getting nothing back in return. You're selling yourself, ye whore!'

Lizzie was trying to get a word in edgeways, trying to get it into his head that she'd bought the lighter for his Christmas box. But the more she tried to make him hear, the deafer he got.

Then Robbie went to lift his blackthorn stick again, and Lizzie got into a panic. She raced for the door, and nearly had it open. But Robbie was too quick for her this time.

I don't believe he rightly knew what he was doing. I don't think he meant what he did. It was the temper in him, roaring far out of control. That and the jealousy. 'Stop there, you whore!' he roared, and he lashed out with his stick. I think he didn't see just where he was aiming. He swung out hard and wild, and he hit wee Lizzie a wallop over the head.

She was down on the floor with the blood streaming out of her before either of them knew what was happening.

It was enough to bring Robbie to his senses. Next thing he'd dropped the old stick, and down on his knees beside Lizzie, bawling like a wean and trying to get her to speak to him. But man dear, it was a bit late in the day for that. He went on trying though, the tears streaming down his face.

And it was there Sarah found him, when she went over a bit later to borrow a paper pattern from Lizzie to cut out her new dress.

They had Lizzie away to the hospital in an ambulance, as soon as Sarah got her wits together enough to go out to the phone box and call for one. But for all the good it did, she needn't have bothered.

Lizzie came to for a wee bit in the ambulance, and it was then she gave Sarah some idea of what had been happening. But before long she slipped back again into unconsciousness, and she was dead the same night.

The peelers came for Robbie the next day, and they found him still sitting on the floor by the back door, where Sarah had left him when she went with Lizzie in the ambulance.

Folks reckoned Robbie was lucky, for he got off with a lifer because the jury thought it had been halfway to an accident. But it was all one to Lizzie what he got. It didn't make a tap of difference to her.

Or to Robbie, for that matter. I don't think he was ever right in the head afterwards, and he died in prison before he'd half completed his sentence.

My great uncle Jimmy paused and looked past me out of the window, at the hills shining in the distance, where the day lay dying, spread out in great bloody streaks against the coming darkness. The retirement home was on the edge of the town.

Looking out of the window I could see fields stretching for long distances until they ended in low green hills; fields of barley turning to gold with the moving fringes of the tall stalks painting waves full of a driving and impatient anger across their surface; fields with brown wounds slashed throughout their length to cut deep ridges where the thin spikes of potato plants thrust weak fingers up to grasp the air; fields dark green with cauliflower or the lighter shade of grass where cows were lining up to be taken willy-nilly to the milking shed. Hedges of blackthorn, white thorn, hawthorn and the burning yellow flames of whin barred the fields in, keeping them in their place, their harsh branches closing round to prevent escape.

Beyond lay the hills, green with the illusory colour of freedom, green and light and promising more than they can give, hills which looked as if they could be reached without a struggle, hills within walking distance if it were possible to press on through the thorny hedges. There were dark, purply black mountains further away in the distance, too far to come to easily.

Above them all, the sun bent closer, still sending out its promise of light, enriching the gold of the corn, increasing the deceptive loveliness of the hills even now at the end of its time. But now great gushes of orange and pink and red were spurting out from the helpless and damaged sun as it came falling down the edge of the steep sky to its death, sending reflections to stain the massy clouds which crammed the air full to suffocating.

Last night I'd hit Moira hard across the face in one of our stupid arguments. I'd never get to be as bad as Robbie White, I was sure I wouldn't. But some day would she leave, like Lizzie? Why did I treat her that way? 'Why? I burst out. 'Why did she go back, no matter what her ma said? She'd got safely away.'

'I mind wee Lizzie White well on her wedding day,' my great uncle Jimmy said. 'A quare good-looking wee girl she was, and that happy. And that fond of Robbie.' Jimmy sighed heavily.

He peered past me out of the window again. 'Day's nearly over,' he remarked. 'Soon be dark. Time to switch the lights on.'

He turned back to me. 'Lizzie wanted to make a go of her marriage. There wasn't much anyone could do about that. She wouldn't have gone back to him whatever her ma said if she hadn't really wanted to. She didn't want her marriage to be destroyed and she was ready to take a risk to make it work out. In spite of it all, and brute though he was, thon big Robbie White, the one thing that couldn't be changed was this. Lizzie, poor foolish wee girl, couldn't get rid of the idea she had in her head. She still thought she was in love with him.'

3 – Shadows

published in *Brazen City,* Belfast 2008

It was cold tonight, and Danny found that he was shivering in spite of the leather jacket. He began to walk faster, pulling the jacket tightly round his thin chest. He passed the empty buildings where Mackie's used to be, listening all the time for the sound behind him that would signal the success of his job.

Suddenly the night was full of it, a whoosh and a roar that poured over all his senses and made it hard not to cower down with his hands to his ears.

No time for that.

He broke into a run, looking back over his shoulder now and then to make sure no one was watching or, worse still, coming after him. The streets were empty, but in a few minutes the sound of the sirens would follow the roar of the explosion, and they would be on him.

In the seconds before then, he needed to be at least round the next corner and looking for the car.

The sirens pierced his ears as he reached the turning.

Where was Jacky?

A voice sounded out of the darkness. 'Danny. Over here!'

He fled across the street. The car door swung open, and he piled in. They roared down the middle of the road and went skidding round the next bend. Then it was the West Link, and on to the M1, and mingling with the other fast traffic.

Danny's breathing slowly returned to normal.

'Got a feg, Jacky?'

'Sure.' Jacky tossed the packet over. 'Ye did well, boy. I heard the bang.'

Danny laughed. 'Yeah.'

'Give them something to think about. Gotta keep up the pressure.'

Danny felt a sudden, wild exhilaration. He couldn't remember when Jacky had last praised him. More often it was, 'Get a grip, kid. Catch yerself on and don't be so daft.'

All through his childhood, Danny had felt diminished, put down, knowing that Jacky despised him.

There had been the time at school, his first year at 'big school', when Charlie Flanagan's gang had been picking on Danny most days, just because he'd got a prize for maths at the Christmas exams. Swotty Pants, they'd called him, and other names he didn't want to remember even now. He'd stopped going in to school dinners, and hidden out in one of the cloakrooms, because it was as they were coming out from dinner that Flanagan or one of his mates usually started in on him. It left him feeling hungry and miserable, but not so miserable as he would have been if Charlie Flanagan had beaten him up.

It worked at first. But after a week or so, they tracked him down anyway, no matter where he went to try to dodge them. Then there would be the making fun of him, and after a while the pushing, and then the slapping. And then the punching. Danny didn't want to think of himself as a coward, but it was getting to the stage where his life was so miserable that he just wanted to stay away from school.

That had led to more trouble, when the truant catcher came round to the house and spoke to his ma about it.

Ma didn't want to get Danny into trouble with his da so she'd asked Jacky to see what he could do about it. Make sure his wee brother went to school and didn't mitch off.

Danny hadn't told anyone about Flanagan and his gang. He knew it wouldn't do any good. But now, in despair, he told Jacky – Jacky, five years older, one of the big boys – hoping maybe he could help. Instead Jacky had laughed, and insisted on him going to school. 'You stand up to the gits, Danny,' he said. 'Can't have our Danny letting these boyos get away with beating him up. You hit back, kid.'

Danny had tried before. He told Jacky so. But how could a smallish, underweight boy like him stand up to half a dozen hefty louts who didn't hesitate to lash out at him on any excuse, and never seemed to get caught?

But Jacky insisted. He made Danny go to school dinners and let the gang catch him. Then Jacky stood round the corner out of sight and watched as Danny tried to fight back. Only when he saw that there was no way Danny, bruised and battered with a bleeding nose, on his knees on the ground, was going to chase off the Flanagan gang, did he come round the corner, saying casually, 'You there, our Danny?' scattering the gang by his very appearance.

'Just you keep standing up to them, kid,' he said. 'They'll soon get sick of it.'

Jacky didn't understand.

Over the next few months Danny faked sickness so many times and missed so many classes that he dropped badly behind at school. Then, whether from stress and worry or just coincidence, he took seriously ill, with some sort of bronchial thing, and was off for several months.

It was the answer to his problems: when he was able to go back, they put him in a lower class, and Flanagan seemed to have forgotten about him.

At the end of the year, which wasn't long after this, Flanagan left, and Danny began to enjoy school again for the first time in what seemed like years.

Jacky said, 'See, our Danny? You stood up to them, and they gave up, right? Like me with our da.'

Danny knew it was nonsense. But Jacky didn't understand.

Jacky didn't really care.

Tonight, driving down the motorway, smoking one of Jacky's cigarettes, Danny felt, for the first time, accepted by Jacky on an equal footing.

He had achieved something that even Jacky was bound to admit had been pretty spectacular. He hadn't been scared, had gone straight ahead. He was one of the boys now. Just like Jacky.

At the safe house, there was a girl he had never met before called Maire, who gave them a cup of tea. Danny leaned back, inhaling deeply, and watched her move about the room, her long red hair sweeping her shoulders, her body swaying, as she bent to take the teapot from the low cupboard, then stretched up for the mugs and the jar of sugar. The familiar actions were reminiscent of his childhood, when his mother would move about the kitchen providing food and safety. A sharp pang shot through him. He could remember few nights like that.

Too many memories were of weekend nights when the temporary peace had been disturbed by the arrival home of da. Roaring drunk, usually. In a foul temper. A big, powerful man, red-faced from the drink, running to fat, hot and sweaty and looking for a fight. Swinging out at whichever of them was the nearest.

Danny shivered. He remembered the worst evening.

Da had taken a swing at ma and sent her sideways. Danny had ducked under the table. Out of sight, he hoped.

Jacky was just turned fourteen. Getting to be big for his age. He grabbed at Da's arm. 'Stop that, you effing git!' he roared at the top of his voice, and he took a swipe at Da's ear. A hard blow. Da felt it.

Da turned round slowly, shaking his head as if to clear it. He seemed unsure at first what was happening. 'Is it you, you wee bastard?' he said. 'Think you can tell yer da what to do, do you?' He thrust his face close to Jacky's.

Jacky was still hanging on to his arm. Danny, from under the table, caught a glimpse of Jacky's face. It was white with fear, but riddled with hatred too. Hatred and stubbornness. 'You leave my ma alone!' he yelled.

Da shook his arm, trying to free himself. Then he took a swing at Jacky's head with his other fist. Jacky staggered back. His hold on the arm was broken.

'I'll show you who's boss around here!' said Da softly. He went over to the fireplace and bent to pick up the poker.

With a howl, Jacky sprang away and went belting up the stairs.

Da was slow and cumbersome. He tripped over a chair, came down heavily, then went raging up the stairs after Jacky as soon as he had his balance.

But by that time Jacky had locked himself in his room.

Danny, crouched beneath the table, listened to Da thumping on the door until it seemed impossible that it would survive the attack. But the door held.

Other nights, he had managed to crawl away to bed unseen while his da took out his anger, his disappointment and frustration, on the other two. But tonight Jacky was in the bedroom he and Danny shared with the door locked. There was nowhere for Danny to go.

Ma, partly recovered from the earlier blow, bent down to him. He could see her face, at a funny upside-down angle, red all along the left cheek and jaw where a dark bruise would soon be forming. She was just visible beneath the edge of the tablecloth where it was hanging down.

'Danny,' she said softly, 'crawl over and get yourself into the coal hole – quick, now!'

Danny did as she said. The door of the coal hole opened off the other side of the room, under the stairs. He had only just reached it safely when Da came back downstairs.

There was only Ma left now. Danny, shut behind the door of the coal hole, couldn't hear much of what went on then. He was very glad of that later. As it was, he heard more, much more, than he ever wanted to remember.

He had expected that next day Da would take it out on Jacky, who couldn't stay locked in his room for ever, after all. But it didn't work like that.

Da must have realised he'd gone further than usual that night, further than he'd meant to, in his anger at Jacky. Ma had been taken to the hospital, and wasn't back home for several weeks. During that time Da was more subdued than usual. He steered clear of Jacky. Danny could almost have thought he was a bit frightened of him. And he cut down the drink, for a while at least.

Then Ma came home from hospital, and after the first few weeks, things went back to normal. What was normal for their house, anyway.

But Da left Jacky alone, and when Jacky was around, he was a bit more careful of how he treated Ma. Jacky was around a lot less, though. He took to staying out late himself, and Da said nothing.

Da was drinking as much as ever, by now. Which meant that Danny had to take the worst of it. Or so it seemed to him.

He heard the voice again in his ears. 'It's all your fault, ye wee skitter! Can't you do anything right?'

But what had he done? Knocked over a glass on the draining board so that he'd cut his thumb and bled over Da's newspaper. Or forgotten to pass on a message from one of Da's mates, Arnie Fleming, about a fancied horse for the two thirty on Saturday. It seemed to Danny sometimes that it just wasn't possible to please Da, no matter how hard he tried.

None of the things he did seemed all that bad.

But Da thought different. 'It's all your fault, ye wee skitter!'

And Danny would cry between thumps, 'It's not my fault, Da! It wasn't me!'

But there was nobody else that it could have been. He knew that. And Da knew that.

He hated his life. His family.

And yet the secure atmosphere of the safe house still made him think of his home. His home when Da was out, his mother moving around in peace. A place to shelter, to feel protected from the outside world. For a while, at least.

'Better stay the night,' Maire advised them. 'If there's no problem, yis'll be able to get home tomorrow.'

Later, she and Jacky disappeared upstairs together, leaving him to the sleeping bag on the sofa.

Maire looked a bit like Bernie, he thought. Red hair, anyway. Bernie was Danny's first girlfriend. Only girlfriend, so far. He had met her when he was in hospital, and they had kept up through their early teens, going for coffee together, later to the pictures. He had kissed her tentatively in the back row, and she had seemed happy about it. One afternoon, they had been having a chip together in McDonald's when Jacky came in with a couple of mates.

He saw Danny and was about to ignore him when his eye fell on Bernie.

Bernie was sixteen now, with a slim, nicely rounded figure, big brown eyes, the red hair curling down to her shoulders. She was looking very pretty, Danny realised. Jacky seemed to think so. He came over. 'How's about ye, our Danny?' he said, in a casual, friendly voice. 'And who's the talent?'

'Bernie, this is my bro', Jacky,' Danny said. He tried to be equally casual, but knew his voice was squeaking.

Jacky pulled out a chair from the next table, and drew it over. He straddled it and leant easily with his arms across the back.

Danny felt his heart sinking.

'So, a good-looking chick like you should be able to do better for herself than our kid, Bernie!'

That was the beginning of it.

Laying himself out to be funny, sexy, attractive, and taking every opportunity to put Danny down, Jacky dominated the conversation for the next half-hour. Then he offered Bernie a lift home on his motor bike. 'Save you getting the bus, right?'

Next time Danny saw Bernie, she was standing beside Jacky in a pub, leaning against him. There was a glazed, adoring look on her face as she stared up at him, and Jacky's arm was draped round her shoulders. As Danny watched, Jacky bent over to give her a long, open-mouthed kiss. His hands were all over her.

Danny, who shouldn't have been in the pub at all – he was under age – and was expecting any moment to be turfed out, forgot about the bouncer and the need for a low profile, and started impulsively forward. Then he stopped. What was the use? If Bernie would rather be with Jacky than with him, what could he do about it? He didn't even want to do anything. He didn't care about Bernie any more. The relationship had turned sour on him.

Jacky didn't stick with her long. He never stuck with any girl more than a few months. He just wanted the pleasure of achievement, of showing he could have any girl he fancied.

Danny heard about the split at second hand, and he could have asked Bernie out again, but he didn't want to. He had hardly thought about her since, he told himself. It was only seeing Maire looking so like her, and Jacky taking Maire off upstairs, that had reminded him, and brought back some of the pain.

He lay awake on the sofa in the safe house for some time. Funny to think that the big, half-built office complex must be rubble now. When he had walked past it in the morning, it had been solid, immovable. It would have been empty at night. He had got in quite easily, scaling the security fencing, untroubled by the alarms and broken glass. By the time anyone decided to take the signal seriously, he had already left the bomb and gone. He had been cool, organised. It was only now, beginning to shiver uncontrollably, that he knew he had been under strain.

Well, he had done it. He had set out to achieve something, and he had achieved it. Jacky would think of him as an equal now, not as the useless kid brother.

He remembered the evening, not very long ago, when Jacky had first spoken to him about joining the local unit. They had all been told, Jacky said, to get as many more men recruited as possible. It was to be the biggest recruitment drive yet. They were to start with their own families. Brothers, cousins. That had been why Jacky was speaking to him about it.

When he realised that Jacky had approached him under orders, Danny was at first disappointed. He had thought it was a bit more personal than that. But Jacky would never have considered him, wouldn't have thought he was up to it, otherwise. 'You'll need to come to the next meeting, let the unit commander see you, take the oath, all that,' Jacky said.

'Okay,' Danny agreed. His voice had shaken slightly.

The meeting was less than a week later. Jacky took him along. It was the middle of the night, and the meeting place was a building a good way up into Andersonstown. Jacky gave him a balaclava to put on just before they went in.

The unit commander was impressive, tall, loud-voiced. He spoke with a broad Belfast accent, which Danny thought at first was put on but afterwards decided was genuine. Danny listened carefully as the man outlined what they would expect of him. It was frightening, but exciting too. Later, he took the oath, and felt a mingling of pride and terror at knowing he had now joined up. He was one of the boys.

As they came away, Jacky told him he would be expected to prove his worth fairly soon, that he would be given some sort of job, nothing too important very likely, but something that would prove his commitment to the cause. The day before yesterday, the instructions had come through Jacky. A city-centre building was to be bombed. During the night. The plan wasn't to kill anyone, just to destroy property. Let people know they meant business.

If that wasn't important, Danny didn't know what was. Maybe he'd been given such a big first job because he was Jacky's brother. At the meeting, it had become clear to Danny that Jacky had a much more senior position than Danny had known.

Jacky gave him the details. Told him where and when to collect the bomb. A getaway car would be waiting for him. Jacky would be driving it. 'Gotta look after you, our Danny!' he joked. 'Can't let anything happen to you or Ma'd skin me!'

But Ma would have skinned him if she'd known Jacky had got her wee son sworn in, Danny thought.

Eventually he slept.

Maire turned the radio on while she cooked breakfast the next morning, and they heard the report while they ate.

'A sixty-eight-year-old night watchman, Mr Billy Handley, was burnt to death last night when a bomb destroyed the new city-centre office block under construction for Dobson and McClarin ...' Danny stood up and stumbled upstairs. He reached the bathroom just in time to be sick into the toilet. Why hadn't they known there would be a night watchman? Why had they told him it would be empty?

Later, Jacky shrugged it off. 'Sure, how can ye know everything in advance? He wasn't seen when the boys were lookin' the place over. Didn't see him yerself, did ye? Reckon he was havin' a wee doze somewhere outa sight.'

'I shoulda looked better.'

'Don't be daft! You did yer job – get in and get out quick, that's the orders. Anyway, it's all the more publicity, see? So maybe it's not so bad.'

That night there was an article about the night watchman in the *Telegraph*. With a photograph. Danny had looked at the photo before he took in who it was. An elderly man, they called him. Maybe he looked young for his age. To Danny, he looked very much like Da, who was at least ten years younger than this Billy Handley. Big, wide face, still plenty of hair, high red colouring in his cheeks. Danny didn't read the article. He didn't want to know any more. He wished very much that he hadn't seen the photo.

It was more than a week before Jacky contacted him again. He dropped in one evening after work, and Danny was glad to see him. He found the house lonely, these days, since Jacky had moved out. His mother had little to say – she had grown quieter and quieter in the years since his father's accident. As for Da, he sat in a corner, smoking and staring at the television, though it was a mystery whether he ever understood a word. He'd done nothing else since the day he'd come home from the hospital after his fall from the scaffolding on the building site.

He had been a skilled bricklayer when he could get the work. Now he was nothing.

Danny had been in the last class of the day at school when he had been called out to go to the headmaster's room. He had been worried, naturally, but only about himself. He had been working hard since Charlie Flanagan had left and the rest of the gang had dispersed and stopped their bullying. Surely it couldn't be another complaint about his work He'd had plenty of those in the past, in the dreadful days when Flanagan's gang was still his worst nightmare.

'Very sorry about this, Danny,' the headmaster had said. 'I'm afraid it's bad news. Your dad's had an accident. He's in hospital – in the Royal. Your mum wants you to go there straight away and be with the rest of the family while they wait to hear how he is. Mr O'Malley will give you a lift over, if you go and collect your things now.' Mr O'Malley was a maths teacher who had always treated Danny well, and whom he liked.

The head waited to see if Danny was going to be upset, maybe cry, but Danny felt only thankfulness that he wasn't in trouble. 'Okay, I'll go now, sir,' he said. 'Where should I meet Mr O'Malley?'

Da had been working on one of the new construction sites scattered round Belfast. One good thing that had come out of the continuing Troubles was the amount of building work available, with the money for reconstruction, after each bombing, pouring in from England. It had been a high building, intended for offices, probably insurance, Da had said. Danny remembered him sitting by the fire, just after he got the job, in an unusually pleasant and expansive frame of mind, talking about it.

'The whole city centre's getting covered with insurance offices, these days,' Da had said. 'Can't say I like it much, but there, it's all work, eh, Kathleen?' He drew Ma down on his knee and gave her a squeeze. Danny watched him and shuddered. But Ma let him kiss her, and giggled in a childish way, clearly pleased that he was in a good mood and affectionate to her.

'Now we've got some money coming in, maybe you and me'll go away for a wee break, eh, Kathleen?' Da said, nuzzling into her neck. 'Long time since we've had time to ourselves without the kids, right?'

Not long afterwards, he had taken her upstairs, and Danny, however much he stuffed his hands over his ears, couldn't help hearing the noises from the front bedroom where Ma and Da slept. Laughing, the bed banging against the wall, groaning.

Jacky was out.

Since he was working on a high building, Da, with a skilled job in his own bricklaying line, had had to climb the scaffolding every day to carry out his work. Danny wasn't entirely sure what had happened. Whoever had put up the top piece of scaffolding must have made a mistake: it hadn't been attached properly. When Da and his mates had reached the highest level and stepped out on to the planking to begin the next layer of concrete blocks, the scaffolding had given under their feet. They had gone plunging down with nothing to save them.

Why wasn't there a safety net? Danny wondered. There should have been. Someone cutting corners, he supposed.

One of the other men had gone straight to the ground and been killed outright. Another had managed to land on the next level of planking down, and had ended up with a broken arm, but nothing worse.

Da had fallen most of the way. He had banged against more than one level on the way down.

But he hadn't fallen right to the ground. The strap of his overalls had caught on a projecting steel bar, and he had hung there – for a long time, Danny was told – until the rescue crew had managed to reach him.

His injuries were mainly from the times when he had bumped onto the other levels of scaffolding as he came down.

He had broken both legs and his right arm. But the more serious injuries were from concussion, in spite of his hard hat, which had been knocked askew, and the damage to his neck and back, which, the doctors thought, might leave him semi-paralysed.

Danny hung about in the hospital corridor with Ma and Jacky for what seemed hours, drinking innumerable cups of sweet, milky coffee from the machine, sometimes sitting down, but more often prowling restlessly about, waiting to hear the results of the operations being carried out on Da.

The most surprising thing was that Ma and Jacky were seriously upset. Why should they be, after the way Da had treated them all? Danny, feeling slightly guilty, was glad. Glad that Da would never again raise his fist to them, that there would be no more nights with Da arriving home drunk and laying into them.

That first night, when the family finally went back home, leaving Da in the hospital, Danny fell into a deep sleep, from which he was woken in the middle of the night by the sound of Jacky weeping.

'What's wrong, Jacky?' Danny whispered. 'Is it Da?'

'You wouldn't understand, wee lad. You never got anything but thumps from Da. But before he started the drinking he used to play footie in the street with me ... and one Easter Monday, he took me up the Cave Hill to roll my egg, while Ma was making the dinner, and carried me home, because I hurt my leg ...'

Danny said nothing.

'If you ever tell anyone you heard me crying,' Jacky said, 'I'll kill you, see?'

'I won't,' Danny promised.

'I know he's a right bastard now,' Jacky said, 'but he used not to be.'

Then he was quiet, and after a while Danny got back to sleep.

It was several weeks before they let Da come home from hospital.

Danny couldn't believe it when he saw him.

Where was the giant of a man who had terrified him? Instead, there was a pathetic, broken figure who had to be helped from his chair to the bed made up for him in the corner of the downstairs room, who never spoke, who seemed not to recognise any of them.

It was like the day Danny had heard that Charlie Flanagan had left school. He felt like shouting with delight. Only the knowledge that Ma and Jacky felt differently stopped him showing his feelings.

That night, he had a nightmare. He was about to step out on to scaffolding that would collapse, unable to stop himself. He felt the planking shake, and then he was falling, screaming – and woke to find that he really was screaming.

Ma came in to comfort him, and gave him a painkiller to help him sleep.

He got used to seeing Da sitting in the corner, looking blank, and learnt to behave as if his father wasn't there.

Jacky never made any attempt to speak to Da. The sight too much – the strong father of his childhood reduced to this. Instead he ignored him. As he did on the night he called in, a week after the explosion, to see Danny.

Jacky went up with Danny to his room, filled him in quickly about a new job he had for him, then left.

'Has Jacky gone again?' his mother asked, coming out of the kitchen as the front door slammed. 'Oh – I was makin' him a cup of tea.'

Danny went back upstairs. It began to get dark. Shadows crept about his room.

The wind whistling in the chimney sounded like a voice from far away. Danny! Danny! He didn't know what it was. Or who. He didn't want to hear it.

He got up quickly and turned on the light.

The new job was straightforward – picking up a suitable car and then waiting to act as a getaway vehicle while Jacky and someone else raided an off-licence. He suspected Jacky had deliberately given him an easy one to help him get his nerve back, and was glad to accept.

He wasn't going to let what had happened the last time get to him. He wanted to help Jacky – well, to help the cause, he supposed he should say. If he was honest, the cause didn't mean that much to him. He'd never had time to worry about politics. Enough going on in his own life, right? But he did want to prove himself, not to give up after only one job.

It wasn't his fault that the night watchman, Billy Handley, had been killed. It was the fault of the fellas who had checked out the building beforehand, and had said there wouldn't be anyone there. Well, they'd been wrong, hadn't they? But it wasn't Danny's fault.

He had a couple of strong drinks before he went to collect the car and felt okay.

He had marked out the right vehicle in advance. A newish, but not too noticeable model which was usually parked in front of the owner's house a few streets away from where Danny lived. He knew the owner's name, O'Brien, that he worked in a city-centre office and seldom took the car out after work. But O'Brien wouldn't know Danny well, if at all, and wouldn't suspect him of taking the car. Danny had a local reputation as 'a nice, quiet, wee lad, not a trouble maker.'

But, like all his mates, Danny had known since he was ten how to hot-wire a car's ignition. He hadn't done much joy-riding, but there had been a few occasions. He was fully confident of his ability to get quietly away in O'Brien's car, without attracting attention.

Soon he was driving smoothly across town to the designated off-licence.

It reminded him of the time he, Barney Scullion and Dinger Bell had borrowed a flashy BMW from one of the big houses up the Malone Road. That had been a wild night.

They had almost been caught when they heard the owner coming out of his house and heading down his drive, just as they were about to begin work with the wires. They'd had to scarper briskly out of sight, further down the road, and vanish into someone else's driveway, behind some bushes. But it turned out the owner was on his way to the local pub, walking, not driving.

Five minutes later, they had passed him in the BMW, as he was turning in at the pub door. He hadn't spotted them, hadn't even looked round as they'd driven past.

They had almost burst themselves giggling. It had seemed to Danny one of the funniest things he had ever seen.

Then, heading for the motorway, Barney had raced up the gears to top speed, and Dinger, beside Barney in the front, had turned the radio up loud and opened all the windows, so that the night air rushed through their hair and lifted their spirits to crazy heights.

The other car had come out of nowhere. A Honda. Crawling along in the slow lane, then suddenly pulling out in front of them without a signal. It had been the driver's own fault, not Barney's.

Barney had tried to brake, tried to swerve into the inside lane round the Honda, had knocked into its back on the left-hand side and sent it careering into the central reservation.

The BMW was spinning out of control. Barney wrenched at the wheel, trying desperately to straighten up, to get back into his lane. Too late.

Danny wished he hadn't remembered that ride.

He had unfastened his safety-belt (he had had enough sense to put it on, not like those other two eedjits), and clambered out of the back of the crashed car, diving across the lane and over the hard shoulder, taking refuge in the bushes and trees that edged the M1, staying concealed until it was all over. Until the ambulance had taken away Barney and Dinger and the Honda driver.

He got home in the small hours, limping and exhausted from the long trek back to his house. He seemed to have hurt one leg, banged it against the car door in the crash, but otherwise had escaped unharmed.

Ma had fussed over him. She had been lying awake, worrying, and was too glad to see him back to scold.

Danny told her nothing. He carried with him the mental pictures of Dinger's head bashed in against the dashboard, the bones protruding from his cheek, the blood spurting out of Barney's face and neck where he'd been hurled against the windscreen. They wouldn't tell anyone that Danny had been there too. They wouldn't tell anyone anything ever again, he thought.

It wasn't a good memory to rake up, tonight. He had been trying to think of something other than his last job. And how it had gone wrong. How the night watchman, Billy Handley, had been hidden somewhere in the dark building. How he had been killed by the explosion Danny had set off.

It hadn't been Danny's fault that an old man had been in the building.

Any more than it had been his fault that Barney and Dinger had been killed.

He tried hard to banish the memories, and to concentrate on getting safely to the agreed meeting place, to managing the strange car without making mistakes.

Jacky was waiting for him, and explained where he wanted Danny to park. Then he slipped round the corner to join his mate.

It seemed a long time before the boys showed up. There were too many noises and shadows about. Danny was finding it hard to relax. When they came belting along, he almost forgot to have the door open, and skidded badly at the first corner.

'Whoa, boy!' Jacky said, and laughed. Danny managed a sort of grin.

A second later, he swerved wildly across the street, and Jacky made a grab at the wheel.

'Sorry – but I thought I was into him, there.'

'Into who? I didn't see nothin'.'

'The old fella crossin' without lookin' round. I only just missed him.'

Jacky said no more.

'Fancy a trip down the country, Dan?' he asked, after a few minutes had passed. 'Get a bit of fresh air, relax a bit, pick up some useful stuff?'

3 – Shadows

'Fine by me. When do I go?'

'I'll let ye know.'

The word came a few weeks later. He was to meet up with a fella he had never seen before, Teddy MacCartney, and go on a trip out Fermanagh direction to pick up some things that were needed. No point in asking what it was – Jacky kept very close-mouthed about details. Danny was glad to be doing something.

It was a bright, clear day, late spring, but still very cold, the sky a pale frosty blue, when they set out in the early afternoon.

The drive down the M1, past Dungannon and out into the beautiful low bushy country to the west, soothed Danny's spirit. Teddy McCartney was silent most of the way, and that suited Danny fine.

MacCartney was a thin, wiry man, with a grim face. One of the hard men and no mistake. His head was smooth, shaved. That, and his bleak, forbidding expression made him seem much older than Jacky, but Danny knew he wasn't. Jacky had told him he and Teddy were mates from way back.

As evening came on, they stopped at a pub for tea, and by the time they had finished, the light was going.

Danny felt a heavy weight descending on his shoulders as he got back into the car. Long shadows stretched out from the trees at the edge of the car park, and a cat, brushing silently past his leg, made him jump.

Teddy MacCartney continued to drive without speaking.

For some reason, this was no longer soothing. Danny wanted a friendly voice, chatter about nothing much, something to occupy his mind.

The pick-up went smoothly. Teddy knew where he was going – a lonely farmhouse out of sight of its nearest neighbours, up a narrow, twisting lane. It was a white, two storeyed building with a slated roof, a typical Northern Ireland farmhouse, with the usual country smell, a mixture of pigs, manure and silage hanging in the air about it. There were no roses round the door, yet there was something attractive about it, Danny thought, something solid and secure. It didn't seem like the right place for Teddy MacCartney to be calling to collect ... whatever it was he'd had to collect.

The car pulled in beside a dilapidated outhouse, and two shadowy figures, who must have been waiting for them, came out quietly from the dark area at the front of the buildings.

It was as much as Danny could do not to scream.

Teddy got out and went round to open the boot. 'Come on, gie's a hand there, can't ye?' he growled. 'What d'ye think I brought ye for?'

Danny went to help him. There were two heavy sacks to be stowed in the boot. Danny wondered what was in them, and what they would do with it.

As Teddy slammed the boot lid, someone spoke softly out of the shadows: 'Danny. Danny.'

He swung round, not sure which direction the voice had come from. 'What?'

The voice came again: 'Danny, Danny.'

It died away in a soft whisper.

Danny felt the hairs on the back of his neck stand on end. He moved slowly, awkwardly, towards the darkness thrown by the looming buildings of the outhouses surrounding the old farmhouse, towards the sound of the faint voice.

'You did it, Danny.'

'Who is it? What do you want?'

No answer.

'Leave me alone, can't you?' He was half sobbing, half whispering.

Quickly he turned away from the shadow of the buildings, from the shadowy shape beneath them back into the brightness cast by the car's headlights.

Teddy and the two strangers had noticed nothing. They were talking quietly, checking that everything was safely stowed away.

For a moment he stared back into the blackness.

'Right,' said Teddy's voice briskly, in his ear. 'Time we were heading. Hop in the car, then.'

Danny climbed slowly, awkwardly, back in at the passenger side, pulling the door after him but failing to make it click as it should have done. Teddy, with an annoyed grunt, leant across him to slam the door shut, before driving quickly off.

They were stopped just outside Ballygawley at an Army checkpoint. Teddy was calm, showing his licence and cracking a joke. The soldier waved them on without a search.

3 – Shadows

When they had driven some distance, Danny asked, 'What happens if they search the boot next time?'

'We get in trouble, sunshine, that's what.'

It didn't seem a satisfactory answer. Danny wondered if MacCartney had a gun handy. And if he would use it.

Soon after, they turned off the main road. It was a part of the world strange to Danny: he was lost by the third turn-off, and had an idea that this had been done deliberately. Teddy MacCartney didn't trust him.

They bumped slowly along a road that was little better than a country lane. It was dark, not like the well-lit motorway. The surface felt rough, as if it had been tarmacked so long ago that there was nothing of its original smoothness left, only potholes and ruts. Branches of overhanging trees brushed against the windows with a strange, swishing sound.

Danny felt himself shuddering. Was it just branches he heard?

Presently they jerked to a halt.

Something moved in the bracken at the edge of the lane.

A rabbit, maybe, or a cat hunting late. Obviously. Not any other sort of hunter. Not someone hunting for him, someone who held him responsible, someone who wanted to punish him.

Somewhere quite close he could hear the noise of running water. It was a peaceful sound.

'Sit where you are,' MacCartney said. 'Don't be making any sound, now.' He glanced at his watch, twisting his arm up to see the numbers in the faint moonlight coming through the window. 'We don't want any mistakes to be made about this.'

They sat silently in the car, while all around them the night was full of soft, animal noises. Suddenly a stick snapped, and a shadow loomed up beside the driver's door.

'Teddy?'

It was hardly more than a breath.

MacCartney opened the door and got out. 'Stay here,' he ordered Danny. 'That's what you're here for, right? Keep an eye on the car while we're away across the fields to the side road. Make sure and warn us in time if anyone comes poking in, anyone looking to see what's up.'

He went round to the boot and opened it. By the sound, he was poking in one of the sacks for something.

Danny sat silent and resentful. Something more was planned, and he was being kept in the dark. Jacky might have told him. He wasn't a kid any more. He had shown them what he could do, hadn't he?

Teddy and the other man slipped away into the darkness.

It had been a mistake to let himself think about what he had done, about the way he had proved himself. There were too many shadows and rustling noises. Something was moving in the undergrowth beside the car, an animal. Not someone who was angry about what Danny had done.

Danny felt carefully along the compartment under the dashboard. His fingers touched something cold and metallic, but it was only a spanner. He reached further.

A gun.

Holding it carefully, Danny checked to see if it was loaded. He knew quite a bit about guns: he had always taken an interest in them.

Dinger Bell's father Tommy had had a gun.

Tommy Bell was in the police, one of the minority of Catholics to join the RUC. He had a gun, a belt and holster, and a box of ammunition, which he kept carelessly in an unlocked drawer in his bedroom. Sometimes, when his Da was off duty, and had gone out for a drink, Dinger had sneaked the gun out to show to his mates.

Danny had envied him. If only he had a gun, he could shoot Charlie Flanagan, he thought.

Later, when Flanagan had gone out of Danny's life, the thought had changed.

If only I had a gun like that, I could shoot Da.

He knew it was wrong to think like that, but there were nights, lying awake, or sobbing himself to sleep with his arms, legs and face still aching from Da's kicks and punches, when he did.

He pictured how it would be. Da coming up to him, about to lash out. Danny coolly producing the gun from beneath his bomber jacket. 'Take what's coming to you, big man!'

Da's big, red, flabby face horror-stricken. His automatic retreat, arms flung up across his face to protect himself. Danny pulling the trigger, and Da falling.

He didn't allow himself to visualise the wound he would inflict. There were no spurting arteries, like Barney Scullion's. There was no smashed-in face like Dinger Bell's.

He shut his mind to the details. He didn't want to create the material for another set of nightmares. He just wanted the unmitigated satisfaction of pulling the trigger, and knowing that Da had gone out of his life for good. That he and Ma would never be kicked and thumped again.

Once Dinger Bell had allowed him to hold the gun. It wasn't loaded, but the smooth, cool, heavy feel of it in his hands – he needed both hands to steady it – made Danny feel like a king. He pointed the gun at Dinger and laughed.

That was the end of it. Dinger snatched the weapon back, and never allowed Danny another turn with his father's gun.

After that, Danny had had to make do with weapon comics whenever he could spare the cash.

He read avidly when he was supposed to be asleep. One of the few advantages of Jacky moving out was that Danny had a room to himself. He could read for as long as he wanted, instead of hiding with a torch beneath the bedclothes, frightened that Jacky would wake up and take his torch, with a punch or two for good measure. He took in detail after detail, delighting in the methodology, in the perfection of the design, the smooth skill that produced these killing machines. Of course, after Da's accident, there was no longer any need to dream about killing him. He was near enough dead as it was.

With the loaded weapon in his hand he felt safer. The night noises were less threatening. The shadows were only shadows.

He could see the wavering outline of the blackthorn hedge drawn on the moonlit lane, stretching out its pattern of black lace beside the car. The shadows of leaves and branches. That was all it was. There was no one there.

What was that? He jumped, on edge again. Over past the low hedge, half-way across the next field, he could see movement. But whether it was a man or a beast there was no telling. Danny gripped the gun tighter.

He peered into the blackness. After a while, his eyes grew accustomed to the dark. He could see where the barley grew, already showing as sharp moonlit spikes above the dark earth. He could see the path round the edge of the field, shadowed by low bushy blackthorn and hawthorn hedges and the occasional high growth of an ash or sycamore tree, and lower down the masses of wild flowers. He could almost imagine he saw the outline of sorrel, of vetch, of dandelions.

No one was moving, only the wind ruffling the barley.

There it was again! A shadow, looming across the field, blocking off large patches of the springing barley from the moonlight.

He must keep calm. He was imagining things. It was just the branch of an ash tree in the hedge, waving in the breeze. And that faint echoing sound – an owl or a fox.

'Danny! Danny!'

It was surely the voice he had heard before, calling to him out of the dark at the lonely farmhouse where he had helped to collect the two sacks. Sacks that might hold someone else's destruction.

'Danny! What are you doing?'

He knew now whose voice it was: it was Billy Handley's – the man he had killed.

Blaming him.

Blaming him for something he hadn't meant to happen.

'I didn't mean to – I didn't know you were there!'

'Danny! Don't do it, Danny!'

He pulled the handle of the car door.

The bitter cold of the late spring night stung his face as he plunged out into the darkness.

The shadow moved again across the field. He could see now what it was: a man, a huge, menacing shape, coming nearer.

Danny clutched at the uneven hedge, found a gap, began to push himself through. Thorns drew blood from his hands and face, but he couldn't feel them. Nothing was real to him except the figure coming towards him across the field. He started through the darkness, running across over the barley, the ground rough and uneven under his feet.

'I didn't mean it! It wasn't my fault, Da!'

He hardly noticed that the voice in his ears had changed, that now it was his father's voice, a harsher voice than Billy Handley's, a voice remembered from early childhood.

'Danny! What did ye do that for? It's all your fault, ye wee skitter!'

Danny looked up at the wavering figure, and saw that it was coming nearer.

'I never touched the scaffolding, Da!'

He didn't know if he'd spoken the words aloud, or if he'd heard them in his mind, as he had heard them in his nightmares for so long. He knew he hadn't touched the scaffolding. But he had wished he had done. And he had been glad that someone had fixed it wrong.

The huge figure lurched nearer.

Danny's hand tightened on the gun. The cool, smooth, heavy gun. The gun that protected him.

Something was warning him, telling him to stop.

As hatred and fear rose in him, he blocked his ears to the warning.

He raised the gun and pointed it at the movements he could see across the dark field.

'Leave me alone, can't ye?' he yelled. 'I tould ye it wasn't me!'

He knew he was in danger. He knew he had to protect himself.

He could feel the cool, heavy weight of the gun in his hands, and as he steadied it he became aware of a sense of safety, of power over his enemies.

He knew what he had to do.

He pulled the trigger, and went on pulling.

There were screams in his ears, now, and the sound of something falling.

Danny sank to the ground.

The tears were streaming down his face.

He was lying there when the man who owned the field came by in the morning, passing by the barley field on his way to bring out the cows. He found Danny with the gun still clenched in his hand.

Two men were sprawled out not far away. Both had been shot.

The police had no trouble confirming that the bullets which killed them had come from the gun Danny still held. Their only difficulty had been in getting the gun away from Danny's fierce grip to test it.

The reporter on the news said, 'The two men were identified as Teddy MacCartney, twice convicted of terrorist offences but currently free, having served sentences of one year, and eighteen months, and Seamus Donnelly, wanted by the police for his part in the murder of two members of the RUC. It appears that the two men may have been engaged in setting up a booby-trap bomb on the nearby road, which is frequently used by Army vehicles on patrol. The booby-trap has been dismantled without damage.'

They found the rest of the explosives in the car boot, and guessed that all three men had been together.

They would have liked to get more information from Danny. It would have made his trial easier.

But when they tried to question him, Danny would only mutter one thing, over and over again.

'It wasn't my fault, Da! It wasn't my fault! It wasn't me!'

4 – Giving Up

Commended in the *Seán O'Faolain Short Story Competition*, Munster Literature Centre, Cork, 2009, and published in *The Stinging Fly Press* anthology – *Sharp Sticks, Driven Nails* – in October 2010.

The afternoon sun blazed through the front room window. I moved forward, and pulled one of the heavy cream curtains halfway across.

June. A beautiful day. I used to love days like this, sitting out in the sun on Portstewart beach, with the kids playing happily round us, and Kathy stretched out in her bathing costume, drying after her quick dip.

As I stood there I found myself remembering one particular day, and it came up in my mind as fresh as if it had just happened. I had rolled over towards Kathy on the rug we had spread out on the sandy beach. There was just about room for both of us to stretch out, what with the towels, the beach ball, and the bag of picnic things, sandwiches, juice for the kids, and a flask of tea for Kathy and me. I pushed the stuff to one end and reached out for Kathy. I put my arms round her and kissed her, a long, long kiss. I remembered the happiness, the love, the desire I felt for her.

Something was tugging at me, spoiling the memory. I tried to block it, but the rest of the picture began to emerge, like a photo developing in the dish of fluid when I used to process my own snaps.

We'd kissed for a long time before Kathy began to wriggle free and try to sit up.

'You've been drinking again, Artie,' she murmured drowsily. She was still half asleep from the sun and the kissing.

Well, I had been, but so what? I didn't want her going on at me about it. Not that she did, all that much, in those days.

'Time the kids had something to eat,' she went on. 'Throw us over the bag, like a good love.'

I grabbed her again and kept her lying down, with my arms tight round her. The two of us were laughing, and the kiss this time was even better. But she pushed me away again.

'Maggie, Kevin, Dominic!' she said, as she sat up. 'Come and get your juice and sandwiches.'

Maggie and Kevin came bounding over, chucking down their buckets and spades – they'd been building a castle. The sand in the buckets went everywhere. They'd piled the castle high, digging spadefuls and scooping up bucketfuls until they had a great heap, and then they'd patted it smooth and made ramparts by filling the buckets and upending them carefully all around the upper rim. Maggie had gathered up ribbons of seaweed and shells and was busily decorating the castle, while Kevin dug happily with spade and fingers, excavating a moat that ran round the foot of the mound.

'Careful with that sand, yous'uns!'

'Where's wee Dominic?' asked Kathy sharply.

'Dunno, Mammy,' Maggie said. 'He went off with his bucket to get water for the moat.'

'You let him go off by himself to the sea?'

The note of fear in Kathy's voice pierced all of us.

'I'll go down after him, love.'

'We'll all go.'

We headed away down the beach to the water's edge. There were crowds of children paddling and splashing in the shallows, but no one who looked like Dominic. I set off grimly to follow the shoreline as far as I could in one direction, while Kathy and the kids went the other way.

Kathy was crying, and I wasn't far off it myself, if the truth be told. We'd read a story in the newspaper a few weeks ago about a child who'd drowned on a popular beach, just like this one. I reached the outcrop of high dark rocks that cut off the beach from the next bay. I was for turning back – surely the child couldn't have clambered over there, all the size of him – but then I heard something. A thin, keening sound, helpless and heartrending. I scrambled over, wading through the force of the hard waves that were spraying in and sending the white foam up in the air as they struck against the grey rocks coated in the green and brown of the seaweed, and there he was. He was lying spread out halfway up the ridge, and his right leg was stuck at a funny angle. I felt my heart leap up into my throat.

'Dom, love!' I pushed myself forward through the green, silky water and knelt down beside him on the slippery surface.

'I slipped, Daddy. My leg's sore.'

'It's all right, son. Daddy's got you.'

I grabbed him up trying not to hurt his leg any more, and started back, without giving him the good scold he well deserved.

It was heavy going. The waves pounded against my shins as I splashed through the water, trying to hold Dominic above their reach. Climbing over the rocks was no joke either. I pushed on, and found myself back on the hard-packed, damp sand at the edge of the sea where the tide swept in and out, dumping its cache of pebbles and shells as far up the beach as it could reach. I stumbled on, clasping Dom and hurrying to get back to Kathy. My head was starting to spin. Too much whiskey earlier, and too much stress in the last half-hour.

There was Kathy coming towards us, struggling across the dry, difficult sand further away from the shoreline. I tried to run to meet her. Suddenly I was on my knees, and Dominic had flown out of my arms. I saw him land on his head yards away. Then everything was a blur, and I was face down in the rough, stony sand, oblivious to the world around me.

I heard later that Kathy had got Dominic to the hospital with no help from me. The extra fall hadn't caused any more damage, but the jerk it gave to his leg had been painful enough to make him black out. People who saw what was happening flocked to help. Someone phoned for an ambulance, someone else carried Dominic to the promenade, and from there he was taken in a stretcher to the ambulance and the hospital. He had a broken leg, but was otherwise fine. 'No thanks to you,' Kathy said, but only once.

Nearly twenty years ago.

I don't know if Kathy ever rightly forgave me for it. There's no question it was my fault, drinking too much and getting randy, distracting us both from our rightful job of keeping an eye on our children.

Or maybe it was herself she was never able to forgive.

Somehow things were never the same afterwards.

Yes, we had some more good times. But Kathy was often cross and snappish with me, and more often than not she would put the children first, saying she didn't have a baby sitter when I wanted her to go out with me for a drink.

A long time ago, now.

The kids were grown up and gone, Kevin to Australia, Maggie (I must remember to call her Margaret) to Scotland, wee Dominic to Belfast. He was the nearest, but I seemed to see less of him than either of the others.

The June sun was still blinding me.

I twitched the curtain farther over, irritation in my movements. The room darkened now that the light was partly shut out. I glanced around. Everything looked much as it had when Kathy and I were first married. Dusty, now I came to think of it, but so what? Green and cream patterned carpet, pretty well the worse for wear after thirty years, big comfortable sofa in green tweed with two matching chairs. The photo of Kathy and me on our honeymoon, and the framed enlargement of a snap I'd taken of the kids when they were none of them very old, were still perched on top of the shelf I'd put up when we first moved in. The TV sat on a specially designed table with room for the video on the shelf below. Reception still wasn't too good, maybe it was time to get a new model, if I could ever put aside the money for it. Funny how the money disappeared so fast. As soon as the giro came in it was pretty well gone.

I threw myself down on the sofa, forgetting to watch out for the broken spring, and got up quickly again with a yelp as the end dug into me. Comfortable, did I call it? Maybe it was, at one time.

Instead of settling down to watch the rest of the racing, I found myself gravitating to the kitchen, to the wall cupboard.

The bottle was empty.

I couldn't remember finishing it, but I suppose it wasn't the mice.

Now the struggle.

To buy more? Or to have the sense to cut back a bit?

It didn't take me all that long to decide.

I sighed, patted my pocket to check that my wallet was still where it should be, opened the front door.

I had the key in my pocket as usual.

Okay.

My house was part of a wee Housing Executive estate on the outskirts of Bangor. A quiet enough area, except for Saturday nights, when the bottles were flying and the happy families were playing games. Many a night Kathy and me got woken up by the gulders of them. Three bedroom houses, most of them, with a bit of garden front and back, some of them with a good crop of dandelions and others with roses in the summer and daffodils earlier on, like ours. Well, mine, now. The dole paid the rent – otherwise I'd have had to move out a while back. There were a few flats, as well. Apartments, they'd starting calling them these days. The off-license was about a half-mile walk.

Good for me, the walk, wasn't it? Better to be out taking exercise than sitting in the house all day.

Yes, of course.

The giro had come in, so no problem there.

By habit, I changed into my work boots before leaving the house, though why, I couldn't have told you. It was several years now since I'd needed them – not since I'd been turfed out of my job.

I struck out across the grass behind my house. It was bright with daisies and buttercups, lit up by the sunshine, like sweet hopes for the future.

My feet in the thick boots crushed them as I walked.

Never saw any clover, these days. White and purple, there should be. Purple vetch, too.

Halfway across the stretch of grass there was the beginning of the pile for the bonfire. The kids had been collecting early. When I was a youngster, they didn't start until July.

There were piles of good pallets, like they would use on the building sites. How they got hold of them, I didn't know. Nicked them, likely. Valuable stuff, not just rubbish.

I knew all about pallets. Spent most of my working life shifting them about with the fork-lift, loading and unloading them when the lorries came and left.

Until I lost my licence, and the job with it.

Maybe if I hadn't had that fight with the foreman, they'd have given me some labouring work.

But he was a right git, deserved all the names I'd called him.

Ended up punching him in the face.

I'd been picked up for drunk driving a couple of months before. I'd not been that bad. Well, many's the time I'd been a lot worse, I can tell you. Been out for a few pints with my mates, Peter and Niall, ending up taking a bit more than I should, but the boys needed a lift home, and sure I wasn't going to leave them to walk. I wanted to do the decent thing by them. I'd dropped them both off and was heading back when this police car screeched to a halt in front of me, flashing its lights. Big Marty Rafferty got out and waved me down. I knew Marty – known him since we were kids, for heaven's sake – so it was a bit of a shock when he came the cop, acting like he didn't know me, him and his mate, and making me blow into the breathalyser. After that, it was just a matter of waiting till it came up in court, and there was my licence gone down the tubes, just like that.

I had to explain to them in work, of course. I told Barney O'Hanlon, the foreman, that I'd been doing a favour for my mates, running them home, and didn't he up and say, 'More fool you, Artie O'Donnell. You could have killed somebody, kids or old people or anyone, driving in that state, you gurt eedjit! Well,' he said, 'you'll not be able to take the forklift out on the road now to unload the lorries, you with no licence, so what use will you be to us, tell me that?'

What right had he to talk about my state?

I lost the rag, I don't deny, and punched out at him, and next moment he was flat on his back on the concrete and blood spurting out of his nose. Serve him right!

I grinned at the memory. Then wondered what was so funny about getting myself fired.

That was a long time ago, too.

Nothing to do with me, if the kids nicked the pallets for their bonfire. Served the bosses right.

The off-licence was open.

'Morning, Artie.'

'Morning, Kenny.'

The youngster behind the counter smiled at me. He was about twenty, neat looking, in a shirt and tie and good trousers, not like most kids his age, but maybe the company had a dress code. He had longish fair hair and a thin face with a lot of freckles. I counted him a friend. He was always cheerful, happy to see me, I thought.

Of course, I was a pretty regular customer. He'd need to look pleased.

I dismissed the thought.

'A bottle of your cheapest, Kenny,' I said.

'Whiskey, right? No problem, Artie.'

He took the tenner, winked at me, and got the change. 'Beautiful weather we're having, Artie. Reminds you of when you were my age, I bet. Right, Dad?'

'Yeah.'

'So you've told me many a time.'

I wasn't entirely sure how to take Kenny sometimes.

I grabbed the plastic bag and headed home again across the grass.

It was my evening for calling with Niall O'Hanlon and going to the *Horseshoe Arms* for a quick pint.

Niall gave me a funny look when he came to the door. Niall's been a good friend for a long time. Smaller than me by four or five inches, so he's about five eight or so, with mousy brown hair and a round sort of face, though he's not so fat in the body. I get on well with Niall. He respects me, always has done.

'Are you all right, Artie?'

'Never better, Niall.' I had tripped slightly over the step, but nobody would have noticed.

'Thing is, Artie, I've got a friend here with me ...'

'Sure, bring him along, Niall!' I said cheerfully. 'The more the merrier, right?'

'It's not a him, it's a her,' Niall said. He seemed a bit annoyed.

A good-looking wee red-haired woman appeared behind him in the doorway. 'What's up, Niall?'

Niall turned round and whispered to her.

Although I couldn't hear what he was saying, I heard her answer clear enough. 'Sure, there's no problem. We'll all go down the pub for a pint or two. No need to stay late, eh?'

I saw her give Niall's arm a squeeze. Then he turned round and grinned.

'Fair enough, Artie. We'll all go. But Bridie and me won't be staying late, right?'

We headed off down the road.

The pub was in walking distance. Just as well. Neither Niall nor me had a licence now.

There was noise and music coming from the open door. It was going to be a good evening.

I took a sideways look at this Bridie.

Quite a look of my Kathy, she had. Small, neat, cheerful, and the red hair. The way Kathy had looked, just before she ran off with her big American.

I didn't even know where she'd met him. Kept very quiet about it, but she must have been seeing him for a while. She left me a letter when she went, but I threw it in the fire as soon as I'd read it. All about the hell I'd put her through, and she couldn't take any more of it. How knowing Ryan had been the only thing keeping her going, and what a help and support he'd been to her. I nearly puked.

Four years ago, it must be. Just after wee Dominic moved up to Belfast.

I wondered suddenly if she'd been meaning to go for years. Just waited till the wee one had moved out and set up his own life.

It was a hard thought.

I turned my mind from it. 'What'll you have, Bridie?' I asked. 'Half pint? And a pint for you, Niall, my old mate?'

I went off to the bar. Better get a whiskey for myself. Didn't do to change your tipple halfway. Best make it a treble, in fact.

I could feel Bridie's eyes on my back. She fancied me, I could tell.

Sure, Niall was a good lad, but not one to get far with the women. He was my best friend, these days, I supposed.

Ever since that row with Peter McBride, a year or two ago.

Peter.

We'd been best mates since primary school.

What was it we'd fought about?

I couldn't even remember.

Maybe I could give him a ring sometime. See if we could make it up. I had a vague notion that I'd been slagging him off, just joking, like, telling him he should lose a bit of weight if he wanted the women to fancy him. I'd said something about Alma, his wife. She'd died a few years before that, cancer of the liver as far as I could remember it. I shouldn't have mentioned her, sure. I couldn't rightly remember just what I'd said. That if he'd not been such a ton weight maybe Alma'd have wanted sex with him more often while he still had her. Way out of line, okay. I could see it now.

And then before I knew it, he'd said something about Kathy and her big American, and I'd lashed out at him, and we'd been rolling about on the ground, punching each other out, until Peter caught himself on and scrambled to his feet and took off. I know I was left flat out on the ground for a good while. Passed out, I reckon. Some of the lads got me on my feet and started me off towards home, and I must have got there, because next I knew I was lying with my head on the bathroom floor in a pool of vomit. Not my best memory. I hadn't seen Peter since.

We'd met and got on great our very first day at primary school. I can well remember the times we had together, racing about the playground, pushing each other and laughing, doing each other's homework – I was always good at maths, and Peter could do stuff like learning dates for History – then mitching off school when we were a bit older.

There were times we went away up stream and tried our hands at a bit of fishing, not that we ever caught anything worth talking about. There was one great day, the sun was splitting the trees just like it was doing today, and we'd been out for hours without a bite. We'd each of us pinched some bread and cheese from home, and I'd nicked a few apples from old Flanagan's apple tree as we'd passed it earlier – I climbed up the wall, and lifted half a dozen or so from the branches that stuck out into the street, and dropped them for Peter to catch, so we weren't starving or anything.

But we'd our hearts set on having a fish for our lunch, cooking it over a wee fire if we could, and I tell you, I can still feel the jump my heart gave when there was a tug on the line and I knew we'd got something. Peter jumped into the water to help land it, and I kept pulling on the line hard, and we got it out on the bank. It was only a tiddler, when we got a proper look at it, but we were that proud and pleased. We'd matches with us, and it wasn't a problem to gather up a pile of bits of wood, and between us we got a good blaze going.

We stuck the fish on the end of a long thinnish bit of wood and took turns holding it over the fire till we couldn't bear waiting any longer. Then we broke it in two and ate it with our fingers. It was roasting hot, and we got the hands and the bakes half burnt off us, but it was great. We felt like *Swallows and Amazons*, or *Robin Hood*. I thought we'd always be friends.

Meanwhile, there was Niall. But he wasn't Peter.

I wouldn't want to say anything against Niall. But, sure, he'd never had the gift of the gab, like me. And as for his looks, he was an ugly sort of a critter, when all was said and done. Not one that the women would fancy.

I was just over fifty, okay, but I still had the pull.

I was in good form, that night, if I say it myself.

The two or three whiskeys in the afternoon had helped me. Or maybe it was four or five. Hard to keep track, sometimes.

'Well, Bridie,' I said jovially, 'it's not often I meet such a good-looking woman as yourself!'

She smiled.

Niall didn't seem so pleased, but he was always a bit of a sour one, come to think of it.

I ignored him, and went on talking to Bridie.

After a while, I got her up to dance.

She was a warm, cuddly bit of an armful. I pressed up close to her, enjoying myself.

Then Niall tapped me on the shoulder. 'My turn, Artie.'

I was in two minds about letting him away with it. I was sure Bridie didn't want to stop. But, there, another fight mightn't be the best idea. I went to sit down.

The room was swimming round a bit The heat, maybe, and the loud music.

Bridie and Niall came back to the table, and I pulled myself together. I started to tell funny stories. For once I found myself remembering them. Some of them were a bit blue, but I didn't think Bridie was the type to mind.

I edged closer to her along the seat, and after a while I put my hand on her knee, under the table, right, so Niall wouldn't see. I gave her a wee squeeze.

Then Niall got her up to dance again.

I sat on.

After a while, things began to get blurred. The room seemed brighter, but farther away. It seemed to me that they had come back, and Bridie sat up close to me, put her arms round me, and began to kiss me. Her hands were all over me. She put her leg over my thigh, twisting round to face me, rubbing herself against me. I responded eagerly.

'Ah, Kathy, baby,' I muttered. Which one was it? It seemed as if it was both of them.

Someone was shaking my shoulder.

I swam up out of my dream, and heard voices in the distance.

Then they got more distinct.

'I'm sorry, Bridie.' It was Niall's voice. 'Sorry I let you in for this. He used to be a decent mate.'

Then Bridie's voice. 'Sure, never worry, Niall, love. Dear help him, he's nothing to take seriously. Just a joke, so he is, nothing to worry about.'

I noticed that my head was on the table, resting on my arms.

I don't remember getting home, to tell you the truth. Niall must have helped me.

One thing I do remember, though.

When we came out of the pub, there were people singing on the far side of the road. There were about half a dozen of them, all young and dressed in jeans and casual jackets. Some of the guys had acoustic guitars. There were three girls, and about the same number of guys, maybe one or two more. One of the girls, the lead singer, had a voice so sweet it felt as if it was cutting into my heart, so deep I felt the pain. She was dark haired, pretty, but I couldn't take in much more, with the distance there was between me and them. I wanted to stop and listen, but there was a drag on both my arms, and I went with it.

'What a friend we have in Jesus,' they were singing.

I remembered it from years ago. Kathy picked it to sing at our wedding.

There was something urging me to stop, to listen. But the hands on my arm were forcing me to totter on. There was no strength left in me to resist them.

Next morning, when I woke up, I was lying on my sofa.

I didn't feel too good.

Kathy's chiming clock, striking, told me it was afternoon already.

I lay about until teatime, then made myself some baked beans on toast, and had a whiskey or two. After that I felt better.

I watched some television, had a few more drinks.

It helped me to forget the things I had heard when I came up out of my dream.

Which had been the dream, and which the reality? Bridie couldn't have said those things, could she?

Bridie had liked me, I was sure of it.

So why would she say what she had said?

A joke. I was just a joke.

I must have dreamt it.

It would have been near half-ten when the phone rang.

I got to it just in time, tripping over the carpet where there was a bit of a rip.

'Yeah?'

'Dad? Is that you?'

'Maggie? Is it yourself?'

'What? Dad, I can't make you out. Is that you?'

I pulled myself together. 'It's me, Maggie.'

"Just thought I'd give you a ring, Dad.'

'I'm here, Maggie.'

'What? Dad, you're mumbling. What did you say?'

'Maggie, I love you, my wee girl ...'

'Dad, you've been drinking – I thought you'd stopped!' Her voice sharpened.

'Just a bit, girl.'

'I can't make out a word you're saying. Oh, Dad, can't you get a grip on yourself?'

'Maggie, I didn't mean to ...'

Her voice grew even sharper. 'It's Margaret. Not Maggie. Margaret.'

'Sorry, Maggie.'

'You're useless, Dad. I wanted to talk to you tonight. But it's just useless if you're still on the booze, you old eedjit.'

The phone was slammed down at the other end.

I staggered back to the front room.

It seemed as if there was nothing I could do.

Next morning my head was sore.

I was still lying on the sofa. Hadn't made it to bed, last night.

What was I to do?

I didn't want to drink. Hair of the dog – yuk!

The idea revolted me.

Memories kept coming back.

Young Kenny laughing at me up his sleeve.

Niall looking angry. I suppose he didn't like the way I was getting off with his girl. Another friend on the way to being lost, was it?

Bridie calling me a joke.

But over and above all these, there was Maggie.

Of all my children, Maggie had always been the closest to me, maybe because she was a girl. I remembered her supporting me more than once when Kathy had been laying into me for the drinking. And many a time she'd turned to me for advice. Not recently, though.

What had I done?

She'd wanted to talk to me. But she'd rung off. Thought I was useless.

Had I lost her for good?

The song came back to me from last night.

'What a friend we have in Jesus,

All our sins and griefs to bear ...'

I stood up.

Made it into the kitchen.

Took the remains of the whiskey bottle from the cupboard, and poured it down the sink.

I felt better.

The day wore on.

About the middle of the afternoon, I thought I would phone Peter McBride.

'Are you there, Peter?'

'Yes, who is it?'

'It's me, Peter. Artie O'Donnell.'

I heard Peter draw breath sharply.

'What do you want?'

'Well, Peter ...'

'What?'

'I just thought ... You and me's been pals for a long time, Peter. It's a shame we never see each other these days ...'

'Artie, you know fine why we don't see each other. After that night, I told you I never wanted to have anything to do with you again!'

'Ah, Peter, if I spoke out of turn, I can only say I'm sorry ...'

'Artie, I put up with you for long enough, but it was just too much in the end. After the things you said to me that night, I reckoned we'd be better apart. It was you raising your fist to me that finally did it, you know that rightly. I walked out before I ended up beating the hell out of you. Spoke out of turn, did you? That's one way of putting it. Ah, don't remind me! It's the drink does it, Artie. Are you still drinking?'

I hesitated.

Do your friends despise, forsake you ...?

'Maybe not, Peter. I'm thinking about it.'

'Well, when you're doing more than think about it, you can ring me. Till then, I don't want to hear from you.'

Another phone slammed down.

It was a glorious day. The sun was blazing in through the window again.

I headed for the kitchen. After the way Peter had spoken to me, I really needed a drink.

It was only when I reached the cupboard that I remembered pouring the remains of the bottle down the sink.

Great.

Okay, wait, it had been the right decision.

If it wasn't there, I couldn't drink it.

I sat down again in front of the television, but after a few minutes I got up and began to wander round the room.

I couldn't seem to settle.

I'd be better out in the fresh air, I thought.

Maybe a short walk would be good for me.

But not to the off-licence, right? No sense in that.

Still and all, what harm did the occasional drink do, if it wasn't a matter of overdoing it?

Maybe if I just strolled up that direction, and made my mind up when I got there?

No harm in having a bottle available.

I didn't need to go overboard with it.

I could be a moderate drinker, for sure, like most people, if I just put my mind to it.

It was the overdoing it that was the problem.

I patted my pocket to make sure my wallet was there.

My key was in my pocket as usual.

I set out across the grass behind my house. It was bright with buttercups and daisies, lit up by the sun, like sweet hopes for the future.

My feet, in the heavy work boots, no longer any use to me, but still worn out of habit, crushed the flowers as I went on walking.

5 – Slipping

published in *Ulla's Nib* magazine, Belfast 2009 – a publication of the *Creative Writer's Network, Northern Ireland* – winning the Star Prize in that issue

Thin slivers of ice cracked underfoot in the puddles. Faint and tenuous, the moon slanted long fingers of light through the trees, to touch and illuminate stones slippery with frost. Anna shivered and pulled her thick woollen jacket more closely about her. She picked her way slowly and carefully, fearful that a slip would send her, without warning, over the edge of the narrow wooden bridge into the fiercely rushing stream below.

Her mind, victim of its own fantasies, thrust forward a vivid picture. Herself plunging sideways. The crack of the flimsy handrail as her weight struck against it.

The icy shock of the deep waters, seizing her, pulling her down. Her saturated clothes trapping her slight body, like chain mail or concrete –

'Stop!' she told herself sharply. 'You're not going to slip. Stop it, now.'

But the images in her mind were beyond her control.

Then she was over the bridge, and making her way quickly across the rough ploughed field.

Was someone following her? No, of course not. Imagination.

There was the barn. It loomed above her, dark and somehow threatening. But there was nothing to be afraid of. Dominic would be there, waiting for her.

She felt suddenly safe, uplifted even.

Dominic.

How strange to remember that it was less than a year since she had met him.

That evening at Dylan's pub. A Friday, the place buzzing. A young crowd, people with jobs, glad to see the weekend arriving, ready to kick up their heels and celebrate. The pub had been recently renovated, in a style that suited the old stone building with its slated grey roof and white-washed walls both inside and out.

71

There was an open fireplace with a roaring turf fire, very welcome on that cold October night, a long oval bar in the middle of the sizeable rectangular room. Mirrors lined the wall behind the bar at the far end of the room – Anna liked the reflection of the rows of bottles.

She was laughing and talking with Peggy, Mary and the rest of their crowd at a table near the fire when the tall, fair-haired young man came in with Kevin Doherty. The noise level rose as the musicians tuned up and began a lively reel. Anna noticed the newcomer staring at her across the crowded space. She felt herself blushing, even after she had turned her eyes away.

She had only looked at him for a few moments, but it seemed to her that she had taken in every detail of his appearance. Taller than the stocky Kevin, maybe six feet, well built, his muscles straining against the short sleeves of his white T-shirt, blue jeans encasing slim hips and legs. A tweed jacket slung casually over one shoulder, his finger hooked in the tab at the collar. His eyes were a startling blue in a face still tanned on that late October evening, although the sun had been on extended leave of absence.

Perhaps this was a man who travelled, who was not confined to this chilly northern country. His face was long and lean, already scored with a few lines, which spoke of action and experience, although Anna thought he couldn't be more than twenty-five or -six. Something about him – his self-possessed, confident air – had caused the eyes of every woman in the place to turn to him.

Then she heard Kevin's voice in her ear. 'It's yourself, Anna. Looking good, girl! This here's my mate, Dominic McBride.'

'Hi, there, Anna,' said Dominic softly.

'Hi.'

Anna was blushing again.

Dominic hooked out a chair with one foot and dropped into it easily.

'Can I buy you a drink, Anna?'

She found it only too easy to respond to his slightly crooked smile.

Now she remembered how Peggy and Mary had flirted with him for the rest of the evening. They were her friends. They must have seen the spark that had leapt between her and Dominic. But that hadn't stopped them. First one, then the other was vying for Dominic's attention. They laughed, joked, played with their hair ... Mary Carney, a thin-faced girl with crimson streaks in her otherwise dull brown hair, had a first-class figure. She had no boyfriend – but not, thought Anna, spitefully, for want of trying.

She'd watched Mary stroke Dominic McBride's arm, edging closer to him, making comments with an edge that were meant to be amusing.

Anna wasn't laughing.

As for Peggy Flaherty, she should have known better. Her boy-friend, Spike, was glaring at her across the table, as she leaned towards Dominic, giving him every opportunity to admire the curves displayed by her low-cut top. Finally Spike stood up, pushed his stool back, knocking it over, and said loudly, 'That's it! I'm away home!' He marched out, slamming the door behind him.

Peggy giggled. She knew she could whistle Spike back any time she chose.

Anna's anger grew. Peggy was her best friend. She had thought they really liked each other. She wanted to tear at Peggy's long dark hair, scratch her red cheeks, blacken her sparkling brown eyes. Until, when they were all saying goodbye, she found Dominic McBride's arm around her. 'Walk you home, Anna?'

That had been the start of it.

They had stopped at the old barn – where her father stored hay. It was some distance from farmhouse where the family lived. The white-washed building stood up against the blackness, looking somehow taller than it did by daylight. It loomed up from the night sky, outlined against the pale grey gloom, where the mountains were a hard black etching topped by a few stars and the remnant of a declining moon. Silhouetted pines swayed in the wind which beat them from the sea beneath the cliffs. Dominic pulled her closer. His body was warm against hers, his mouth urgent. Anna's legs felt weak.

Afterwards she had no clear memory of how it had happened or what he had said. They went inside the barn. She could smell hay, straw – and a feral animal scent. Then she was aware only of his strength, as his body pressed hers against the rough straw.

Afterwards, there were cigarettes. Anna took one from Dominic's hand, put it to her mouth, drew in the smoke. There was something strange about it.

'What is it? It's doesn't taste like ...'

'Weed. Try it.'

There was a floating sensation. She felt an immense peace. The dirty barn took on a luminous radiance, the hay sweet in her nostrils, the dark beams soaring overhead, like the arches of a cathedral, haunting and overwhelming in their exhilarating beauty. She could feel the roughness of each thread in Dominic's tweed jacket against her cheek.

She had wanted to stay there for ever.

Her father had been angry when at last she came home, still floating. 'You're late.' A respectable farmer, whose wife had left him some years back, Matthew MacPherson had strict rules for his only child. He was a sturdy hill farmer, short and stocky, like his own sheep, with the red, weathered face of a man who worked outside at all hours and in all seasons.

He had told Anna many times that, like his countrymen, he believed that a man should be master in his own home. He had grown up, he had said, with a strict set of rules, passed on to him by his own father, and he saw no good reason to abandon them. The new ideas and attitudes mystified him. He could see nothing good in them. Anna had tried to argue with him, but knew she was speaking to a stone wall.

'You're too like your mother. Running round, out till all hours ...'

Anna could only just remember her mother. She remembered angry voices, day after day. The child Anna had found them frightening. Alone in her bedroom, she burrowed under the blankets, trying to keep the noises out.

'I can't trust you an inch, ye bitch!' she heard her father shout. Anna wasn't used to hearing her father swear, even when he was fighting with her mother. This was a particularly bad quarrel, she could tell. 'As soon as you set eyes on a man, you're off flirting with him! Don't tell me you weren't making up to that fella this evening at your cousin's house – I saw you with my own eyes!'

'Michael Donnelly was being pleasant to me, that's all.' Her mother sounded furious. 'He's a good friend to me – and it would never be anything more if you'd treat me like a human being! I can't live like this much longer, Matthew, I'm warning you!'

Now Anna heard her mother weeping.

Much later, she came into the room and sat on the bed. Anna pretended to be asleep. Eyes tight shut, she felt a soft hand gently stroking her forehead.

'Anna.' There was a pause. Her mother sighed. 'I would have liked to explain to you. I can't stay with him any longer. And I can't take you with me tonight. I don't even know where I'll find a bed for myself. But I'll send for you as soon as I can, pet. I promise.'

Anna felt something wet fall on her face.

5 – Slipping

'I'll write to you and try to explain,' her mother said.

Anna felt her cheek warm to her mother's kiss. Then she heard her stand up.

A moment later the darkness was empty again.

There was no letter, explaining. There was no word from her mother, sending for her. There was only her father, kind enough in his own way, but retreating more and more into himself.

And the photograph.

Her father had thrown out all the photographs of her mother.

Anna had sneaked out to the bin and rooted frantically around until she found the only one that wasn't torn. She had washed off the rubbish and dried it carefully with her best silk blouse. Then she had hidden it under her mattress.

She took it out only when she was positive her father was far away in the fields, tending the cows or checking the wheat.

A beautiful woman, with delicate features and fair hair that flowed round her shoulders. Anna couldn't help seeing the resemblance whenever she looked in her mirror. Sometimes in her dreams, her mother came for her. But never in reality.

She had learned to say little while her father talked on, as now. She was still floating in her dream.

After that first night, she was careful to come home at a reasonable hour. Later she would slip out again.

How many times had she and Dom met now? She didn't know.

The heroin had come early in the relationship. She had been reluctant at first, influenced by the things she'd heard, but Dominic had laughed at her.

'Don't be daft, Anna. Time you tried the gear. It's great. Just like you, girl.'

Lying back on the straw, she had let him roll up her sleeve, press the needle into the vein in the crook of her elbow. A warm uplifting sensation flooded through her: the rush. She was detached from her body. Her feet and hands felt heavy. Time stretched. She rolled towards Dominic, overwhelmed by excitement, and pulled him close. She was powerful, a conqueror. Her mind was illuminated. She knew everything, could do anything.

'Dom, we've been here all night. I'll be in major trouble.' But she was on a high. It didn't matter.

Dom laughed. 'We've been here an hour, Anna.'

It seemed impossible.

The pattern had been established, had taken in new threads and colours.

The excitement of taking the money from her father's wallet, or from the locked drawer in the big oak desk in what he called the office. Stealing in quietly when he was asleep. The key was hidden on the shelf behind his notebooks. A few months ago, when he'd had flu, he had told her where to find it – she'd needed some housekeeping money. He had been unable to crawl out of bed to fetch it.

She remembered how he had muttered in his feverish sleep: 'Jamie ... Jamie...' Her mother's name. Over and over again.

And then the broken sentences. 'I've stopped, Jamie, I've stopped ... not like that any more ... please ...'

What had he stopped?

She didn't really care.

Her childish love for her father had evaporated.

It was exciting to poke around in the locked drawer, to find papers, sometimes, that he thought he had hidden.

Records.

Letters.

What she had found had turned Anna's feeling for her father into something near hatred.

Her mother had written. The bundle of letters, held together with an elastic band, began only months after the night she had left. There was a repeated theme: 'I want to have Anna. We can arrange to come for her'; 'Please, Matthew, let me have Anna. I have a home now, with Michael. He's a good man. If you'll divorce me, Michael and I want to get married'; 'Won't you let me have Anna? A girl needs her mother.' And letters addressed to her, too. Kind, loving letters, saying she wanted Anna to come to live with her. Asking Anna, as she got older, able to decide for herself, to come to live with her, to allow her mother and Michael to come to fetch her.

5 – Slipping

The letters had stopped two years earlier. Jamie had given up. Her final letter said that she and Michael planned to emigrate to Australia. There was no Australian letter, no new address.

Anna read them all. Then she went back to her room, and wept. Tears for what she had lost. Tears of anger against her father He had let his daughter think that her mother didn't love her. She realised dimly that he must love her in his own reticent way, saying nothing to her but wanting to keep her. It wasn't an excuse. His cruelty in hiding that her mother had written was unforgivable. Bitterness welled up inside Anna. He deserved anything she did to him. Taking his money wasn't enough.

He had never changed the hiding place for the key. Had he forgotten that she knew it? Anna thought he must have done. He usually kept money in the drawer, and never seemed to notice if some was missing. Dom needed money. He had no job.

The gear cost, he told her repeatedly. 'If you want it, you've got to help out, Anna.'

She didn't know, any longer, what she felt for him.

But only a few months into using it she was sure she needed the gear. The first rush, the high which followed, the feeling of power, of control, of understanding everything, being free, detached from pain and problems: she couldn't imagine living without all this.

There was the barn at last, cold and immense in the slanting moon-light. Anna went inside to wait. He was late.

She stood in the middle of the high, empty building, keeping away from the walls – rats might be scurrying through the straw. She never worried about them when Dom was there, but now she stood, shivering, hugging herself.

At last!

At the sound of his footsteps, she rushed towards the open door.

'Where have you been? What kept you?'

'Hush!' He slid in quietly, putting a finger to his lips. 'Don't make a sound. Someone might be listening.' He put his arms round her and drew her down on to the straw. All her fears disappeared.

Afterwards she handed him the money, and he gave her enough of the sweet brown sugar to last until she saw him again. At least, she hoped it was enough. The effect wore off so quickly now.

He seemed edgy, uneasy. 'Did anyone see you come?'

'No. What do you mean?' She stared at him, suddenly frightened again. 'Do you mean my father?'

'No.' He was impatient. 'I'm not worried about him. It's Red. He's gone crazy!' He stopped, and his face took on a strange expression.

He didn't mean to say that, Anna thought. It slipped out. Something he wasn't going to tell me.

He hesitated, then went on. 'Have you heard of Red Murphy?'

'The one who used to be in the IRA?

'They chucked him out. Then he came up here, up the coast. Don't know why he ended up in County Antrim. Now he's into drugs. Kevin told me he'd heard –'

'Heard what?'

'Oh, it's probably nothing. Just ... Kevin heard there's a word out on me. Red Murphy thinks this is his patch, right?'

'But you don't deal, Dom,' Anna said. It seemed important, all at once, to get that clear. 'You're only a user, like me.'

'Well ... A man has to get money somehow, Anna. I don't do all that much. But Murphy thinks ...' He trailed off again.

'Just be careful when you come here next,' he said eventually. He slipped quietly out of the barn.

She knew that she was always to wait for five minutes after he'd gone before she left. Dom had warned her to be careful they weren't seen together. Until now, she had thought it was because of her father.

They wouldn't meet again for three nights.

The days crawled for Anna. Her father was unusually surly. The work on the farm seemed more irksome than ever. She could only vaguely remember the time when the low white farm buildings and the old stone house, a storey higher, had seemed to her the most beautiful place on earth. Her home was set against green slopes rising to dark purple hills dotted with sheep. In spring the perky tails of new lambs stuck into the air as their owners bounded over the grass, full of youth and freedom.

Anna's sense of attachment to the place had dissipated like smoke in the wind. She would be glad when she could leave home. Dom had talked about it at first, how they could move in together, but it was months now since he had mentioned it.

Matthew MacPherson was unusual among the farmers of County Antrim in that he had some good pasture land, not just the rough hilly country suitable only for sheep, so he was able to keep some cows. It was one of Anna's jobs to get up early to help her father with the milking. Even with all the expensive new machinery, he and Peter, the cowman, couldn't manage on their own.

He was getting old, Anna realised.

So what?

Half dreaming, she stood in the milking shed manipulating the machinery while her father and Peter herded the cows in and began to take them through the process. Unthinkingly Anna pressed the wrong switch. Chaos.

'Careful!' roared her father.

He hurried over, sorted out the mess.

'More like your mother every day,' he muttered. 'Can't get anything right.'

Everything seemed unreal to Anna, as though it was hidden under a thick, insulating blanket. It was hard to care about anything in this unreal life.

That afternoon, she took out the Mini and drove over to see Peggy. Her father had given her the car on her eighteenth birthday, just six months before she met Dominic. It had been new – bright scarlet with a powerful engine, a built-in stereo and cream upholstery. No one else among her crowd of friends had anything halfway approaching it for style. Funny to think how pleased she had been, how grateful to her father. That was before his illness had given her access to her mother's letters.

She drove briskly across the hills. The narrow road, only just wide enough for cars, stretched across the high plateau covered with coarse grass, sturdy reeds and patches of purple heather. The sun was out, and Anna's spirits lifted. It was good to be in charge, to press her foot on the pedal and feel the mounting speed as she bucketed round bends and flashed past the woolly white sheep.

She enjoyed being with Peggy. They talked about Dominic, and about Peggy's boyfriend, Spike. Peggy and Spike had made it up long ago.

Anna had decided not to hold a grudge against Peggy for flirting with Dominic in the pub that night. It was good to be able to have some happy, normal talk. The days were too full of shifting, insubstantial thoughts and visions.

'You all right, girl? You seem sorta ... weird.'

'I'm fine, Peg. Just happy. Lit up.'

Sometimes she thought she was seeing things that weren't really there, hearing noises that intensified to screaming pitch, feeling presences she couldn't identify.

Presently Mary arrived.

Anna had never liked Mary as much as Peggy, but she was part of the scene. One of the gang.

'Are you still seeing Dominic?' Mary asked after a while.

'Yeah.' Anna tried to seem nonchalant, but inside she was exulting. Dominic! Everybody wanted him. But it was Anna who had him.

She decided to drive back by the coast road, alongside the Atlantic. It seemed a long time since she had been near to the sea. She could smell it before she came close, a sweet, sharp scent made up of seaweed and salt water. She pulled up, parked in a lay-by, and scrambled down to the beach. The surf pounded relentlessly against the shoreline, pushing forward then drawing back.

Further out the huge ocean waves gathered momentum, rising high, then crashing to the sand a few yards from Anna's feet. The water close to her was green and silken, trimmed with creamy lace. Anna slipped off her trainers and began to run, half in the sea and half on the hard-packed sand.

The sky had turned grey, like the deeper stretches of the ocean, harsh and threatening. Ahead the cliff surrounding the bay seemed to grow higher as she approached it, towering above her, a stained white hulk with a scarf of green grass thrown about its head. Sheets of golden whin bushes were just coming into bloom, setting the surrounding hills on fire. Sea birds flew in and out of their cliff-side nests, holes carved out by the wind storms for the black and white guillemots with their bright red beaks and the gulls that cried harshly as they swooped low, then flew ever up and out over the waters.

Anna focussed on one large grey and white gull as she ran. She wished fiercely that she could fly out over the ocean, fly forever – endlessly. Her head began to whirl. The blanket of mist that had hovered over her for days had lifted with the sharp sea air and the fresh wind that buffeted her face. Now it descended again, blotting out her surroundings with its thick, muffling odour of stale cupboards and unwashed clothes. She found herself tripping, then stumbling to a halt.

She raised her eyes to the gull again. Its wings spread wide, and it uttered a loud squawk. It flew defiantly, forcing itself into the wind.

Anna felt herself plucked up to fly, free, far above the vast ocean, cold and alone.

5 – Slipping

When she returned to herself, she staggered back to the car, picking up her trainers on the way. They were drenched by the waves, half buried in the sludgy sand. Anna turned the heater on as soon as she started the engine. She felt cold and frightened, not sure if she could drive home safely. It was a relief to reach the farm without incident. Even the rough voice of her father, wondering why his tea wasn't ready, was a welcome anchor to reality.

She took the last of the heroin that night before she went to bed.

Hours later, it seemed, she was in the depths of a vivid dream. She was on her way again to the barn, as she had been so many times recently. It was dark, except for a frail moon. She walked slowly, carefully, across the rough wooden bridge.

Her foot slipped, and as she grasped desperately at the handrail, she knew that someone was coming up behind her. She hung there, half over the edge. The footsteps grew louder.

They came nearer.

Then there was a thundering in her ears, a searing pain in her chest and she fell into the rushing, icy water. She had been shot. The water seeped into her clothes, turning them to concrete ...

Anna woke up.

It was some time before she dared to risk going back to sleep

Tonight she was to meet Dominic again.

In the morning the remnants of her dream clung round her like the ragged clothes of a diseased beggar, spreading the infection of fear. At intervals her whole body shook in shivering fits.

She went up to her room early, telling her father she was tired. She sat on the edge of the bed, waiting until she could escape from the house unheard.

Presently she heard her father's door close, heard his light click off.

Outside it was cold. There was frost on the ground again. Anna hurried along as fast as she dared, fearful of slipping. Suddenly she stopped and looked over her shoulder. She had heard something.

Or had she?

Nothing moved.

Anna went on again. There was no one there, she knew that.

Soon she could see the barn and hurried on. She gave a final shiver, as much of anticipation as of cold, as she stepped over the threshold.

At first she thought it was empty. Then she heard a groan – so weak that she almost missed it.

Anna moved slowly forward.

On the ground, over to the left.

A dark bundle.

Dominic was lying in a huddled mass, his eyes clenched shut, his arms clasping his chest. A dark mess oozed from a hole in the front of his jacket.

Blood.

'Dominic!'

He opened his eyes briefly. 'No – no! Don't!' Then he focussed on her face.

'Anna ...' he muttered. 'Go away ... quick ... It's not ... safe ...'

His head lolled back. Blood trickled from his mouth. His eyes closed. Anna put her ear to his lips. She couldn't hear him breathing.

She stood up. For a moment she remained where she was, dazed. Then she began to run.

Out of the barn.

Across the ploughed field.

Her breath came in gasps, and she heard someone say, over and over again, 'No! No!' It was only when she had almost crossed the field that she knew it was her own voice.

When she reached the bridge, frosty and dangerous, she slowed. Putting out shaky hands, she took hold of the fragile rail.

All at once she knew that someone was behind her.

Coming closer.

Footsteps, growing louder.

Anna knew what would happen next.

The shot. The searing pain in her chest.

The plunge over the edge of the bridge into the icy, drowning river below.

The water soaking into her clothes, turning them to concrete.

But this time there would be no waking.

6 – Ballystravey, 1988

Published by *Luciole Press*, California, 2009

Cool sandy grass patches, rough under her bare toes.

Pebbles.

Bits of broken shell that hurt a little.

That was how she remembered the place.

Mostly there was a cold wind, lifting the sand in skiffs round her feet.

Other times, she could remember the sun blazing hot on her shoulder-blades, and she capering about on the beach, flinging the big coloured beach ball for Daddy and young Tommy to catch. Sometimes her two older cousins, Olive and Markie, had joined in, too.

Piggy in the middle, that was what they'd played; she'd have been six or seven, maybe.

A dozen years ago. Near enough.

The beach didn't have a name, not that she knew of. But the town-land, and the nearest village, was Ballystravey. It wasn't too far from Belfast, just down the coast of Strangford Lough a bit. Sheila could see Scrabo Hill, with its single stone tower high above the dense green covering of whin bushes, which would be bright gold in the spring and summer.

As she watched, the tower was lit by an unexpected streak of sunlight. There were clouds floating behind it on this wintry day, only a few clouds, with the rest of the sky a pale fine blue, and the sharp fresh air that whipped against her cheeks was clear for miles around. If she turned her face towards the wind and looked in the other direction she could just glimpse the Mournes in the far distance, standing dark purple against the sky which paled from faint blue to white as it touched the horizon.

Waves splashed against the rocks that surrounded the little bay, their creamy froth scattering drops on the rough sand. Strands of green and brown seaweed trailed across the shoreline, making patterns wherever they went. Sheila could remember playing with the seaweed, popping the bobbles, using the long strands to decorate her sandcastles.

The fellas were late.

Sheila gave a shiver and pulled her denim jacket tighter. The wind was cold today. She jumped up and down, flapping her arms.

Last night it was cold outside the bank. Dark, too. If there was one thing she hated, had always hated, it was waiting around in the cold, and here she was doing it again today. Some girls wouldn't stand for it, and no wonder. If it had been anyone but Davy, she wouldn't be standing for it herself.

The bank was an old stone building, tall and elaborately Gothic, a Victorian creation far too impressively large for the small country town it dominated. Davy's friend Billy, he had told Sheila, knew a lot about breaking into banks. They needed money to buy explosives and guns. The other side had them, plenty of them. Time things were evened up, Davy said.

The break-in had been approved by higher up, who were keen to have money for more weapons. Billy would use his skills to get the side door open, and then the strong room, but he needed Davy to help carry stuff. Sheila's job was to stand guard outside and let them know if there was any sign of the cops.

The bank stood on the main square. It was a magnificent detached grey edifice with a high cornice running along the front above huge windows, carved with figures from Greek and Roman mythology. The great wooden front doors, brass hinges and locks looked, and probably were, impregnable – but a small dark alley with a tall fence on its other side ran down the left of the building. It led to a much smaller door where the bank staff left at the end of the working day, when the big front doors had been shut to customers.

'You stay out of sight inside this alleyway, Sheila,' Davy instructed her. 'If the cops come along, get back quick as you can and tell us. Don't be letting them see you, now – that would just attract their attention, the last thing we want. Got it?'

'Got it,' Sheila agreed. She wondered, not for the first time, why she had let herself in for this. But when Davy had talked to her, his words tumbling over each other, about 'the cause,' and the need for action, she'd found herself becoming equally excited and eager. It had seemed like a great adventure, but also like something important and right, which they had to do.

It had been Sheila's idea to use the cottage where Auntie Beattie had lived to store the money until it was safe to move it. It wasn't more than ten miles from the town. They'd agreed to make their way there separately this afternoon, Sheila by bus from Belfast, the fellas by car.

Not the one they had all travelled in last night – that had been dumped after they had dropped Sheila home. It would be easy enough to pick up another one. Or they could come on a different bus. Anyway, they were to meet up on the beach.

Her auntie's cottage was just up that loaning – Sheila turned her face away from the sea to look at the narrow sandy lane. It was years since she'd been there, not since Auntie Beattie had gone to Markie's in Australia after Uncle Jimmy'd died. Markie was Beattie's youngest, and always the pet, but it had been a surprise to the family when Beattie, so set in her ways, had taken off for the other side of the world.

The cottage had been sold. Sheila'd never heard who got it. She'd often thought of coming back to it someday. She'd had so many happy times there as a child. A little whitewashed stone building, with a roof of grey slates, and a bit of garden front and back, not very big by today's standards, but it had been big enough then for her grandparents to bring up four children.

There was a big kitchen downstairs, with an open fireplace where at one time most of the cooking had been done. The hobs were still there on either side of the fire, ready for someone to put on a kettle for tea or saucepan of spuds and swing out over the heat. But Sheila's grandmother had insisted on a proper stove, with an oven and gas rings, as soon as the gas connection reached Ballystravey. Daddy told Sheila he remembered it arriving when he was ten.

There were two rooms upstairs, crouching under exposed beams, one for Daddy's parents which had held a big double bed with a warm patchwork quilt, folded back in the summer, and a cot for the youngest child. The other room had another big double bed and a wee single, and this was where the three older children slept. To get into the double bed you had to crawl over the small one.

In summer, the heat under the beams made the rooms stifling, and in winter the family had sometimes had to throw their coats over the blankets for extra warmth – the cold penetrated everywhere. When the youngest brother, Albert, was too big for the cot, Beattie had moved downstairs to a truckle bed at the far end of the kitchen, where she complained that the light from the oil lamp on the table and the talk of the grown-ups kept her awake until all hours.

The toilet was at the far end of the garden, down a path that had seemed to the child Sheila to be miles long, twisting its way between the blackcurrant bushes and beans that grew on either side. Now the taste of blackcurrants reminded her of how she had hurried along that path, nipping berries from the bushes – in spite of warnings not to eat them: Auntie Beattie had wanted them for making jam.

Daddy had lived there with Beattie and their two younger brothers, until after their had parents died, when the two younger boys had had to go across the water to Liverpool to get jobs.

Daddy had landed on his feet with a job selling furniture in a big Belfast shop. He'd worked there for about thirty years, now, and been promoted to manager when Sheila was eight or nine. Beattie had lived on in the cottage at Ballystravey, and married Jimmy Thompson, the postman from down the road, who'd been courting her for years.

Sheila hadn't liked Jimmy all that much. He was a big, hearty man, red in the face, always cracking jokes about Catholics or worse, about women, which made Sheila embarrassed. She could remember once when she was nearly four she had stayed with Auntie Beattie for most of a week. She'd been told that Mammy wasn't well, and needed a bit of a rest, and that it would be a nice wee holiday for Sheila, and so it had been, apart from Jimmy.

She had been frightened of the loud-mouthed man who came home from his work to Auntie Beattie late in the afternoons. She'd run out of the house and hidden behind the old chestnut tree in the back garden when she'd heard him coming, squeezing herself down small to try to keep out of sight behind the scratchy tree trunk, until an angry Beattie as calling her in for her supper.

That was the only time Sheila had visited Auntie Beattie by herself, but the family – Daddy and Mammy, Sheila, and the new baby boy Mammy had got while Sheila had been in Ballystravey – often came for a family holiday in the summers that followed.

One summer there had been a heatwave.

Sheila came out into the garden before breakfast. She could feel the heat cutting into her.

There was a bee buzzing round one of Auntie Beattie's red roses.

Sheila stared at it. It was fatter than any bee she had ever seen.

It was bright, with black and yellow stripes. Pretty to look at. Sort of furry, maybe velvety.

Would it sting her if she didn't move away?

The roses were a deep, dark red. Crimson, that was called.

Sheila knew the colours from her school paint-box. The brighter red, like blood, was called scarlet.

The roses had a strong sweet smell. The heat made it stronger.

The bee started to move away from the flower, hovering in mid-air.

Sheila was frightened.

With a swift movement of her hand she knocked it to the ground and stamped on its body. When she lifted her foot in the brown strapped leather sandal and the short white ankle sock, the bee was still moving about. She had to stamp again and again before it was dead. Afterwards she felt sick, but when Mammy asked her why she didn't want any breakfast, she wouldn't tell her.

Bees were harmless, Daddy always said. It was wasps you needed to look out for. Wasps would sting you if they saw you anywhere near.

But a bee would leave you alone if you didn't touch it.

There were smooth round pebbles on the beach. Sheila picked one up and skimmed it across the surface of the water, counting the bounces the way she and Tommy used to do.

Six: that was pretty good.

'Sheila!'

There they were at last, running over the beach towards her, Davy and his friend Billy with the ginger hair and the squint in one eye that gave him a mean expression.

'What kept you?'

Davy spoke quickly, not answering the question, tripping over his words the way he always did.

'Come on, we haven't time to hang about. Have you got the key?'

'It's in my pocket.' She dug it out, handing it to him.

'Over this way. You'll have to hop the stream.'

They followed her over the sand, scuffling about and shoving each other like kids.

Davy was carrying the big sack. Sheila recognised it from last night: it had held most of the money they'd got away with. Billy had a battered leather satchel like a school bag.

'Up here.'

The loaning looked neglected. There were brambles and thistles which must have grown up in the years since she had been here last. No one had been cutting them back or keeping it trimmed, the way Daddy or Jimmy used to do. Sheila was glad she had her jeans on.

She caught her hand on a thorn and sucked at the scratch. It made her aware that there was an unfriendly feeling to the place, as if she was intruding, as if the cottage wanted to keep her out, to protect itself from her plans for it. This wasn't how she remembered the place. She had always been happy here. Was someone angry at what she was doing? How silly. But that was how it felt.

'Is it much further?'

'Just a step.'

The cottage seemed smaller than she remembered. The garden, gigantic in memory, was hardly more than a patch.

Sheila pushed open the gate, and Davy went in past her. He had the key out ready.

'Get in, quick, the both of you. Dear knows who might be passing any minute.'

The door creaked badly.

'Sit down on the floor, Sheila,' Davy ordered, 'and keep well out of sight of the windows, now. Billy and me's going down into the cellar to see where we can put this stuff. The less you know about it, the better.'

The floor was covered with dust. Auntie Beattie's big sofa and the two soft chairs were still there, looking faded and scruffy. There was no reason for Sheila to sit on the floor when there were chairs but she knew Davy was worked up so she sat on the floor to please him, and leaned back against one of the familiar armchairs.

She remembered Beattie sitting in the evenings, just before bedtime, in the one nearest the fire, with Uncle Jimmy on the other side of the hearth, his big feet stretched out to the heat. Mammy and Daddy would be on the sofa. Markie and Olive were sometimes outside, sometimes playing at the other end of the kitchen. Tommy had been put to bed earlier, but Sheila was allowed to stay up until a bit later.

She would sit quietly reading one of Auntie Beattie's books, books Beattie had had since her own childhood, *The Girls' Book of Heroines* and *Mattie Goes to Boarding School*. If she didn't interrupt the conversation, the grown-ups would forget about her. The words sort of drifted over her – but sometimes she listened rather than reading, the discussion grew heated, Then Uncle Jimmy and Auntie Beattie would talk about the Fenians. How they were taking over the place, and no one to stop them.

'Now, Beattie,' Mammy said in her soft voice, 'what harm have they ever done you?'

'Harm!' Beattie exploded. 'What harm, you're saying, and Dublin rule just round the corner! If we didn't have the big man to stand up to them, we'd be under the South long ago.'

Even Daddy, who didn't often say much, joined in with his sister. 'Beattie's right, Sadie. The country's in a bad way, and somebody needs to stand up to the Fenians before things is worse.'

Uncle Jimmy, his red face growing redder every minute, said, 'It's a terrible state of affairs when O'Neill's wanting to take the jobs away from honest working Protestant men and give them to the Taigs. They're doing their best to overrun us, the whole country knows that. Soon there'll be more of them than of us. I remember when I was a youngster there were only a handful of them living in Ballystravey, and now every second letter I deliver goes to a house with Taigs living in it that used to belong to decent Protestant folk.'

'I'd never trust one of them,' Auntie Beattie put in vigorously. 'Their eyes is set too close together, you can tell one just by looking at them. It's a sign that they're out to deceive the rest of us, so it is.'

'Some of them are all right, now,' interposed Daddy. 'I'd some good friends who were Catholics when I was growing up here, Jimmy. Still and all, you can't trust most of them. They never wanted this country, ever since it was set up, and they've been trying to take it over for years now. At the end of the day, a Taig's still a Taig.'

'Hush, Tommy!' Mammy said sharply. 'Don't use words like that. Sheila, it's past your bedtime.'

Sheila was puzzled. Why did Mammy not want her to hear? Sure at school everybody said those sort of things all the time. Even the teachers, when they were in a good mood and ready for a chat, on a Friday afternoon when all the sums were done.

Mr Magilligan, Sheila's teacher, used to tell them stories about times in the past when the Troubles were going on, back in the twenties. The boys were expert at starting him off, with a question or two, and sometimes he'd go on for ages and forget about the lessons they were supposed to be doing. History, it counted as, and even Mr Magilligan – or Shorty, as they called him behind his back – didn't remember it, but his dad had told him about it. There'd been shooting in the streets of Belfast, he said. That was hard to believe.

'And if it ever comes to that again, boys and girls,' Shorty used to say solemnly, 'I hope you'll all be brave enough to stand up for your country and not let it be overrun by those whose dearest wish is to destroy it. Things aren't looking too good right now. If we had a few more people like the good doctor to tell the truth in the circles where it needs to be heard, it might help.'

Shorty never talked outright about Taigs or Fenians, like Auntie Beattie, but everybody knew that was what he meant. Some of the other teachers, like Miss Kilmaine – known as Meany – who took them for singing, would come right out and talk about the dreadful things that would happen if we let the Fenians take control of the country.

Everybody knew it was the truth, so what was the use of Mammy saying it wasn't?

A few years later, when Sheila had moved on to big school, it began to happen, all the things she'd heard the grown-ups warning each other about, but never doing anything to stop. Shooting in the streets, and bombing. Why did they talk so much about it, and then let it happen?

In the big school, Davy Craig sat behind her in class. Sheila thought he was very good looking. He had dark hair and grey-green eyes, that held a reckless look: it said there was nothing much he would stop at. Sheila fell for him straight away. Often he would pull her hair. Sheila didn't mind, but sometimes it hurt.

One time she couldn't help squealing.

The teacher came down to see what had happened.

'I gave my finger a nip in the desk,' Sheila lied.

Davy had been pleased with her. She was on her way home from school when she heard him calling her from behind the three bombed houses up the street. 'Sheila! Would you like a drag?'

It was her first taste of a cigarette. Only for it being Davy that was giving it to her, Sheila wouldn't have been that keen.

After that, the girls teased her about going with Davy Craig. Most of them fancied him, but it was always Sheila whose hair he pulled, whose scarf he nicked in the playground, Sheila who shared his cigarettes.

Mammy and Daddy didn't know anything about it – not for years. Sheila was well on at the grammar school, and going with Davy properly, before they ever heard about him. They were neither of them too pleased. 'A clever girl like you, who's passed your eleven-plus and all!' Mammy had grumbled. 'I don't know what you see in that eedjit.'

'Davy passed his eleven-plus, too. He's just as clever as me.'

'But he doesn't do well at school, from what I hear. Doesn't bother to work at it. Thinks he can sail through without trying. He'll be leaving school when he's sixteen and ending up on the dole, you mark my words.'

She had been right but that wasn't Davy's fault.

He couldn't make a job for himself when there were none, could he?

Daddy hadn't been pleased either.

'I don't trust that fella an inch,' he said. 'You look out for yourself, Sheila. He'll come to no good, and you with him, if you don't watch out.'

They'd been glad when Sheila and Davy lost touch, when he went off to England looking a job.

Sheila had been working hard for her A-levels by then, and kept herself busy.

Then there had been the excitement of starting Queen's.

Davy had been far from her thoughts the day she bumped into him again, coming up Royal Avenue.

They went into McDonald's and Davy bought her a milkshake. They sat side by side on the tall stools, and when Sheila glanced at him she found that he was staring at her. She felt her face going red, and quickly asked him what he had been doing. He didn't say much.

It was strange to see him back.

'Hey, do you know something? I've missed you, funny face,' he said after a bit. Sheila waited for him to say more, but instead he began to talk about the country. The state it was in. 'That's why I've come back. It's time somebody did something, Sheila!'

He sounded a bit like Auntie Beattie, but Sheila knew better than to say so.

'You remember Morris Skinner and them boys at school? They had the right idea.'

'Morris Skinner's in the Maze.'

'But at least he did something! I tell you, Sheila, I can't bear any more to sit and watch it.'

Sheila looked at him. His dark hair falling over the white face. His eyes bright.

'I'll say no more now. But I can count on you, Sheila, can't I?'

Yes, he'd always be able to count on Sheila, that was a certainty. That was why she was sitting on the floor of Auntie Beattie's cottage now.

A draught blew up the cellar stairs from the open door. Sheila shivered.

It was cold enough inside to skin you. She was getting dust all over her new jeans, too.

Davy was shouting something, but she couldn't hear what it was. He was likely talking to Billy, anyway.

Last night, at the bank, he had shouted out every now and then. Each time she had thought it was for her, and gone running up the alley to the door, but it had always turned out that it was for Billy. To help lift something heavy. To hold the torch so Davy could see what he was doing.

It had been a waste of time her being there, she'd grumbled afterwards, but Davy would have none of it. 'Sure, we needed a look-out, didn't we? If the fuzz came just when Billy and me were coming out with the money, where would we be now? In the Crumlin, wouldn't we?'

He was worried. He needed somewhere to put the money, he said, until the boys got word to him about where to deliver it.

Auntie Beattie's cottage had been a great idea.

'You're sure it's sitting empty?'

Sheila was sure. Mammy had been talking just the other night about the shame it was, such a waste. She still had the key in the top drawer of her dressing-table. But it would be dishonest to go down there when it wasn't even in the family now.

Sheila had felt a bit mean, sneaking into Mammy's room and taking the key when Mammy was out doing the shopping. She wouldn't have done it for herself. But doing it for Davy was different.

Feet clattered on the cellar stairs.

' Okay! Job done!'

Sheila couldn't remember seeing Davy in such tearing high spirits before. Usually he was serious-minded, moody even.

'Come on, let's get out of here!'

Billy spoke – for the first time to Sheila's knowledge: 'Sooner the better – don't want anyone to see us here with them weapons.'

Davy grabbed her arm, and hustled them all out of the door.

'What does he mean, weapons?' she asked. 'It's only money, isn't it? Or did you buy some stuff with it already?'

Davy laughed.

'Sure, when would we have had the time for that?'

Last night, after I went on home, and you and Billy went somewhere else with the money, Sheila thought, but she said nothing. She shivered. Davy couldn't really be planning to shoot someone, could he? Or maybe the guns were for Billy. It occurred to her that even if Davy and Billy didn't fire the weapons themselves, they'd got them for people who would have no hesitation in using them.

'Come on!' said Davy.

He almost ran her down the lane to the beach.

'Sheila, you make your own way back like we said. Don't want you to be seen with wild boyos like me and Billy here!' He put his arm round her and gave her a quick kiss. 'I'll give you a ring later.'

Then he was away racing across the beach.

The news was always on at night, in Sheila's house. She didn't listen to it much. It was always the same.

It was the next Thursday night, that young Tommy said, 'Another bloody Taig shot. Good riddance!'

Tommy had been bitter since he'd lost his leg in the bomb at the *Horseshoe* pub. He hadn't even been inside, still far too young for that, just passing by too close at the wrong moment. Two years ago, now, but he couldn't get over it.

Mammy didn't tell him off, the way she would have done once. 'Whereabouts?' was all she said.

'Ballystravey. That's not far from thon cottage my auntie Beattie used to have, right, Ma?'

'Ballystravey was the nearest town to your auntie's. We used to have some quare good times down there, before she flitted. D'you mind the time your daddy fell into the river trying to land a trout? I must tell him when he comes in from the pub. He'd maybe know the fella that's shot, with coming from those parts himself.'

Daddy knew him, sure enough.

'Kevin Bradley? You're joking me! Sure, him and me used to hang around together – before I came up to Belfast, that is. You wouldn't know him, Sadie. It was before you and me got acquainted.' He sat down heavily in the nearest chair and started to take his shoes off. Then he paused with one still on.

'I thought you might know him,' Mammy said.

Daddy went on talking, shoes temporarily forgotten, and Sheila listened. There was an expression of horror on her father's face as the reality sank in.

'So Kevin's been shot, is it? Well, well! Many's the game of footer Kevin and me had. He was a great goalie. A harmless crater. Coulda played for a team, I'd a thought. What would anyone go shooting Kevin for? He never did anyone any harm. What's this country coming to, can anyone tell me, when the likes of that can happen?'

Sheila had nightmares that night, worse than any time since Tommy lost his leg.

It began with a bee coming for her face, and getting larger until it seemed about to smother her.

And there was a noise like a loud explosion, and her father's voice in the background, saying over and over again, 'Harmless! Harmless!'

And through it all, the heavy scent of roses, and their soft scarlet petals showering over her head and face.

'But they're the wrong colour! The wrong colour!'

'Sheila! Sheila, petsie, what is it?'

'What?' Sheila sat bolt upright in her bed. Her face was drained of colour by the harsh electric light.

'You were having a nightmare, pet. What's wrong, my lamb?'

But Sheila only stared at her, and said nothing. Presently she began to cry. 'I can't tell you, Mammy. I can't ever tell you.'

7 – Stevie's Luck

Shortlisted for the *Brian Moore Award*, Belfast 2008 and for the *Cúirt Award*, Galway 2010 – published in the *Bridge House* anthology, *Crime After Crime*

Okay if I sit here, mate?

Ta.

Nice quiet place this, I like it. Fuller than usual tonight, or I wouldn't butt in like this, see?

Buy you a round?

Ach, no problem, lager is it?

Bit quieter than the dive I was in a few weeks ago. Fights breaking out all the time, so they tell me. There was a bad row even the once I was there, I'm telling you.

Bad.

I missed out on the worst of it, I'm glad to say.

Let me tell you about it. Don't mind, do you?

Don't usually go to this Drummond place – like I say it's a bit of a dive, never know what might be happening, bad stuff, maybe. It was Marie wanted to go – my usual's the King's Head, a bit more upmarket, but Marie says the Happy Hour in the Drummond's real good value so, hey, I goes along with it.

Place is jumpin' when we gets there, Thursday night. Wouldn't expect it, but maybe news about this Happy Hour stuff's got around. They've done it up since I was last there, lotta red paint, hanging baskets, coupla tables outside – like, who's going to sit there more than a coupla days a year in our climate? Oh, right, it's for the smokers, isn't it?

You see them outside all the pubs now, shivering and smoking away, must think it's worth it. I'll smoke outside on a fine night, but not the sorta weather some of them put up with. The flowers in the hanging baskets inside are a bit droopy – not getting watered much, I'd bet. You need to look after flowers, water them enough and not too much. Nobody gets it right. That's the sort of thing I care about. I'm sensitive, me.

I used to look after the flowers and plants when I was a kid. Mum never bothered, or she'd drown them and they'd be dead in a day or two. I told her not to do it after a while. I took care of them.

Mum wasn't much good at any practical stuff, come to that. She was a lovely woman, not very tall, slim, delicate sorta girl. I've got some snaps of her here, you wanna see? Lovely, right? Coulda gone on the films, I used to think. She and me got on fine, especially when I was a kid. She was a popular lady, always some fella or other chasing after her, but none of them mattered to her like I did, or that's how it seemed to me, right?

Sometimes one or other of them'd move in for a while. I didn't mind, long as he didn't cause me no pain. She kept them in line, made sure they behaved. One guy, I'll never forget him, he was called Bernie – he lifted his hand to me one day when I'd been giving him a bit of cheek, called him a baldy ould git, as I remember it. Well, Mum was down on him like a ton of bricks, and he was outa the house, bag and baggage, the same afternoon. That's what she was like.

Money? Well, I don't know, she managed okay, never seemed to be short, don't really know where it came from. The dole, I reckon, and maybe my da sent her some from time to time. It wouldn't have been anything else, see, if that's what you're getting at!

She changed a bit as I got older. Stopped being so protective. But there weren't so many of the men after her by that time. She was getting a bit rough looking, tell you the truth, by the time I was sixteen or so. Musta been all the drinking. Lines on her face. Hair needing touched up, and she often didn't bother, so the grey was starting to show every now and then.

Couldn't seem to talk to her any more, way we used to. She'd get angry, right out of the blue sometimes, and turn on me. She was the only one I could trust from when I was a kid, and then I couldn't trust her either. I moved out a year or two after that. Hey, sad story, right?

My da? I dunno where he was. Don't even remember what he looks like. Only what Mum used to say. Saw him just two or three times, when I was the size of sixpence.

Mum said we were well rid of him.

Okay, so here we are in the Drummond, Marie and me.

Marie's looking all about, seems to be expecting someone. She's dressed up real nice, short, narrow skirt, lots of eyeliner, fluffy blonde hair pulled up on top of her head and a few curls hanging down on her smooth neck that's all brown from the sun, and this sharp, spicy perfume. Top so low cut you could see gleams of white flesh where the suntan ended. Maybe she'd like me to tell her it makes me fancy her, but, hey, it's not good for chicks to think they've got you going. Gives them a big head, makes them think they can push you about.

I wasn't looking bad myself, mind. I'm not all that tall, but so what? I look a bit like Sinatra, the chicks tell me, before he got old and wrinkly, in the first pictures he made – you see them sometimes on the late night movies on the telly, or you get them on DVD – slim figure, thin bony face, smooth good looks. When all the chicks were howling for him, right? Not saying they're all howling for me, but I get my share, see?

Mum used to say I looked the image of my da.

Before she went into the home, that was. When she could say anything that made sense. She came round to see me one day, maybe ten years ago now, and started ranting and raving and threatening me. Seemed to think I was my da. Didn't recognise me. Didn't talk any sense. End of it was I had to call the doctor, and he said she needed to go into an institution, for her own safety. Not to mention mine – the look in her eye when she started shouting at me and lifting the kitchen knife and coming at me, well, I had to get out quick, I'm telling you. Nothing else for it.

Senile dementia, they called it.

But she wasn't that old.

I always remember her the way she used to be, when I was a kid, when she made a fuss of me and told me how handsome I was, just like my da. Showed me a photo of him once, but when I asked to see it again, she'd burnt it, she said. When I try to picture it, all I get is Frank Sinatra in his younger days. But I reckon that should be close enough.

I like to dress right for the look, dark shirt with the turned-down collar and a real smooth light-coloured tie, blue to show up my eyes, see?

So, when Marie started looking all round, I says to her, 'Hey, what's up, babe?' Not that I was really that worried, but you gotta make an effort, make them think you're interested, it's half the battle.

'Nothing,' she says. She gives me a look, and I squeeze her bare knee under the table, and I can see I've got her going, right? Then she says, 'See Porky anywhere?'

I don't. Don't want to.

'How would I know where Porky is?' I says.

'Thought you were talking to him on the phone the other day?'

'Hey, that wasn't Porky,' I said. I laughed. 'You've got Porky on the brain, kid! Waiting for your next fix, right! You mustn'ta heard me right. That was my bookie!'

'Oh, right,' she says. 'Just, I was hoping to see him. I've got the cash for some gear,' she couldn't help telling me, though she knows I don't like that sort of stuff.

I'm getting sick of sitting there without a glass in front of me.

'Buy me a drink,' I says.

She's still looking all ways, like, but she heads off up to the bar

That's what chicks are for, right?

Totally.

Porky, I have to tell you, is a guy I can do without. Full of shit, okay? In both senses. See me, I'm not into all that stuff. The odd bit of blow, yeah, but the gear, like, that's another whole bag of trouble. Not for me.

What Marie does is her own funeral. Totally.

Hey, that wasn't a bad sort of joke, right?

He does other stuff, Porky, beats people up to order, I'm told, but that's not something I'd have anything to do with, either, right? Gotta look after yourself, keep clear of all that stuff, right. I look after myself, always have done. Nobody else's going to do it.

So I'm waiting for Marie to get back over with my drink, when this fella comes up to me. 'Stevie McCartney?' he says.

I give him a look.

'You owe me big-time,' he says.

I know who he is. Joe Murphy, from the bookie's.

Big red-faced guy with a crooked nose. Used to do some boxing.

So I know he's been waiting to collect from me for the past month on account of I missed out on last month's payment, but what I don't know is how he knew to look for me in the *Drummond*, which is like a dump I never go to, and I was starting to wonder about Marie, but, hey, she wouldn't squeal on me, not Marie.

She comes back then with the booze and I can see they know each other.

'Joe.'

'Marie Bas. Hi, babe. Good to see ya.'

It makes me wonder again.

I grabs the drink, and, what about it? It's lager.

So I bangs it back down on the table, so's a big gollup of it spills. Makes a bright goldy sort of pool on the tabletop. 'I don't drink that muck, Marie,' I says, keeping my voice calm. 'You know that rightly. Bacardi. Tequila. Either. Even a good vodka. Not lager.'

What's that, mate? Oh, right, yeah, a tequila'd be great. Ta.

Good stuff, that. Thanks. Feel like I need something tonight, don't know why. Just need a bit of comfort, sort of.

Right, so, where was I?

Marie was looking upset. 'Stevie, maybe just this once – it's a promo offer, see? Quid a pint.'

I just gives her a look.

'Stevie I've only got the money for Porky, and I need it bad. Till the giro comes in. You know. I gotta have the stuff regular. I can't ...' She trails off and tries smiling at me.

Joe, the ignorant git, interrupts: 'Talking about money, Stevie Wonder,' he says with a big ugly grin on his chops.

'All right, all right,' I says. 'You'll get your money. End of the month. Swear it.'

Joe grabs me by the front of my shirt, drags me up on my feet, bangs my legs against the edge of the table, not that he cares less. He's some size, the boyo. 'Know what, rat face? Not the end of the month. Now. Or it'll be too bad for you. I'll have to tell big Shamie you've been a naughty boy, see?'

If you think Joe's a big one, you oughta see big Shamie. My teeth's starting to chatter and my legs is wobbling and I feel sorta sick.

There's people all around, lined along the bar, crowded into booths, standing about with their glasses in their hands. And nobody paying no heed. They turn away, look into their drinks, talk all the louder, laughing about nothing. I could be dead in a second or two for all they care.

Marie grabs Joe by the arm. 'Let him go, you bully, you! He hasn't got no money! You can't hurt him! You said –'

'Hasn't got no money, you're telling me? Then,' says Joe, leering at her, 'I just wouldn't like to tell you what's gonna happen to him, babe. Not the kinda stuff to say to a lady like you, see.'

Marie bursts into tears. Then she starts scrabbling in her handbag.

I can't see too well what she's doing, with the way Joe has my shirt scrunched up round my neck so's I can't hardly breathe, but I can sorta see, out of the corner of my eye, right, that she's taking something out of her bag, a white envelope, maybe. 'Here!' she says, and she pushes it at him. 'There's that fifty quid in there. You know. All I got. Leave Stevie be. Give him a chance to get the rest of it together, okay?'

'Chicken feed! His bill's in thousands!' says Joe. Then he looks at her and he musta changed his mind. Fancies her a bit, maybe. 'Okay, babe,' Joe says. 'End of the week, right? Not any longer!' And he drops me back into my seat, looking sorta contemptuous, like, and brushes off his hands. As if he wants to get rid of the feel of me. 'Don't know what you see in this dirty wee squirt, Marie. A right lump of scum,' he says. 'You can do a lot better for yourself.' And he walks away.

So then Marie throws her arms round me and she's all huggin' me, like, till I has to say, 'Whoa, whoa, girl! Everybody's looking.'

They were, too. Voyeurism, it's called. Anything sexy, they're avid, especially one fat git staring down Marie's top. But, hey, if someone looks like getting beaten up, that's another story, right? Time to look away. And I'm wondering about the stuff going on between Marie and Joe Murphy. How would she think he should know she has fifty quid? And what's with the 'You can't hurt him! You said ...' bit? And I was starting to wonder if Joe'd given her the fifty quid to tell him where he'd find me.

Still and all, she's done a really nice thing, hasn't she, giving Joe her drug money to help me? So I says, 'How's about getting outa here, babe?' and I takes her hand and moves her outside, round the back alley, and I let her kiss me.

The half-moon was out by then, and a star or two twinkling in the navy blue sky, and there was just a sweet warm summer breeze touching our cheeks and lifting Marie's hair enough to make it look like – what's that stuff? – gossamer, and the smell of the creamy honeysuckle and the pink roses in the hanging baskets, and Marie's own scent, sort of spicy and Oriental, and it was really getting to me.

And, I'm telling you, I couldn't help feeling a bit of a stir when I looks down at her with her arms tight round me and putting everything she has into the kiss, and half her acid green top dragged off with the action, like, and I thinks, *Hey, guess what, maybe I could do worse.*

Never reckoned on a live-in girlfriend, and still don't want one, but maybe Marie and me could see a bit more of each other. I knew she'd been wanting to. Things she'd said. Maybe it was time I rethought our relationship. I hadn't thought she cared all that much about me, compared to the drugs, hadn't thought I could trust her – well, you can't trust any-one, can you, specially druggies on H? But maybe I'd got her wrong.

And, hey, if she'd been up to something with Big Joe, sure, she didn't want anybody but me, now, did she?

Then she opens her eyes and looks right up at me, her mouth still fastened on mine. She's smallish, right, Marie, and her body just fits good against me, and I could feel her all the way down pressing close against me, and I have to tell you, honest, I felt my legs go all trembling.

It was, like, something special, see?

Hey, what's this, another tequila? Hey, it's my round, mate. Well, okay then, if that's the way you really want it. Cheers, mate!

Any road, we goes on snogging for a bit, and then I goes, 'Okay, babe, let's do it!' But funny, she pulls back and says, 'Hey, wait a minute, Stevie, I gotta go to the bogs,' so I acts cool, though I'm, like, ready enough. I steps back and I says, 'Don't be long, babes,' and I gets out a fag and lights up while she skips off.

And that's where I might feel a bit guilty if I wanted to, right, because if I hadn't let her go back in there, it would have been different.

But, hey, what else could I do?

I stood there and leant against the whitewashed stone wall and smoked, and I wondered again about Joe Murphy. And about Marie and Porky.

So the fag's about done, but I'm not, like – get me? – and there's no sign of her coming back. I'm starting to wonder what's keeping her, when I hears this racket going on inside.

I goes over to the back door of the pub, with its new bright red paint, and I open it a bit, thinking, like, It'll be a gas to see what sorta fight's going on.

It's not that easy to see, what with all the guys crowding round, but there's Marie, right in the middle of it.

I open the door a bit further, but I make sure to keep well behind it. Out of sight, like. I could see big Porky. I nearly yelled out at him, but I got myself stopped in time. He's a huge guy, hard to miss.

Hard fat, they call it. Muscles as well as bulk, see? And his ginger hair shaved to nothing.

I never liked him. Ex-para military, heavy into the drug scene these days. Not the only one, like. Trouble, for sure. A man to keep away from. But Marie hasn't the sense to do that.

What – you going, mate? Oh, just heading up to the bar, right? Yeah, I'll stick with the tequila, ta.

Where was I? Yeah, Porky's useful in a sort of way, see? Useful to Marie, I mean. Any road, he has the drug franchise, like, for round here. Doesn't bother me. I don't need him. I keep clear. Like I told you, I don't go for the hard stuff.

He's standing there with his hands on his hips like some oul' targe of a woman, his face stuck forward with a glare in his eyes I wouldn't want aimed at me. He's yelling at Marie.

And give it to her, the girl, she's yelling right back at him. Up close and personal, as they say.

'You owe me!' Porky yells.

'Only one bag!' Marie yells. 'Peanuts!'

'Can't do business that way,' Porky grunts. 'Pay on the nail, that's how it goes. If you want some now, you pay up front, right?'

'So I don't have the cash, okay?' yells Marie back at him. 'Whatta you want from me, tell me that? Blood?'

Funny her saying that.

I knew rightly she'd spent her last, paying Joe off for me, and it sorta crosses my mind I should maybe give Porky the twenty-five she owes him. Maybe I should help her out this time. But sure, what difference would it make? She could manage without it for once, right? Do her good! She shouldn't be so hooked on the stuff!

Anyway, I don't want to talk to Big Porky at all. I'd rather just have nothing to do with him.

I've my hand in my pocket, fidgeting about with the roll I won on the scratch card Wednesday, coupla hundred, but I've got plans for that. Horse called *Stevie's Luck*, couldn't lose, a name like that. Mind, I wasn't far off giving it to Joe earlier on, when he was near choking me. Would have if Marie hadn't jumped in.

I'm trying to make up my mind, when the real trouble starts. Billy Moore and three or four of his heavies comes into the pub. You know Billy, right?

Got out on the *Good Friday Agreement*, and kept away from the political stuff. Went for the drug-dealing instead.

A wee shrimp of a man himself, with the wedgie heels on his cowboy boots to give him more of a height. Not just small enough to be in a circus. But the boys with him makes up for it okay.

7 – Stevie's Luck

Another round? Thanks, mate! Like, I'm real chuffed to get talking to you tonight, mate. I sorta felt like I needed someone to talk to. A good listener, right? Anybody ever tell you you're a good listener, mate? Make a person feel like you're really interested, see? Hey, I must be getting a bit bluithered here – listen to me getting all sentimental.

So, Billy Moore and his heavies come into the bar, right?

He was looking for Porky, I heard after. Porky'd been muscling in on Billy's territory, it seems. Not happy enough with his own patch, the big eedjit. Billy and the boys were here to teach him a lesson.

Well, that's what they do, everybody knows that. If Porky'd been cheating on Billy, he was asking for it.

'Hey, Porky!' Billy goes, all friendly like. 'Glad to see you sticking to the *Drummond*, boyo!'

'Yeah, right, this is my patch, Billy, you know that,' says Porky. You could tell he was dying with nerves, but doing his best not to show it. A huge big fella like Porky, and Billy hardly up to his chin, but Porky was shaking in his trainers. It was kinda funny to see. I couldn't help laughing.

Billy's lip was dripping with sweat, and he had a funny grin on his thin wrinkled face with the red cheeks and the droopy pouches at his jaw. He was a lot older, I could see, than he'd like people to know. Oughta get a facelift, like Joan Collins.

'So it's a funny thing, Porky,' Billy says softly, ' but somebody was telling me they saw you dealing blow down the *King's Head* Monday night. That's a funny thing, isn't it, Porky? And an even funnier thing, I'm told you were dealing the gear on the Tuesday night, Porky.'

Every time Billy says 'Porky', his voice seems to go up a bit higher and get a bit louder. He's moving up closer to Porky all the time, and Porky's sorta trying to slide back a bit, without being too obvious about it. Marie's moved away a step or two, I'm glad to see, and I was wishing she'd get herself on over to me at the back door and out of it, but I suppose, like the rest of us, she was too hooked on watching what was going on. A right soap opera, so it was.

'No, Billy, you've got it all wrong,' Porky starts stammering out. He's turned a weird sorta colour, like a dirty white – like his mammy doesn't use Persil.

'Wrong, am I, Porky?' Billy sounds ever so soft and gentle.

For about half a minute.

Then suddenly he's screaming. 'Get him, boys! Take him out the back!'

Then there's a lot of action that I mostly don't see too well, what with everybody crowding round, and what with Billy mentioning the back door, which made me pull my head back, thinking I'd be as well getting away from there myself. I just caught sight of Chippy, the *Drummond* bouncer, out of the corner of my eye, and he was dodging away out of the picture, making for his post at the front door – there's just one of him, see? – and then, like, I think I hear Marie doing a bit of shouting.

Seems Porky's pushing her in front of him, trying to keep away from Billy and the boys.

There's punches being hurled all directions, and a lot of screeching and stuff, and I stick my head round the door again, and I'm just wishing I could see better when there's a gleam of metal and one of the boys is pulling a knife.

So then I'm pretty pleased to be so far back and out of it, and I look round to make sure no one's coming up behind me and I can get away okay if I want to.

It's fine, a clear exit, good enough.

I takes another look round the door, just interested to see what's going to happen next, like, and then for the first time I gets a good view of Marie.

Porky has her by the arms in front of him, with her back up against his fat belly, like one of these human shields you hear about on the news, and she's, like, struggling to get free and not getting any joy out of it, and I starts wondering to myself if maybe I can do something for her, but, hey, what could I do with all these big guys?

It all happened in a minute.

I can still hear Billy shouting, 'Get him, boys!' sounding just like a big baby yelling for sweeties, and everybody else is screaming and bawling away, and Marie's looking round, sorta wild, with her fair hair coming down over her face and her green top dragged lower than ever. Then I don't rightly know but I've a sorta idea she sees me, peering round the door, and her face changes and goes all soft, like she thinks I'm going to come riding in on a white horse and rescue her, but, hey, my shining armour's away this month for a polish, and just as she seems to be catching my eye the fella with the knife kinda makes a lunge at big Porky, and Porky sorta swivels round and drags Marie further in front of him and the knife goes thrusting up right into her belly.

I see her face going white and her eyes dreadful and a big gollup of blood, like, spurting out of her, and then I'm outa there.

Down the back alley and on the first bus back to my own flat, right?

And the door locked and no lights showing the rest of the night.

She died in the hospital, not long after they got her admitted, I heard.

Nobody knew I was ever there at all. Except Joe Murphy, okay, but he was long gone and not wanting mixed up in it. Far's I know, he never said nothing, right?

They were looking for witnesses, but, sure, I couldn't have told them much any road. All I saw, like, lotsa people saw more. Up to them to spill their guts if they weren't worried about what Billy Moore might do to them later.

I kept my head down and no one came near me for a bit.

Sure, I'd missed mosta the excitement with being out the back all along, hadn't I?

One of Billy's guys got arrested, they tell me, but there wasn't anything on Billy – well, naturally. He hadn't even been armed, and no one was saying anything much that would tie him in with it.

And nobody knew Marie had anything to do with me. Well, she hadn't, by then. And, hey, it was her own choice to go there, nothing to do with me. All I did was go along with her. None of it was my fault, not in the way I see it.

See, I'm not a criminal. Never did anything all that bad.

Never had anything to do with big Porky, and less still with that Billy Moore, so my name never got mentioned.

I was right out of it.

Lucky, wasn't it?

Yeah. Totally.

Like, I've had a lot of luck, see? Mind you, the flippin' horse came in sixth. Still, you can't always be lucky, can you?

But, hey, I was lucky meeting you tonight, like. Dunno why, but I felt like I needed someone to talk to. That's not me, not usually, right? Know who I am and what I'm doing, don't need anybody else propping me up, not me. Got my life organised the way I want it.

See, I'll tell you a secret. You don't want to let anyone else get too close. Not so's you start caring too much about what happens to them. Start that, and you find yourself getting right and messed up. Look out for yourself, make sure things go your way, that's the thing. I've been doing that since I was a wee kid, and I'm telling you, it works for me.

Why're you gettin' up? What, chucking out time, is it? Give me a tick, I'm trying to get up, here. What was it I just said, don't need anybody to support me, like? Got that wrong, didn't I? All those tequilas, mate!

Going my way?

Well, maybe you might give me a hand. Looks like it'll have to be a taxi for me, this time. What was it you said your name was? Bas?

Hey, just like Marie. Nothing to her, are you?

What did you say? It means 'death' in the Irish? Funny, that.

You want to turn off down this alley?

Right, mate, whatever you like. It's a shortcut, a bit dodgy, right, but hey, there's two of us, okay? You'll not be needing that knife you've got there, mate, but does no harm to have it ready, yeah?

It must be my eyes, mate, that last Tequila, maybe? But you're looking sorta funny all of a sudden.

Yeah. Must be my eyes.

Listen, mate, you're my friend, right?

It's really good I met up with you tonight. Lucky, that's what.

But see me, I'm always lucky.

8 – Dark Night

**Extended into the full-length historical novel –
Johnny McClintock's War – published August 2014**

John Henry McClintock met Rose Doherty when she was sixteen, and he a year or so older.

They met at a tent mission, which meant a gospel meeting in a large tent, in a field miles from anywhere.

It was a soft, warm summer night. Music poured from the tent as John Henry drew nearer to it, one of a large crowd of people, stepping cautiously through the long grass at the field's edge – soon to be trampled flat by the hordes of visitors – and trying, not always successfully, to avoid the still wet sticky cowpats laid down that day, and the big purple thistles which grew everywhere. The huge dirty beige tent had no ribbons or other decorations, only a cardboard placard set up at the entrance, giving the times and the dates of other meetings, in bright red against the whitey-yellow background, with the name of the speaker in a bold dark green. There was a similar placard attached to the gate at the entrance to the field, where a blossoming hawthorn hedge spread its white, sweet-smelling flowers close enough almost, but not quite, to obliterate the writing.

John Henry hadn't seen Rose yet. He had gone along to the tent with friends of his own age, just as she had done a few minutes earlier. A tent mission was one of the free entertainments on offer in those days just before the First World War. You could be sure of meeting a large crowd of young people, who would seldom be gathered together in one place otherwise.

John Henry had left school a few years before, at his father's insistence, in spite of his evident ability. And in spite of the desire of his teacher that he should stay on, even try for teacher training eventually. (The idea of university an impossible dream in the minds of most.)

He had taken a low-skilled job in a linen factory, and was therefore contributing to the family income, like his older brother, and helping to support his younger sisters to his father's great satisfaction.

John Henry was philosophical about it, but he wanted quite fiercely to get out of the linen factory, to do something that mattered with his life. He knew his abilities – his quickness to learn and to understand. He had been top of his class by a mile every year since he first started in the small local school. He wanted to make use of the intelligence he had been given.

Rose Doherty was also working, as nearly everybody of their age and social class was; helping, mainly in the kitchen, at a nearby farm, fortunate in that she had been able to find work near her home and could return to her parents' cottage most nights.

They went in separately, greeted at the flapping doorway of the tent by a beaming, friendly man who had lost most of his hair. This man was holding out sheets with the words of the choruses, and the huge crowd had already begun to sing, as a warm-up to the meeting proper. As they stood near to each other at the door of the tent, taking the sheets in turn from the friendly man, John Henry and Rose each noticed the other. They were strangers, but through the mind of each went the fleeting thought, Perhaps – not for long?

They went on in, and found places with their own friends, in different parts of the tent.

Gradually the singing drew to a close, and the meeting opened.

The speaker was a gifted orator.

'Friends,' he began, in a soft, gentle voice, 'you all know that there's someone out there. Someone who made you. Someone who loves you.'

A collective sigh went round the tent. John Henry stirred uncomfortably. He didn't much want to be moved by this man, to respond. He was only here for a bit of fun, for company.

The speaker went on: 'Yes, friends, it was St Patrick who first opened our eyes, as Irishmen and women, to the presence of God in all nature. But St Paul said it before him, and David said it in his psalms, the songs he wrote from his shepherd's heart, "The Heavens declare the glory of God!" '

The speaker's voice grew louder, more emphatic. John Henry's attention wandered.

For a few moments he was back in his early teens, experiencing again the wonder of the beauty of the earth in springtime. The freshness of early morning. The pink and white of the apple blossom all around. The still nights. The feeling of something – something. A presence that was trying to speak to him. Which he longed, but was afraid, to listen to.

When he came back to the here and now, the speaker was quoting the Irish poet Joseph Plunkett, the young Christian Brother who had recently joined the republican movement.

'I see his blood upon the rose
And in the stars the glory of his eyes.
His body gleams amid eternal snows,
His tears fall from the skies.

I see his face in every flower;
The thunder and the singing of the birds
Are but his voice – and carven by his power
Rocks are his written words.'

The speaker dropped his voice, which had been soaring to the skies a moment before, and went on, speaking quietly:

'All pathways by his feet are worn,
His strong heart stirs the ever-beating sea.
His crown of thorns is twined with every thorn.
His cross is every tree.'

Something caught at John Henry's heart, stirring and exalting him. He no longer wanted to resist; to fight whatever it was that was drawing him, reaching out to take him captive.

The speaker went on. He was quoting from the Bible now, referring with all his eloquence to the death of Christ, to the need for surrender to him. All at once, John Henry knew what he was going to do.

In another part of the tent, tears streamed down Rose's face as she listened with her whole heart to the speaker's emotional words. She was miles away from that place, wandering in a bright garden, hand in hand with someone who loved her so much. The pain and the joy were intermixed to an unbearable extent. The need for action, for response, over-whelmed her.

The speaker, dropping his voice to its initial softness, drew to the end of his message.

For a moment there was silence.

Then came the final prayer, and the appeal.

At its close, when the speaker called for people to come forward, as a sign that they wanted to give their lives to the Lord, Rose Doherty stood up and walked to the front.

While she was waiting afterwards for her turn to pray with one of the counsellors, she noticed someone standing next to her, also waiting. It was the young man she remembered seeing as she came into the tent before the meeting started.

Coming out of the tent, he spoke to her. 'Beautiful evening, isn't it?'

Rose agreed. The clear starry night, the dark navy blue sky studded with its distant silver stones were very beautiful.

'Come from round these parts?'

'Dromore,' she said. This was a village some five or six miles away.

'A fair distance,' said John Henry. 'If you'd like some company for the walk home, I'd be glad to go along with you.'

Rose had plenty of friends who had come with her and would have kept her company on the way back. But for all that, she accepted the offer.

Over the next months, they saw each other regularly. John Henry made a point on the first Sunday of going to the church that had organised the tent mission where they had met. But he found that Rose, like himself, didn't belong there, and had come only for the mission. From then on, having found out which was Rose's own church, he went there.

He would wait for her afterwards, and they would walk together through the country lanes, like other young courting couples. John Henry picked the spring flowers, especially the early wild roses, 'Your flower, Rosie,' and the bluebells whose scent filled the air for such a distance around their full bursting beds. He gave them to Rose, who pressed a single wild rose in her Bible when she returned home that night and kept the withered petals safely there, between the leaves.

Both their families seemed happy enough with the understanding that had come about between Rose and John Henry.

Then John Henry went away to fight in the war.

8 – Dark Night

For over five years, Rose waited for him.

He was a volunteer, for Irishmen, even in the north of the country, were not conscripted.

It was the first real disagreement Rose had had with him, and although it was made up before he sailed, it left a sour taste in her mouth. She could see no reason for John Henry to go, and indeed held a strong conviction that all war was wrong.

But John Henry held to his equally strong belief that it was his duty to go and fight. And although Rose was no moral weakling, and was not to be persuaded out of her conviction, John Henry, a man of great strength of purpose, remained firm in his.

'You, of all men, Johnny,' Rose said to him, when the subject first came up, one warm September evening as they walked arm in arm through the woods near Rose's home, stepping on the first of the fallen leaves, and hearing them crackle underfoot. 'You who's such a firm Christian! Why should you want to fight? What about turning the other cheek, and loving your enemies?'

'Ach, ach, Rosie, you're getting it all mixed-up,' John Henry said. He spoke the more vehemently because he wasn't completely convinced that Rose was wrong, for her words had touched something in him. As he walked, he reached up above their heads, and pulled down a thin branch, whose slight attachment to the mother tree made it dangerously easy to snap off. John Henry broke it quickly, and held it in his left hand, while his right arm still encircled Rose. He began to swish with it angrily at the trees and bushes they were passing, knocking the leaves from bramble and whin alike.

'Turning the other cheek, that's about private fights, quarrels with people who do you down some way. It's nothing to do with a whole country going to war. If we didn't fight, we'd have Kaiser Bill over here, forcing us to do things his way, before you could turn round. Is that what you want for your country? If the Irish don't fight for the country's freedom, can you tell me who will? We're the bould fighters, and proud of it, Rosie!'

'Most of us think we should be fighting for Ireland, not for England, Johnny,' Rose retorted, but he would have none of it.

'That's a different matter, Rosie,' he said firmly. 'I don't deny there are problems enough at home, now they've passed the Home Rule Act, and are promising that it'll be carried out as soon as the war's over. But we all need to pull together here, girl! This war is against the Kaiser, and we need to put our private differences aside, and stand shoulder to shoulder, or we'll have no country left, either England or Ireland!'

'I still think fighting's wrong, Johnny,' she said, not trying for a new argument, but simply sticking with what she was sure of, for all his efforts to change her.

But there was something fighting against her, which she wasn't even aware of, and that was John Henry's ardent desire to get out of his dead-end job, to go somewhere, to do something, to make a success of his life. He told himself that the desire sprang from a need to do his duty, as a Christian and an Irishman. But if he had looked a little deeper, he would have had to recognise the burning need to get away from the daily round that was trivialising his life. And which, day by day, he hated more.

Joining up, if he did it, would create an opportunity for him to escape.

So all at once he was angry at his failure to bring Rose round to his point of view, and near to throwing up the whole understanding.

It was the sight of the tears beginning in Rose's eyes, as she murmured, 'Oh, Johnny, I don't want you to go away to war! Suppose – suppose –'

She couldn't bring herself to put into words what she feared, but John Henry didn't need them.

Rose feared, and with good reason, that if John Henry set off to go to war, she would be left, like the heroines of so many sad Irish songs, with only his memory, and the announcement, some day, that he had died 'gloriously, for his country.' And what use would that be to anyone?

The following day, John Henry enlisted.

He went up to Belfast to do this, and found himself surrounded by eager crowds of boys of his own age, mostly not old enough yet to be called young men. John Henry was just turned eighteen, but he recognised some faces in the milling crowd of boys he knew were younger than him. There was a medical, and John Henry was pleased to come out of the embarrassing experience (he had never stripped in front of anyone before) with a grade of A2. 'Why "two"?' he asked, and was told that his eyesight wasn't quite perfect – but it would do.

There would be twelve weeks' training before anyone could be sent to France. The two Northern regiments, the sixteenth and the thirty-sixth, would be sent to Aldershot. To John Henry, who had never been across the water, it was an exciting prospect. The first, he thought, of many new experiences. He was a bit nervous, too, but by now he had put Rose's views behind him, and was sure he was doing the right thing.

8 – Dark Night

He was kitted out with a new uniform, given a rucksack to carry his belongings, and told that he would sleep overnight in Victoria Barracks. He would sail, with the rest of the new recruits, on the following day.

Early next evening they left. It wasn't many minutes out from Belfast, in fact they were still sailing down the Lough, when a dreadful, demoralising sea sickness made him question his sense in letting himself in for this.

'I'm dying, Paddy!' he gasped, to a boy standing beside him, who had shown himself friendly. 'What'll I do?'

'Hang over the side,' Paddy advised, 'and bring up everything you can. You won't feel just as bad then.'

Paddy O'Connor, who had worked with his father on the family fishing boat at Ardglass, was used to the sea and although well past sickness himself, he had seen enough of it to be reasonably sympathetic to others.

John Henry took his advice, but it didn't help much. For what seemed like hours he hung over the side of the ship, retching continually long after there was nothing to bring up. At some unidentified time, he staggered away from the rails to the corner of the deck where he had piled his kit, wrapped his greatcoat round him, and managed a few hours of disturbed sleep.

Liverpool looked grey and gloomy, teeming with rain, when the ship drew in to harbour next morning. John Henry, however, had no sooner stepped onto firm ground again than his spirits began to rise. Presently, when the sun came out, watery at first but soon growing in strength to light up the strange docks, with piles of boxes and coils of rope spread everywhere, he even found himself whistling.

'Rock of Ages, cleft for me!' whistled John Henry.

Paddy, struggling over the roughly concreted dock at his side, weighed down by rucksack and greatcoat, looked at him. 'Religious, are you?'

'Aye,' said John Henry, always a man of few words, and they left it there.

The next stage of the journey was by train. John Henry was surprised to see the platform filled with cheering crowds, most of them women, many from Liverpool's large Irish population.

'There's the brave lads!' called one woman. 'Shoot lots of Germans for me, ye boys, ye!' She was red-faced, dressed in too-bright colours, and swaying dangerously from side to side. If they had been at home, John Henry would have known what to make of her, but being in a strange place, he gave her the benefit of the doubt. Maybe respectable women dressed like that over here. He'd been told that you could believe anything of people who lived in England.

However, one thing he was in no doubt of at all, and that was that she was drunk. He thought it was sad.

Inside the train, it was the lucky first-comers who got seats, crammed tightly into the carriages, while the rest sat on rucksacks in the corridors. John Henry had hung back to help Paddy, who was struggling more than ever with his load, and now he found himself condemned to the corridor. He didn't really mind. At least like this he could stretch out his long legs. Unlike the soldiers in the carriages, who could hardly move, packed as they were like sardines in a tin, but without the lubricating oil.

As soon as the train had started, someone who had a mouth-organ started to play, 'Pack Up Your Troubles In Your Old Kit Bag' and all around, people joined in enthusiastically (in so far as they knew the words, and even a bit further.) After that came, 'It's A Long Way To Tipperary,' and then, 'The Mountains of Mourne.'

A boy sitting in the corridor not far from John Henry joined in, softly at first, then with growing confidence. He had a sweet Irish tenor voice, high and piercing. Like John McCormack, whom John Henry had once heard sing at a concert in Belfast. As his voice soared up into the words of the last verse John Henry listened and felt as if his heart was being squeezed: 'So I'll wait for my wild rose, who's waiting for me ...'

The words brought him a painful vision of his own Rose. Only a day gone, and he was missing her already. Maybe he would never see her again. Then he gathered up his courage. Never mind, he thought. We'll certainly be home by Christmas, if not before. The recruiting officer had told him so and, anyway, everyone was saying the same. I'll see her then, John Henry thought.

The twelve weeks of training dragged.

John Henry, used to an indoors job in a factory, found himself pushed to the utmost to carry out each day's programme of long marches, drill, practice with gun and bayonet, early rising, confinement to the training camp except for a few hours on a Saturday evening. And above all, the constant sharing of a limited space with nine other people, the other members of the ten-man unit to which he had been allocated. He was used to some degree of privacy, if not during the working day then at least after it. At home, he had spent quite a lot of his free time wandering around the countryside, through the woods and fields, often with Rose, but more often still on his own. The removal of this freedom was the thing he found hardest to come to terms with.

As a substitute for his freedom, he learnt to enjoy the sense of comradeship that grew steadily among the boys in his hut. As he grew stronger physically, and found he could manage the increasingly strenuous daily training programme without falling into bed exhausted at the end of each day, so John Henry found himself with time available to take part in the chat and banter of his companions, and to join in games of football and other sports with a pleasure he had not experienced until now.

He even found time for a few walks in the open air, discovering more beauty in the English countryside than his insular Irishness had led him to expect. Autumn was fully present by now, but the multicoloured leaves, with their melancholy voices sighing of death had their own beauty for John Henry. As he walked through them at his ease, he thought.

There was more blasphemy from his companions than he was used to, although his time in the linen factory had to some extent inured him to that. Whether because it came naturally to them, or because they thought this was how real soldiers should talk, his companions used more foul language, too, than John Henry found comfortable.

However, after the first few weeks, he noticed a considerable drop ing off in this. He suspected that the reduction was only in his presence, that when he was not there, they spoke as crudely as ever. But he was happy to escape the worst of it.

His friendship with Paddy O'Connor grew. The red-haired young fisherman from Ardglass was generally to be found in the middle of any practical joke, but he spent some quiet time with John Henry too, questioning him about his beliefs and listening avidly to the answers. John Henry usually found it hard to talk about such personal things, often struggling to put his meaning into words, but he did his best, because, like most people, he couldn't help liking Paddy.

'So, what do you think about this story that the troops saw angels at Mons, before the battle?' asked Paddy.

'I don't see why not,' John Henry answered slowly. There were some things he still had to work out for himself. He was never ready with quick, glib answers. But that did him no harm in Paddy's eyes.

Then one evening Paddy asked, 'What do you think of this?' Each of them was stretched out on his own bed, speaking in low voices just before lights out. Paddy produced a string of rosary beads from beneath his pillow, and held it out for John Henry to see, keeping it scrunched in his own hand, so that it stayed out of sight of people passing. 'My ma gave me it just before I left to sign up,' Paddy said. 'I suppose, you not being a Catholic, you would think little of it.'

John Henry took a few minutes to decide. 'If it helps you to pray, Paddy, and to concentrate on what you're praying, I don't see how it can be anything but good,' he said at last.

Paddy laughed. 'Well, I don't know about that,' he said. 'I suppose I think it's a kind of good-luck charm. I mean, my ma wouldn't think like that, but me, I'm different from her, see?'

'I suppose you are,' John Henry agreed.

'But when I have it in my hand just before going to sleep, it gives me a good feeling, that's all.'

'Well, we could all do with something like that, these days, Paddy,' John Henry said. 'Here comes Corp. It's lights out.'

There was another plus, during this time of training, which made up to John Henry for all the rest. As part of the training, they were each given the opportunity to follow courses, to learn things which would better fit them for their return to civilian life after the war, and John Henry eagerly chose to extend his curtailed schooling.

He quickly gained certificates proclaiming his successful qualification in mathematics and English, and went on to add French and German to the list. It meant working for most of the few hours that would otherwise have been leisure time, but John Henry rejoiced in the opportunity to make use of his talents at last.

During this time, and especially over the first weeks, when the physical work and the mental strain of never being alone were at their height, John Henry lived mainly through the letters Rose sent him regularly.

Rose was missing him desperately. Without the full programme that filled John Henry's days, she had too much time to brood, to wonder if he would come safely back, if he would stay faithful. She worried less about this last than about his survival. She knew he was a man of his word. He would not easily break the promises he had made to her.

But as she stood by the farmhouse sink, with her arms plunged into the greasy water as she scoured the pots and pans, or as she peeled endless potatoes or kneaded the dough for another batch of soda bread, she found herself continuously wondering how soon it would be before Johnny was under fire, and how soon the war would be over, and if he would then come safely back to her.

She prayed for him every night; it was all she could do for him. She wrote him long letters daily, and in them she enclosed a wild flower, an autumn crocus or a Michaelmas daisy, and, as winter drew on, a holly berry or the leaf of an ash tree which she found one day still hanging from its branch. She discovered eventually that the official censorship authority removed these tokens before they got to John Henry.

At last the training was over.

One evening a few days before the end of the final week John Henry was surprised to be called to the hut of the camp commander, Major Fitzpatrick.

The major was a tallish man. Although born in Ireland, he had gone to a school in England and there had acquired an accent that to the troops under his command sounded English, although his English friends would have said he had a definite brogue. He had a fair bushy moustache, slicked back, light-coloured hair, which was mostly hidden under his uniform cap, and the beginnings of a pouch above his Sam Brown belt (which he hoped would diminish once he was out in the field again away from the fleshpots of the training depot, and the officers' mess there).

In so far as he had seen anything of the man at first hand, John Henry quite liked him.

Formalities over, the major said, looking at a paper on the desk before him, 'I understand, McClintock, that you've done well in all your subjects. English, mathematics, French and German. Your sergeant instructor recommends that you be promoted and begin to teach some of these subjects from now on. You'll be corporal at first, and if all goes well, you'll be promoted to sergeant instructor yourself, before too long. Are you willing to take this on?'

For a moment John Henry could say nothing. His delight was too great. Here was the recognition, the opportunity, he had been longing for.

The major, seeing he was dumbstruck, kindly filled the gap for him. 'You realise, of course, that that means remaining here at the home base, instead of going to the front.'

John Henry stared at him. No, he hadn't realised that. His pipe dream burst in his face like a wet, soapy bubble, stinging his eyes. 'I'm sorry, sir,' he said, 'but if I have the choice, I'd rather do what I signed up for. I'm here to fight the Germans, sir.'

Major Fitzpatrick frowned. 'Are you sure, man? It's not everybody who's offered an opportunity like this. Don't decide in a hurry.'

But John Henry had already decided.

A few days later, he sailed for France with his small unit and the rest of his battalion.

They landed in Calais, and started marching.

John Henry's later memories of those first months in France were confused. They marched by day, camped overnight, marched the next day. They covered an unbelievable amount of ground. He was glad, now, that the twelve weeks' training had toughened him up or he would surely have collapsed by the second day. Then came a stage when they were transported by train, packed even more tightly than they had been on the journey from Liverpool. The soldier with the mouth-organ still played to them as they travelled, but the tunes were stale now to most of the men.

The final stage, bringing them up to the line, was by cattle wagon.

Almost before he could register that they had reached the place where they would fight, he and the others were set to digging trenches.

They were in Belgium now, not France, he found when he asked the corporal in charge of his unit. Their job was to defend the line near a town that was apparently called Wipers. There had already been heavy fighting there in October, while John Henry's unit was still in training. Time had moved on, so full of work that he hadn't taken in its swift progress. John Henry realised, with dismay, that tomorrow would be Christmas, and the fighting, for him at least, hadn't yet started.

Christmas Day was some sort of unofficial truce. John Henry found that if he listened carefully, he could hear the German soldiers, entrenched across no man's land, singing carols.

In the end, the trenches were ready. Then came months of cold. Of sleeping on muddy ground, when it was his unit's turn to supply the guard. Of rising in the middle of the night to take his turn on duty. Of near misses from bullets, and often hits. One evening a bullet that just missed John Henry killed his fellow sentry, tearing through the boy's brain.

He lay awake at nights, in the huts where off-duty units were allowed some shelter, unable to sleep for the pain of his blistered hands (still raw from the recent digging) and tried to read the end of Matthew's gospel by the light of a candle stump seeking a little peace.

Then came the attack.

For the first time in this war, the German forces used gas.

Although Major Fitzpatrick rallied his forces bravely, and led them over the edge of the trenches in response to the initial German offensive, it soon proved impossible to force their way on into the gas which polluted the air all around them.

John Henry at first found himself charging after Major Fitzpatrick across no man's land, for some reason wasting his breath by shouting. Bullets and shells flew on all sides of him. To his right, a shell exploded, killing what must have been at least a dozen men. He saw torn pieces of a human body jump through the air, and found more underfoot as he continued to run forward after the major. Some pieces, with sick horror, he thought he recognised as belonging to friends.

Then it was retreat. They were back at the trenches.

But they were still running; and still running.

The Allied line was chased back so many miles that day that a new battle line had to be drawn up, beyond the place where John Henry had completed his journey by train.

'Could have saved themselves the fare,' observed Paddy, the only other member of John Henry's unit, as far as he knew, who had survived.

'I don't think they paid ... ' John Henry realised it was a joke.

How could Paddy still joke after what they had seen that day?

The new line was drawn up, the new trenches dug. John Henry and Paddy were allocated to a new unit, created from the remnants of several others.

To John Henry, one of the worst things about the trenches where he spent so much of his time for the next three years was the absence of all nature's beauty which meant so much to him. Mud, mud, mud stretched on all sides. There seemed at times to be little else. Where, John Henry sometimes asked himself, was God to be found in all this?

He read, in an English newspaper passed to him by Major Fitzpatrick, who knew that McClintock loved to read, an article written by a Sergeant Munro. The major told him Munro was in the Royal Fusiliers, but wrote under the name 'Saki'. The article was called 'Birds on the Western Front'. Munro, apparently, on throwing himself to the ground to escape enemy fire on one occasion, had found his face pressed into a nest of baby larks. Some were injured, but the rest seemed to be thriving in the middle of the battlefield. John Henry wished he could have a similar experience.

And yet, as he began to look around him more carefully, he saw some signs of the nature he loved. Trees, smashed by shellfire, but still standing up as stumps with some ragged leaves. And new shoots growing recklessly, ignoring the repeated lessons that should have taught them how foolish it was to try to survive. And one day, a lark sang high above the trenches, soaring into the heights of the sky, lifting John Henry's heart in the old way.

There must have been a nest somewhere nearby, but though he looked for it, he never found it. The song was enough.

One night when he was on sentry duty he was kicked awake by Paddy, who had completed the shift before him. 'Get up, you lazy blurt!' Paddy said, with a grin to take away the sting. 'Get out there so's I can get to my pit!'

John Henry scrambled guiltily to his feet. He tried, normally, to wake in good time, and to be dressed and ready to take his stint, so as not to keep the man who was coming off his shift waiting. For he knew, none better, how ready a guard was to collapse straight into bed the minute his hours of duty were over. 'Sorry, boyo!' he said. He dressed hurriedly, and took up his rifle.

'I'll just lie down here, mate,' Paddy said. 'I don't have the energy to crawl away over to my own place, when you'll have been keeping this one nice and warm for me. You can have my bed when you finish your duty. Don't be coming back here and waking me up, now!'

'Fine with me.'

John Henry went out to walk up and down beside the trenches, watching for enemy activity. He ducked occasionally as a bullet headed in his direction. No need to report that: it would make itself known without his help. He was there to give advance warning of troop movement, of an attack across the lines. But for most of his shift, with nothing happening but the occasional shell falling well short, or a bullet easily dodged, John Henry felt secure enough.

It was one of those lovely, quiet nights that he had always enjoyed. The stars shone in a clear navy blue sky. The night air felt warm against his cheeks, a reminder that summer was approaching again. John Henry looked up at the sky, and for almost the first time since he had arrived at the battle lines he felt a presence there, someone watching him, loving him.

The shift came to an end. John Henry prepared to go and wake the next man on duty.

Suddenly he heard another German shell soaring through the air towards him. He threw himself down instinctively, and waited.

The shell landed, a direct hit, in the trench in front of him. He heard noises, groans, exclamations. Clambering down into the trench, he looked around. People on all sides were crying out with the agony of injuries caused by shell splinters.

John Henry looked at the spot he had claimed for his own bed, where Paddy should have been sleeping peacefully. Instead he saw blood. Torn, reeking remnants of flesh. The remains of the exploded shell. The unrecognisable remains of a body.

Nothing, no one, alive.

The Germans had scored their direct hit on Paddy O'Connor.

It was Willie Woodbine who helped John Henry through his grief. And through the guilt, however senseless, that he couldn't help feeling at Paddy's death.

Willie Woodbine was a Church of England vicar who had picked up his nickname because he made a habit of offering cigarettes as well as comfort to the soldiers he met. When he offered one to John Henry, he met with a firm refusal. John Henry, very much a man of his time and country, considered that a Christian should neither smoke nor drink. All the same, Willie Woodbine was the first man John Henry had met since he joined up who seemed to share his own beliefs. Talking to him helped.

He soon found that the vicar's own experiences on the battlefield were rapidly turning him into a pacifist. And since the things John Henry had seen were producing in him a bitter hatred of war and fighting, he was glad to meet him.

Since coming to France, he had seen every last one of the unit he had trained with killed. Day after day, there had been senseless death after senseless death. He no longer knew where to find God in the horror and muddle of the fighting. Sometimes he would remember how he had looked up at the sky, and knew that he had felt God there, just before Paddy's death. There was an irony in that which he couldn't cope with.

He shared his sense of guilt with Willie Woodbine. 'It should have been me, see? In that bed. It was my bed. Paddy was only there by accident.'

'That's one way of looking at it,' the older man said slowly. 'There are others. You were where you were supposed to be, out on sentry duty, when the shell exploded. You might like to think you were being looked after but if that only makes you feel worse, think of it from Rose's point of view.' (For John Henry had spoken to his new friend of Rose and of the far-off days when they had walked the country lanes in peace. And of Rose's belief that war was wrong, which he himself was fast coming to share.) 'How would Rose have felt if you had been in that bed at that moment? Be grateful for her sake, if not for your own.'

Gradually, John Henry began to come to terms with what had happened.

It was only by looking at the date on one of Rose's letters that John Henry noticed that he had been on the battle line for nearly two years. Although it was summer, the Flanders plain was turning into a swamp under increasingly heavy downpours. The natural drainage had long since been destroyed by the bombardments of shell and gunfire. The rain had nowhere to go. John Henry and his comrades spent long hours bailing out the water that filled every shell hole and crept higher and higher up the trench walls. Much of the time they spent up to their knees in muddy rain water.

Rumour had it that very shortly they would be going over the top in an attempt to drive the Germans back and retake the ground they had held at the beginning of the fighting.

John Henry, like most of his comrades, looked forward to the day when the advance would begin. The endless monotony of living in the everlasting mud, in company with scavenging rats swollen from feasting on scattered human remains was something he wondered if he could bear for much longer. And yet what alternative was there? Only the advance, when it came.

One day they were lined up in front of the huts, most of them so inundated with rain water that their clothes hung heavily on them and it was an effort even to shoulder their guns. The battalion commander addressed them: 'This is what you've been waiting for, boys!' he said. 'This is where you show your courage, what you're made of! This is your opportunity to join your names with those of the men who have defended our country all down the centuries! With Marlborough! With Clive! With Wolfe! With Wellington! This is your hour, the battle you joined up to fight!'

The men, dizzy with fatigue, tormented with lice, found them-selves cheering, excited and exhilarated.

They were to go over the top the next day.

So, for John Henry, began the long-drawn-out horror of the third battle of Ypres, a battle that was to last, with repeated advances, until, in November, it ended with the capture of the place that afterwards gave its name to the series: Passchendaele.

Next morning, as often before, a mist hung over the Flanders plain, and the summer rain continued to sheet down.

John Henry, woken by the reveille, prepared with his unit for the attack. The moments while he waited for the signal to advance seemed longer than the years he had been away from home.

Then, suddenly, they were charging over the top of the trench, himself and the men, or boys, he had lived with for the past months. Beside him was Charlie, a farm labourer from up near Derry, who last week had shared a bar of chocolate, sent from home, with John Henry and a few chosen friends. On the other side was Geordie, an illiterate Belfast boy, whose letters home John Henry had helped to write.

John Henry followed Major Fitzpatrick's broad, uniformed back in a dream. This had happened before. And, as before, John Henry was uttering strange war cries he hadn't thought he knew, charging at top speed across no man's land towards the German trenches.

He had no time to look around, but he knew that on all sides the line of British troops spread for what must have been miles. Not simply his own battalion, but all the others who had been holding this part of the line were being thrown against the Germans in an all-out attempt to drive them back and retake the ground lost more than a year ago.

He could see only vaguely through the enveloping mist and the clouds of gun smoke like a blanket pulled over his eyes. Over to his left, he was dimly aware that something had exploded – a mine, he thought. He heard men scream, and when he glanced sideways, Geordie was no longer running beside him.

Still he charged on, grimly now, the first exhilaration fading to something like despair. Now he could no longer see Major Fitzpatrick's back in front of him. What was going on?

He continued to move forward. His foot caught against something, and then he was down on his knees, his left hand flung wide to support himself. It came down on something that felt like cloth.

Major Fitzpatrick was sprawled before him. He leant forward. 'Sir! Major ...' It was too late. The major's eyes were wide open, staring.

His commanding officer certainly did not rank as a friend, but John Henry had nothing against him – had often found him kind and helpful.

He looked more closely. Major Fitzpatrick's head was more than half destroyed by the exit wound of the bullet that had killed him. Brains oozed out. Flesh had disintegrated. The blood was already beginning to congeal. John Henry's sadness turned to horror, to disgust.

He stumbled to his feet again.

During the minutes he had knelt by his dead commanding officer, he had been left behind. He looked around, but could see no one.

Aiming towards the sound of the screams and gunfire, he began to run again, in what he thought must be the right direction. He continued for several minutes, but the noises grew fainter, and there was still no sign of his comrades or even of the enemy.

Stopping in his tracks, he tried to orientate himself.

He thought he could identify the direction of the sounds of battle. He began to move again, not so rapidly this time. The moment for speeding up would come when he was sure he wasn't moving further away with each step.

If only the mist would lift. The smoke made it yet more difficult to see, even though the guns seemed now to be further away. Presently he found himself tripping over roots, held back by thick undergrowth. He must have stumbled by mistake into a wood. Clearly, his first move must be to get out.

He turned to retrace his steps. After what seemed a long time, but was probably only five minutes, he found the trees getting thicker about him. He must be going further into the wood.

Ahead of him, an owl, one of the many that frequented the battle-field, screeched, and flew up at an angle away from him.

John Henry felt like giving up, and would have done if giving up had been in his nature. He ploughed on, taking first one direction, then another. After a while, it occurred to him that at the very least he could prevent himself taking the same wrong turning if he marked one of the trees as he passed it with a strip of cloth. He ripped a small piece from his shirt tail and tied it round a branch.

Sure enough, eventually, although he could have sworn he was following a straight line, he came to the tree marked with a piece of his shirt. So, he should try to go back from here.

But when he came to the same piece of shirt for the third time, and then a fourth, even John Henry could not force himself onward.

He sank down beneath the accursed tree, rested his head on his arms, and wept a little. Was he to die here in this wood, not even in the heat of battle, but from exhaustion, hunger and thirst?

He had been sitting there for some time when he noticed that the top of his head, still bent over his arms, was surprisingly hot. He reached up a hand and felt it cautiously.

John Henry raised his head. Through a gap in the trees, the sun was shining down on him with an unexpected power. He stood up.

The mist had lifted, and the sun was lighting the ground in all directions. John Henry realised that if he went about it carefully, he should be able to see enough to find his way back out of the wood.

Still stumbling from time to time over tree roots, he tracked his previous route by broken branches and occasional footprints where the ground was wet. In a surprisingly short time, he found himself back at the place where he had unwittingly entered the wood. It was really not much more than a clump of trees and bushes, he now saw. He was appalled that he had been so completely lost in it. Like someone drowning in a few inches of water, he thought.

He was out on the wide Flanders plain again, and once more his first duty was to find his way back to the battle and contribute whatever he could to his side.

He made his way across the broad space, squelching across the acres of mud, needing all his remaining strength to lift one foot after the other. His ears remained alert for any sound of voices or gunfire.

As he grew accustomed to his surroundings he saw with growing revulsion that what he had at first taken for bumps and uneven places in the ground were people – dead or dying soldiers, sunk into the mud and partly covered, their clothes so caked and filthy with it that many blended into the landscape unobtrusively as human wreckage.

John Henry looked more closely as he plodded on his way. Expecting, yet dreading, every moment to see a familiar face. Before long he had seen more than one, and he wondered if anyone at all had survived the battle except himself. Then he heard a feeble voice crying out to him from a short distance. He made his way across the sea of mud and recognised a boy he had rather disliked.

'Micky,' he said, going down on one knee beside him. 'What can I do for you?'

Micky groaned. He was a farmer's boy from County Antrim, who had made a point of teasing John Henry about his beliefs, and had, John Henry was reasonably sure, been responsible for the disappearance of his Bible before its equally mysterious return. But all that was in the past.

John Henry remembered that he still had some water in his flask. Unscrewing the top, he held it to Micky's lips, and the boy drank gratefully.

'Where are you hurt, mate?' he asked.

'I dunno. I don't seem to be able to move. But I don't feel any pain, 'cept for my left arm. I reckon it's broke. But my legs and all, they don't feel nothin'.'

John Henry, who remembered enough from his basic first-aid training to have a fair idea of what was wrong, tried to keep his voice cheerful. 'Well, Micky, that doesn't sound too bad. Sure, there'll be people along soon with stretchers for the wounded, don't you think? We'll not try to move you until then, see?'

'Don't leave me, Johnny.' The boy's face was white and frightened. 'I'm sorry I hid your Bible, Johnny. Don't leave me.'

'I'll not leave you, Micky. Don't worry about the Bible – sure it was only a joke.'

He knew that Micky's back was broken. It was likely he hadn't long to live. He took the boy's hand in his, and sat down beside him.

'What happens when you die, Johnny?' Micky managed to say. 'Johnny, say a prayer for me, will you?'

So John Henry, still holding the boy's hand, tried to bring him what comfort he could, until, long after, Micky's voice sank below a whisper, his eyes closed for the last time, and, like a flickering candle, his life went out.

John Henry was filled with anger. What was this war they were all fighting, which did such things to men not much more than children?

He wanted someone to blame.

He stood up. 'This shouldn't have happened to you, Micky,' he said loudly.

In the middle of the mud and misery of no man's land, he began to stamp up and down. His feet struck hard against the soggy earth, producing a squelchy, sucking noise. He wanted to hurt, to punish. He waved his fists wildly, and shouted. Someone was responsible. Someone had brought about this vileness.

He went on shouting and stamping for some time.

At last he stopped. He was shaking, hardly able to keep to his feet. He felt as if, after a long drinking bout (something he remembered from his early teens), he was sober again but hollow and sick.

It came to him, standing beside poor dead Micky, remembering Major Fitzpatrick, remembering Paddy, remembering the other boys in his training unit, all gone, that there was no one he could hold to blame but himself.

'Rose told me this wasn't what You wanted,' he said, shouting once more. But now he was no longer speaking to dead Micky. 'You said, "He who lives by the sword shall die by the sword." By the guns and the shellfire, too, then. You didn't want any of this. I'm here, taking part in this damned bloody war, by my own choice, just like all the rest of the poor fools. But it wasn't by Your choice.'

He shook his head and knelt down, took Micky's hand in his again, and began to weep quietly.

At last, he began to speak again, quite softly now. 'You've kept me safe, so far,' John Henry said. 'If you'll bring me home safely to Rosie, I'll tell her how wrong I was, and I'll never go to war again.'

He went on holding Micky's hand for some time, but eventually, stiff and sore, he released it, and stood up.

There was nothing else for it.

Staggering slightly, he continued to make his way across the plain of Flanders. Until at last he heard, in the distance, the continuing sound of battle.

Rose continued to struggle through the years of John Henry's absence. She drove herself hard at work, with the result that she finished for the day, and was ready to go home, all the sooner.

She spent the extra time trying to teach her younger sister Emily to read, with some difficulty, for Rose was not much of a scholar herself. Emily was worse, but with Rose's help she improved a little, so Rose felt she wasn't wasting her time.

One night, when John Henry had been away for more than two years, her older brother Tommy brought a friend home with him after work, expecting Rose to make dinner for them both.

Rose didn't mind. She worked at least as hard during the day as any of her family, but when she was at home it was her job to cook whatever meals might be required.

It was later than usual for Tommy to come home, and the meal Rose had made for herself and her father, her younger brother Sammy, and Emily, was long since over and cleared away. However, she set to readily enough, and began to peel more potatoes and put them on to boil at the side of the fire, swinging the hob out over the heat; then added a saucepan of cabbage. When everything was ready, she mashed the potatoes with buttermilk and a little salt, and put plates from the dresser on the table.

The two men, Tommy and his friend Hughie, sat down to eat, and Hughie at once remarked, smiling at Rose, 'Aren't you the lucky man, now, Tommy Doherty, with a wee sister that's a good cook like Rose, here? Many a man would be happy to take her off you, so you'd better be watching out.'

Rose expected Tommy to make some response, but his mouth was full, and he did no more than grunt, so Rose took it on herself to answer. 'My man went to the war, Hughie, but I've been promised to him for nearly three years now, and when he's safely back we'll be getting wed.'

Hughie's face fell. Rose recognised, with some surprise, that his words, although delivered in a joking manner, had been meant seriously. She was sorry for him, and would have been even sorrier if she had thought him anything but a great lazy lump of a boy, only too like her brother Tommy with whom she had never got on well.

When she leant over the table to gather up the dishes and take them into the scullery to be washed, she was annoyed to find Hughie trying to put his arm round her waist. Rose wriggled free, and gave him a look that she hoped made her feelings quite plain.

But when she carried the dishes out into the scullery, to her annoyance Hughie followed her, took the plates gallantly from her hands, and set them down for her beside the washing-up bowl. 'Now, Rose, see what a good man you'd have, to give you a bit of a hand in the house, if you took me!' he said, giving her what she supposed he thought was a winning smile.

'I've already told you, Hughie O'Hagan, that I've a man of my own already, who's away at the war!' she snapped.

'Ah, but Rose!' insisted Hughie, coming a step nearer. Rose stood with her arms akimbo and her eyes flashing. Beside her stood the tub of water that her younger brother Sammy had brought home from the pump to supply all that day's needs. Rose was unwilling to turn her back on Hughie, and scoop up water from the tub to wash the dishes. She had an instinct that, if she turned her back on him, Hughie would grab at her again. 'Rose, for all you know the man may be well dead by now. Who's to say he'll ever come home again?'

'I hear from him every week, Hughie O'Hagan,' Rose told him, 'so I know fine he wasn't dead when he wrote me his last letter, not so long ago. I'll believe he's not coming home when I get the telegram, and not before. And I'll tell you straight, you're doing yourself no good by making suggestions like that.'

'Well, and I'd no intention of upsetting you, Rose, but I'm just being realistic, see? And I'll tell you what, Rose, you should remember that, for all you know, he'll have been going with any number of other girls all these long years when he's been away from you. What soldier wouldn't? And so why should you stick by him if you can't be sure he's been sticking by you?'

Rose picked up the saucepan that had held the potatoes, and brandished it at him. 'Don't judge everybody by yourself, Hughie O'Hagan!' she shouted, waving the pan in his face. 'And get on out of here before I give you a clout! Johnny wouldn't break his word to me, I know that fine!'

Hughie ducked away from her, laughing. 'My, my!' he said admiringly. 'You're just like my old ma when you shout like that, Rose. You needn't think you're putting me off, at all, girl!'

But at least he went out of the kitchen.

But from then on, he was back in the house regularly, annoying Rose, already tired at the end of her long working day. And, moreover, raising doubts and worries in her mind about Johnny. Not about his faithfulness, but about whether he would ever return to her.

Things came to a climax one summer evening when Rose's father and brothers had gone into the village to an entertainment in the church hall, and Emily had gone early to bed. Rose, too exhausted by a particularly strenuous day, and not especially drawn to the entertainment offered (coloured slides of Africa) had opted to have a quiet night at home.

She had just made up the fire, and settled down beside it to mend some of the shirts and socks that had begun to pile up in her work basket, when she heard someone knocking vigorously at the door.

Who on earth ...? she thought. Then it occurred to her that it was probably a neighbour, short of bread or some other necessity, coming in the hope of borrowing enough to get them through tomorrow's breakfast.

With a sigh, she stuck her darning needle into the top shirt, set it to one side, and went over to open the door.

On the threshold, swaying slightly, stood Hughie O'Hagan.

Rose stared at him.

'Is Tommy there?' he mumbled.

Taken a jar, was all Rose thought at first. 'No, he's not, Hughie, so you may go on away home,' she said.

But Hughie moved forward, over the threshold.

'And so I may, indeed, when I've got my breath back,' he said, sounding quite reasonable. 'You won't turn me away from your door without so much as a mouthful of cold water, will you, Rose?'

'Well, come in a minute and I'll get you a glass,' Rose said, stepping back and opening the door wider. 'But when you've had it, you'd better be going. You can sit down over there while I fetch it.'

'You're a great girl, Rosie.' Rose was annoyed to hear him call her by the name no one but John Henry had ever used. She turned away in irritation, and went to dip him a glass of water from the tub in the scullery.

When she came back with it, she found that, far from sitting down to rest, he was standing, straddling the gap between the table and the fireside chair, which would be the easiest approach to the doorway. 'Come here to me, Rosie,' he said coaxingly.

Then, seeing anger in her face, he went on, 'There's no one here but me and you, Rosie, excepting the wee girl asleep upstairs, so you can't say no to me this time can you?'

Rose backed away.

'Indeed I can, you great lump!' she said. 'I can say, "No!" and I can say, "Clear off!" and I can say, "Have a titter of wit, ye eedjit ye!"' She was still more angry than scared.

Hughie laughed. 'My, my, Rosie, you're a great girl,' he said admiringly. 'Just the girl for me, darlin'!'

Moving forward, he grabbed Rose round the waist and tried to kiss her. Rose was still holding the glass of water in her right hand. Twisting in an attempt to struggle free, she raised her arm and emptied it over Hughie's head.

His face took on an ugly expression. Spluttering and gagging he seized Rose even more roughly.

'That's enough of that!' he said. His furious tone made Rose aware of the danger she was in. Hughie's brutal strength shocked her. Through her head, thoughts ran haphazard. What did he intend? How far did he mean to go?

She struggled and kicked, wishing she still had her heavy working shoes on instead of the soft, flimsy slippers she always changed into when she was at home in the evening. Hughie's red, scowling face, meaty, fleshy, ugly, was very near to her own, and she could feel his hot breath, smelly with the onions from his last meal, on her cheek. And the whiskey he had been drinking. He was pushing her backwards, dragging her down to the floor, while with one hand he attempted to tear at the buttons on the front of her dress.

Rose saw that she would be lost if she let him throw her to the floor, where the weight of his body would pin her and allow him both hands for the purpose of stripping off her clothes.

'Help me!' she found herself praying, as she tripped on the edge of the hearthrug and felt herself borne downwards.

A thought slid into her mind and she acted on it without hesitation.

In her right hand she still held the empty glass. In one instant, she had smashed it against the hearthstone just beside her. Now she was holding a jagged piece of glass in her hand. With an upward thrust of her arm she slashed the sharp edge along Hughie's cheek.

He cried out in pain.

Rose, hardly aware of what was happening, felt blood dripping over her. And noticed, still numb, that her own wrist had suffered in the blow.

Hughie rolled away from her, swearing and crying. His left cheek was ripped from just beneath the eye to the jaw.

You'll need stitches in that, Rose thought automatically.

Then the horror of what she had done came home to her. She had only just missed Hughie's eye. And she thought, So much for my lectures to Johnny! The words she had quoted came to her lips and she spoke them aloud: 'Turn the other cheek.'

'No!' With a howl of terror, Hughie sprang to his feet and bounded towards the door.

'Get out of here, Hughie O'Hagan!' she said softly. She still held the jagged glass in her hand. 'And don't ever come back, unless you want me to tell my big brother Tommy on you. And then see what he'd do! It'd be a lot more than me!'

Hughie found the door handle and blundered out, still sobbing.

If Rose had not been shuddering in every bone, she knew she might have been laughed.

Foremost among her emotions was shame. Why, she didn't know. What was there for her to be ashamed of? But she knew she didn't want anyone ever to hear about this. Least of all John Henry.

She was confident that Hughie would say nothing. He would make up some story for the doctor who stitched his cheek, and for his mates;

probably about an accident while drunk. The story of his failed attack on Rose wouldn't redound to his credit.

Rose shivered at her narrow escape. She knew well that if Hughie had succeeded in his assault on her, her family would have heard about it straight away from him, and would have tried to force her to marry him, brute though he was.

But she was safe enough now.

No one would ever know.

She needed to sit down and recover. But her father and Sammy would be home soon, and she needed to clear up the mess – broken glass, blood, disorder of rug and chair – that Hughie had left in his wake.

Buttoning her dress, thanking heaven it wasn't ripped, she went to wash the scrape on her wrist in the scullery, then wrap some clean cotton round it, pulling her sleeve well down to conceal the signs. Then she fetched a dustpan and brush, and began to tidy the room.

She wished with all her heart that the war was over, John Henry safely home, and they wed.

John Henry survived the war unharmed, and in this he was unusual among the Irish who had fought.

He was demobilised, and finally arrived home in 1920, to find him-self with no job, little prospect of one, and a country torn with passion and violence. This time, he saw eye to eye with Rose, and had no desire to be involved, on either side, in the bitterness that was pulling Ireland apart.

Rose had already seen enough of it.

Until recently, most of the trouble and fighting had been around Dublin and other places far south of her home in Dromore, County Down. She had said little enough of it all in her letters, for she didn't want John Henry to be discouraged by what he might come home to. Among the few things she mentioned was the execution of the young poet, Joseph Plunkett, after the Easter Rising. They had both loved his poem 'I See His Blood Upon The Rose', which the speaker had quoted at the tent mission where they met.

It was not until just before John Henry's return that the troubles reached Dromore. General Gerald Smyth, who originally came from the nearby town of Banbridge, was assassinated in Cork for his speech encouraging the police force to shoot without fear of punishment. Shortly after his death, some Catholics were shot, by way of reprisal, in Banbridge and Dromore.

Rose found it hard to believe. She had known one of the victims well. 'A harmless critter,' as she told John Henry. A bit of an eedjit, but a man who had been a friend of her older brother. A very different man from Hughie O'Hagan.

For Rose, it took away some of the joy of John Henry's home-coming. She sat on the floor at his feet, that first evening, and wept with her face in his lap as she told him of it.

John Henry had come back tired, uncertain of the future, but relieved, in a quiet way, to be free of the fighting and its depressing aftermath. He had seen all he wanted to of death and killings. To meet with it here on his own doorstep, and hear of it from Rose, who for him represented everything he had longed to come home to, was a blow.

But the man who had returned from the war was not the boy who had left more than five years ago. He knew how to handle grief, how to turn from it and replace it with the things that meant happiness. Presently he drew Rose to her feet and wiped her eyes with his handkerchief. 'It's a bad state of affairs, Rosie,' he said gently. 'But there's no need for us to be involved in it.'

Then he pulled her down onto his knee. 'Rosie, Rosie, I've been waiting for this for near on six years! Come here, wumman, till I get at you.'

And Rose laughed, and kissed him with a passion that matched his own, until at last it was John Henry who drew back in alarm. 'The sooner we get married, the better, Rosie,' he said. 'For otherwise, it's not going to be easy.'

Rose agreed wholeheartedly.

But John Henry had no job and only a small amount of money from the army. To marry on that was easier said than done. Jobs, he knew, and Rose was able to confirm, were few and far between. John Henry was only one of thousands coming home from the war. Men who had left the army, and were in search of a job and a regular income. He would just have to search, like all the others.

At first he was optimistic. After all, he had the certificates he had gained during his training, qualifications that should surely be worth something.

But it wasn't long before he discovered that their true value was very low.

He also found, as trouble escalated round him, that it wasn't easy to put aside the death and destruction saying it had nothing to do with him or Rose.

It rolled over them from all sides.

About a week after he had heard from Rose about the shooting of her brother's friend, and others, in Dromore, John Henry went to Belfast for the day to explore the possibilities of getting employment.

He was walking down the Short Strand, coming away from a factory where he had been told that they were not taking on workers, when he suddenly found himself in the middle of an uproar.

There were crowds of people shouting and pushing, and a sound that John Henry couldn't believe he was hearing again: snipers' bullets were singing past his head. He'd thought he had left that behind him for good with the signing of the Armistice. Before he could throw himself to the ground he heard a voice in his ear. It was familiar but at first he couldn't place it. 'Keep your head down, mate. Come on! In here!'

A hand seized his arm, and hauled him into a nearby doorway. John Henry looked into a friendly, grinning face. It was Geordie, the young Belfast boy whom he had helped with his letters home.

'Geordie! I th-thought you were killed!' he stuttered.

'Not me! Got the rest of me eight lives still – a tiger cat, me.' Geordie kicked open the door behind him. 'In here!' he half advised, half ordered, and dragged John Henry into an empty, dusty hallway. 'Upstairs!' Geordie said. They ran upward, their feet clattering on the uncarpeted wooden flights. Geordie pushed open another door, and took John Henry with him into an unfurnished attic room where a man was crouching at an open window, aiming a rifle down the street in the direction of the Albert Bridge Road.

'What's going on?' John Henry asked. 'And, Geordie, how did you get out in one piece? I heard the mine that got you – right beside me, I thought it was.' He was shuddering at the memory.

'Not just in one piece, boyo,' Geordie said. 'Lucky thon auld mine wasn't all that near me, or you'd have been right. But I lost an arm.' John Henry noticed for the first time one of Geordie's sleeves was pinned across his chest, empty. 'I had a bit of time in hospital, but then they reckoned it was a Blighty one, and they sent me home. I wasn't half pleased! Well worth it, I reckon. But I got here to find there was just as much fighting needed as in Flanders.'

Geordie's friendly grin was replaced by a momentary scowl. Then he grinned again. 'But, John Henry, it's good to see you, me old mucker!

But don't go walking down places like Short Strand that way another time. Lucky for you I saw you in time. The papists are shootin' at us right now, and nothin' new in that.'

'Papists?' John Henry repeated. 'I don't remember hearing you talk like that out in the trenches, Geordie. You never spoke like that to young Charlie. I thought he was a good mate of yours.'

'Oh, aye ... Charlie. Nothing wrong with Charlie,' muttered Geordie. 'A dacent wee fella. But Charlie was out there fighting for his king and country, like you and me, Johnny. Not like these scum, trying to destroy the country, with their rebel hearts.'

'They think they're fighting for their country, too, Geordie,' said John Henry gently. 'And since when does a man's religion matter to you, boy? As I remember it, you hadn't much time for religion when I knew you? Did you get converted? And I may as well say, if you've got converted, it's to a very different sort of religion than mine, if it leads you into this sort of bitterness.'

'Ach, now, Johnny, who said anything about being converted?' Geordie protested, half laughing. He ran his fingers through his fine, bright blond hair. 'You know me, Johnny, that's not in my line. But I can't stand back and see my country destroyed, boy, me that knows as much as I do about handling a firearm.'

There was a lot more John Henry could have said. But before he could speak, the shrill whistle of a bullet woke him up to where he was. Geordie seized him and pushed him back from the line of sight through the window.

As they both crouched near the doorway, they heard a scream and a groan, and the sniper at the window fell back, clutching his shoulder.

John Henry was the first to move. Diving low across the room, he took the man in his arms and dragged him to the safety zone. Then he spoke sharply to Geordie. 'Get moving. You can see rightly that this man's injured. Have you a first-aid kit in the house or, better still, someone who knows a bit about medicine? And give me your hankie, if it's clean enough.'

Geordie, looking dazed, obediently handed over his handkerchief, and said, 'There's a first-aid kit in the next room. I'll get it for you. But you'd be knowing as much as anyone here about wounds, and the way to be dealing with them, Johnny.'

John Henry wasted no time on further words. Tearing the shirt from the sniper's shoulder, he examined the wound. Folding the handkerchief into a pad, he pressed it against the fountain of blood that spurted from it. 'Could be worse,' he grunted, as Geordie returned with the first aid box.

He searched in it, and produced some clean lint and bandages – better than Geordie's handkerchief, thank heaven – and a useful-looking ointment. 'Is there any brandy about?' he asked. And then, as Geordie looked blank, 'Any spirits, man? Gin? Whiskey?'

'Aye.' Geordie, suddenly understanding, darted away again, and returned with a glass of whiskey, which he held out to John Henry with a trembling hand. 'I thought you didn't drink, Johnny.'

'It's not for me, eedjit. It's for this poor critter here, to ease his pain a bit while I do what I can for him. What's his name, anyway?'

'Liam McClatchy.'

John Henry gave a snort of amusement at the very Irish name, then controlled himself. Geordie was unlikely to see the joke. 'I don't think the bullet's lodged in him,' he said, 'which is a blessing, for I've little or no experience in getting one out. If it had been, you'd have needed to get him to a surgeon. As it is, I'll do my best to clean and bandage the wound, but you'll still need to get a professional man to look at him as soon as you can, understand me? You don't want to see the wound going septic and developing gangrene, do you now, Geordie?'

He spoke in as menacing a manner as he could, for he was well aware that it would be against all Geordie's instincts to reveal Liam's activities, and his own, to anyone in authority.

He saw that Liam's eyes were open now, and spoke to him calmly and gently. 'You're going to be fine, Liam, boy. If you let me prop you up a bit and drink this wee drop of *uisque beatha*, you'll feel a lot better for it.'

Then John Henry began to clean and bandage the wound, noticing with satisfaction that Liam McClatchy was oblivious to more than a faint sensation of pain somewhere in the far distance. 'Well, Geordie,' he said briskly, when he was sure he had done everything he could, 'you'll need someone to help you with this fella. Get him away somewhere safe, where there'll be people to look after him. I'll have to be getting on home now, soon as it's safe to leave.'

'You'd better stop a while yet, Johnny,' Geordie urged. 'I'd like you to meet the unit commander, see? He could use a good man like yourself, Johnny.'

'Unit commander?' John Henry asked. 'Are you tellin' me you've got yourselves all set out in units like a real army?'

'Aye, Johnny, sure we have.' Geordie spoke proudly. 'Most of the boys fought in the regulars like you and me. The feeling is, they didn't fight the Germans to come back home and find these fellas destroying our own land, Johnny.'

John Henry felt sick. He wondered for a moment if he was going to throw up. Then he took hold of himself. 'Did you not see enough of fighting and killing out there, Geordie?' he asked. 'Why do you want to bring it back here with you?'

'But it's not us that's bringing it, Johnny!' Geordie protested eagerly. 'It's them auld ...'

But John Henry could take no more. 'I don't want to meet your commander, Geordie,' he said violently. 'And I'm not for joining any unit for any reason. I came home to get away from all that, not to get into more of it. Now, have you got that straight? If so, I'll say goodbye. Would there be a back way out of here?'

Geordie, his mouth still open in disbelief, took him to the door.

A few minutes later, John Henry was making his way down the narrow cobble-stoned alley to the main road and the nearby bus stop that would put him on his way back home.

The trouble was, if he was to search for a job, John Henry was bound to spend some time, at least, moving round Belfast, as well as looking nearer home. And since so many of his old army mates were involved in this new fighting, the meeting with Geordie was only the first of many such. He was not often involved in actual shooting incidents, but time after time, when he bumped into an old army comrade, he would find himself, before long, being invited to join what had become known as the Ulster Volunteer Force, a follow-on from the UVF of pre-war days. John Henry found it hard enough to convince his former colleagues that he had done with fighting. That, in fact, it was the very last thing he wanted to think or know about.

Rose was a great strength to him. More than happy that he had changed his view of war, she did everything in her power to encourage him to remain firm. She herself had been the object of many attempts to persuade her – indeed, said Rose indignantly, it would be fair to describe those efforts as bullying – to support the loyalist side, and even to join the women's group of the UVF and make herself available to give whatever help she could. But Rose stuck firmly to her guns – or, rather, her opposition to guns – and had somehow managed to do this without, for the most part, antagonising her friends and neighbours.

The hardest of all was when old Mrs Reilly, the farmer's wife for whom Rose had worked on the friendliest of terms for many years, began to pressure her, along with others less close. Annie Reilly had been a second mother to Rose, especially since the death of Rose's own mother a few years ago, while John Henry was away at the war.

'Sure, Rose,' Annie Reilly said one day, 'I can't understand a good girl like you not wanting to stand up for your country, as is only right.'

Rose tried to speak, but Annie rode over her.

'And you've seen for yourself the savages that these people are, shooting poor young Joe Kilpatrick only the other week, up in Belfast, and him a dacent young fella that never did harm to anyone. I remember wee Joe when he was growing up, went to school with yourself and my Lizzie, and only moved up to the city because he couldn't get the work near here.'

Annie stopped to dab her eyes with the corner of her apron. Rose was indeed upset about Joe's death: like Annie, she remembered him well – he had had untidy fair hair, and a shy smile, and had often offered Rose a bit of his lunchtime piece, when Rose herself had had nothing with her to eat.

But before she could speak, Annie went on, 'Would you not think better of it, and join with the rest of your friends and neighbours and put a stop to all this, for it's plain that if we don't do it ourselves, no one else will?'

'Mrs Reilly, I've thought all I need to about this,' said Rose, firmly. 'I can't see how more killing's going to make things any better.'

But she went home that night and cried herself to sleep, for she could see something very like enmity creeping into Annie Reilly's eyes. It would be so much easier not to struggle any more, to be part of the movement that all their friends were part of.

So far from easy was it for either Rose or John Henry to keep out of the bitterness that even in their church pressure was heavy on them to go with the crowd.

One particularly black day, John Henry found himself cornered at one side of the churchyard, almost pushed up against the low wooden gate that led into the graveyard, and hearing one after another of the young men, Timmy Burke, Steven McBride, Willie Millar and the rest, whom he had thought of as his friends, telling him, first seriously, then angrily, how important it was for him to join them in fighting for their country.

With an inward smile at the irony of it, John Henry heard the voices repeating to him the arguments he had used against Rose when he had decided to enlist. And heard himself using against them the arguments Rose had used to him.

'And what does the Reverend Donnelly say about all this?' he asked eventually, finding it hard to believe that a minister would support such opinions.

'Ach, him!'

'Thon one's just scared to speak out the way he should!'

'He thinks the same as us, underneath, you can be sure!'

'Boys, you just don't know the first thing about real fighting,' John Henry told them wearily. 'If you'd been over in Flanders like me, you'd not want to see the misery of it repeated in your own land, I'm telling you!'

But this only made them angrier.

They knew all about fighting, they said, and about fighting for the things that really mattered.

John Henry was glad to slip away in the end without punches being thrown. At one moment Timmy Burke had lifted his fist, but it had come to nothing, and finally the crowd had given up, turned their backs coldly, and left him to it. Making his way unobtrusively through the low gate and across the graveyard to the path at the far end which led to the road, John Henry decided that before long he would have a word with Mr Donnelly.

The opportunity came about a week later.

John Henry was strolling along at his ease, wandering mostly through fields, with the occasional excursion onto a convenient lane, glad for once not to be tramping round the hot dirty streets of Belfast. As he passed the door of McGilligan's farmhouse, Mr Donnelly came out. He had obviously been doing some sick visiting, for as he paused to say good-bye to the woman at the door, John Henry heard his loud, carrying pulpit voice saying he hoped someone would be much better before long.

John Henry waited politely until the minister came out onto the lane, and they walked along together in a friendly way.

'Still looking for a job, McClintock?' asked the minister.

'Aye, sir,' replied John Henry briefly.

'If you like, I could put you in touch with a man who knows how to pull a few strings,' the minister suggested pleasantly. 'I don't think you know him, but I'm sure he could find you a job soon enough, if he thought you were a man he could trust.'

John Henry looked at him. 'And who would that be, sir?' he asked, still trying to sound polite, even though he had an idea of what was coming.

'This man's name is Peter Moore,' the minister said. 'You'll maybe have heard of him, but I hear you haven't met him as yet.'

John Henry flushed. He came to a standstill in the dusty lane. 'I know that name,' he said slowly.

'You'll know him as a respected leader in the community, I suppose. A man who stands up for what's right.'

It was a while since John Henry had been so angry. 'Don't let me mistake you now, Mr Donnelly,' he said. In his anger he no longer bothered with, 'sir.' 'The man you're speaking of is the district commander of the UVF, is that right?'

'Well, that's right,' agreed Mr Donnelly, beaming. He hadn't yet picked up on John Henry's reaction. 'We don't usually mention that, McClintock. But just between you and me, that's certainly the case. Mr. Moore can get you a job tomorrow, if so be you're prepared to back him in the stance he's taking.'

John Henry's indignation was choking him. When he could speak, he said, 'And do you think it's right, sir, for a minister of the Church like yourself to applaud this man and his comrades? To give at least verbal support to what they're doing?'

Mr. Donnelly stiffened.

'I think, as a minister of the Church, I may be in a better position to judge the rights and wrongs of people's actions than yourself, McClintock,' he replied. 'But if my well-meant attempt to help you to a job is going to be received like this, we'll say no more about it. Good day to you, McClintock!'

He strode off down the lane, muttering to himself.

John Henry kicked unhappily at the white dust round his feet. He was more shocked than he had expected to be by the minister's words. If he couldn't find what he was convinced was the right perspective in his own church, where could he find it? And was his only chance of a job to be dependent on going against his deepest beliefs?

There seemed no easy answer.

In the end, John Henry felt obliged to leave the church he had joined, to be with Rose, after the mission. He threw in his lot with a small group who called themselves 'brothers', later known generally as the Plymouth Brethren, who believed, like Rose and now John Henry, that all fighting was wrong.

John Henry, with his war record, sat awkwardly among them. But the war was in the past, and for the present, he and they were in whole-hearted agreement.

John Henry went on spending his days in the search for work.

In the end, the solution came easily enough. It was after the uneasy truce in July 1921. It was to be more than another year, after the assassination of Michael Collins, and the end of the civil war in the south, before the killings in the north of the country could be said to have ended. During this time there were, if anything, more shootings than there had been in the previous year.

John Henry was trudging through Belfast one day, wondering if things would ever be any different, and reflecting that, truce or no truce, the danger of walking through certain streets in Belfast had not changed, when he was hailed by an old army comrade, Jamie Patterson. Jamie, although a corporal, had always, off duty, treated John Henry as an equal; he had a great respect for John Henry's intelligence and book-learning.

'John Henry McClintock! It's yourself!' Striding heartily over to John Henry, he clapped him on the back with one hand, seized John Henry's hand with the other and shook it vigorously. 'Ye auld rascal! Hey, it's great to see you, boyo!'

John Henry responded cautiously. Too many encounters like this had led within a few sentences to invitations to join the UVF.

'And what are you doin' with yerself these days, me auld mucker?' asked Jamie Patterson.

'Not a lot,' admitted John Henry. 'Mostly looking for a job, like the rest of us. What about yourself?'

'Looking for a job? And you with your certificates and book-learning?' Jamie sounded incredulous. He pulled off his cap and scratched his balding head. 'Well, now, I could offer you something, but it's not a job that's fitted to someone as smart as yourself, Johnny. But, maybe, I don't know, might it do to be goin' on with, like, till you come up with some-thing better?' He wore an anxious look on his round, red face. Afraid, John Henry could see, of insulting his old comrade by a degrading offer.

'Jamie, if it's cleaning the streets, I'd be glad of it!' John Henry told him, and Jamie's face cleared.

'Ah, well, in that case, and seeing as how you've a bit of experience in this line, as you once told me, would you be interested in a job in my family's linen factory?'

John Henry's sense of humour was tickled. He had spent more than five nightmare years in the army, followed by two more years, now, of unemployment, mainly because he'd wanted so badly to get away from the linen factory where he had worked in his early youth. Now the wheel seemed to have turned full circle, and he was being offered the chance to go back.

He controlled his amusement, and clinched with Jamie Patterson's offer gratefully.

The best thing about it, to John Henry's mind, was that the factory was not in Belfast. In fact, it was in Lurgan, not many miles from his home in Kilmacartan, and near enough to Rose's home in Dromore. With the job in the linen factory for security, John Henry and Rose decided to marry. They had known each other for more than seven years by now, and although it would not have been uncommon, in those days of poverty, for a couple to wait for much longer, no one could have accused them of rushing into it.

The deciding factor was the death of John Henry's father, which left him with possession of the family cottage. His sisters were all safely married, with homes of their own, and his older brother had long since gone to America, where report had it he was doing well. None of them put in any claim to the cottage. It was a place, therefore, where John Henry and Rose could set up life together as a married couple.

Rose was glad to be moving away from Dromore. She had lived there all her life, and for most of the time had been happy. But the last couple of years hadn't been so good. There had been a growing cold-ness that blew into her face like a freezing north wind from her former friends and her neighbours. For a time she had almost expected to be asked by the Reillys to leave her job at their farm.

It hadn't come to that, but even her father and her two brothers had spoken coolly to her at times.

There had been one dreadful morning, after a restless night when Rose had several times been wakened by voices whispering just outside her bedroom window, and more than one set of footsteps moving about, when she woke to find that someone had painted on the wall, by the front door of the cottage, the words, *'Taig lover'*.

The paint was bright scarlet, and it had dried leaving trickles like blood from the bottom of some of the letters.

Rose stood by the open door looking at it, shocked almost to tears. She had risen early, and was ready to leave before six o'clock, to walk the half-mile to Reillys' farm and start her day's work. But in spite of the early hour, the scarlet letters stood out only too plain to see, in the slowly growing light of the summer dawn.

There was no time to do anything about it now. She must hurry on to begin her work at the farm. But she knew, without needing to be told, that her family, except her little sister Emily who shared her room, would be even angrier with her than before.

That evening she scrubbed hard at the lettering when she came home, but found it difficult to remove. For months after, the faint pink remnants accused her every time she left the house.

She never did find out who had written the message. There were plenty who might have been responsible. Rose would be glad to get away from the lot of them, and move to somewhere where no one knew her or cared about her opinions.

They had a small wedding in the local parish church: the group of brothers whom they met with on a Sunday weren't licensed to conduct marriages. Their families came, and a few friends. Rose was surprised by how happy she felt to see that Annie Reilly had put aside their differences and turned up on the day.

They married on a Saturday afternoon, each granted a half-day holiday for the purpose. There was no question of a honeymoon. Money was too tight. But they would have the Sunday to themselves before John Henry needed to return to work.

Rose would not be going back to the Reillys' farm. It was too far from her new home. Instead, she would work part-time for a farmer within easier reach.

Neither John Henry nor Rose had made love to anyone before their wedding night.

It would have been considered a strange thing if Rose had come to her wedding bed as anything but a virgin. Custom and attitudes were laxer for a man, but as it happened John Henry hadn't slept with a woman before the night of his conversion at the tent mission, and since then had managed to resist temptation. There had been opportunities and to spare in the army, but he had remembered Rose, waiting patiently for him, and reluctance to deceive her had helped him to hold back.

They came to this first night together excited, but perhaps equally nervous. They had in their separate ways been looking forward to the physical closeness, the sensual experience. Rose was perhaps a little more nervous than John Henry. Like many of her generation, she knew little of what to expect. There had been whispered reports from girls she'd known at school, passed on to them by older sisters and relayed in turn by the younger girls.

Then there had been what she had picked up by simply living in the country and working on a farm, of the breeding and birthing of animals; but she had been given to understand that things were a bit different for human beings.

John Henry, mixing as he had with boys his own age both at school and at the factory where he had first worked, and later unable to avoid hearing his friends and comrades in the army talking about their experiences with women, knew a lot more in theory. But the responsibility rested on him to make sure that everything went as it should – a heavy weight, he had begun to feel.

Apart from the gossip passed on by their friends, they had both read the *Song of Solomon*, and various other parts of the Bible, which spoke without any reticence of sexual matters.

It wasn't, taken altogether, much to go on.

Rose had managed to get together enough money from her meagre wages to buy some white cotton and sew herself a new nightgown. Anything else she could spare had gone on a few ribbons, to turn her spare dress – the one designated as 'good' and kept for Sundays and special occasions – into something more like her idea of a wedding dress.

John Henry wore his respectable Sunday suit to the wedding, but for his wedding night he had nothing new. But he had seen to it that his nightshirt was freshly washed.

Thus arrayed, they confronted each other across the double bed that had belonged to John Henry's parents.

John Henry had changed and washed downstairs in the kitchen, allowing Rose the privacy of the bedroom, with the warm water carried up in the ewer, and the basin on the washstand. Rose stripped, washed as thoroughly as possible, and dabbed on a few drops from a little bottle of perfume, a present from one of her friends on her last birthday, which she had saved until now. Then she slipped the new nightdress over her head. She heard a soft knock on the door, and called in a voice which she tried to keep from quavering, 'Come in.'

Now John Henry stood, his discarded clothes held in a bundle in one hand. And noticing, as he glanced self-consciously round the small room, that Rose had folded hers carefully and placed them on the room's one chair, at the head of the bed, on the side where she was standing.

'Which side do you like to sleep on, Rosie?' he asked. His voice sounded hoarse, and he coughed to clear it.

'I don't mind,' said Rose in a hurry.

' *"For this cause shall a man leave his father and mother,"* John Henry quoted, ' *"and he shall cleave to his wife, and they shall be one flesh."* This is a good thing we're doing, Rosie. Nothing to be ashamed a out.'

'I know it is, Johnny,' said Rose. She held herself back from giggling. She didn't want to make him feel like a fool. But there was no need for quotations from the Bible right now. 'Johnny,' she said, 'why don't you put those clothes down somewhere, and come round here and kiss me?'

So he did.

And as his hands stroked her soft breasts, and they fell backwards onto the bed, he gave over wondering if everything would be all right, because for him, it definitely was.

Not so for Rose. She was surprised, and quite a bit upset, at how much it hurt. Johnny, knowing so little, had entered her long before she was ready for him. In the morning, she found a trace of blood on the sheets, and comforted herself by memories of what friends had said about 'losing your virginity', and supposed that another time, it wouldn't hurt in the same way. She had also woken in the middle of the night to find herself lying in a puddle of what she thought at first was blood, but later realised was the male input. (Seeds for babies, she thought.) She found it surprising, and not really very pleasant. Perhaps she would get used to it. At least it wasn't blood.

These happenings were not what she had hoped for, or known that she should expect, on her wedding night. There wasn't much romance about them. But there was one thing that was all she had hoped of it. Falling asleep, cuddled in her husband's arms, was something she had dreamt of for years, and now that it was happening, she found it made up for the rest.

Things got better, though not all at once. Rose plucked up enough courage to make clear to John Henry that she needed to be ready before he entered her. It wasn't easy. They had never spoken of such things before. But the painful alternative was enough to force her to find the words to explain.

John Henry, while saying little, made it clear that he appreciated her courage, and was far from being offended by any reflection on his skills as a lover. He, like Rose, wanted things to go well, and was ready to learn where necessary.

Rose didn't know how unusual John Henry was in this, but if she had known, she would have seen nothing strange in it. She was quite ready to believe, and indeed was sure enough without telling, that her Johnny was a man in a thousand in every way possible.

They made love most nights, and before long it was a pleasure to Rose as well as to her husband.

Before the first year of marriage was up, Rose was pregnant, and in due course bore a fine, healthy, female child. The girl was christened Mary, and both her parents were delighted with her, although Rose knew that John Henry's heart had been set upon a son.

'Time enough for that,' was all he said to her upon the subject, and when Mary was coming two, and Rose was pregnant again, he made his pleasure obvious. Rose hoped for his sake that she would have a boy this time, though, for herself, she didn't mind one way or the other.

When the second girl, Katie, was born, John Henry said little. He still expressed his satisfaction in public, and indeed he loved the child dearly, but to Rose he said, 'It's the Lord's will, Rosie, and when he means me to have a son, He'll give me one.'

The next pregnancy was slower in coming. After a few years, Rose had almost stopped looking for it, until in the end she was taken by surprise.

This time she prayed for a boy, and a boy it was – but not without a long, hard struggle.

Rose woke suddenly in the middle of the night. She turned over in bed, and either heard, or felt –she could never be sure afterwards which it was – a sort of pop. A moment later she was soaked in water.

'Johnny! Johnny!' she exclaimed, pulling at her husband's arm. 'Johnny, I'm starting!'

'Go back to sleep, Rosie, there's a good girl,' said John Henry, sounding quite wide awake. 'It's not morning yet.'

Although the sound of her voice had brought him just awake enough to hear that she was speaking, he was still more than half asleep, and clearly hadn't understood a word of what she had said.

It didn't take Rose long, however, to shake him fully awake. Once he had taken in properly what she was saying, John Henry sprang out of bed. 'We'll have to get the midwife, Rosie!' he said. 'I meant to send wee Mary for her, if it had been a reasonable time of day. But I can't have the wean running out at this time of night on her own in the dark. Will you be all right while I fetch her myself, Rosie?'

'Of course I will, Johnny,' Rose answered firmly. 'You just let Mary and wee Katie sleep on for as long as they will – it'll be a sight easier for us all, that way. You can go for the midwife yourself, and no harm done. But first,' she added, catching at his shirt tails as he started to leap out of the bedroom door, 'you'd need to get some clothes on you and look more like somebody dacent, boyo! And don't be going anywhere till you help me change the soaking wet sheets on this bed.'

The midwife, who was also the district nurse, came promptly enough. She was still a young woman, though older than Rose by some years, and her round, happy face and plump figure told of a nature which for the most part put all worries aside and got on with things cheerfully. She radiated competence and support. Rose knew her well.

By the time she arrived, Rose had put on a clean, dry nightgown, and got back into the newly changed bed. The first time she had given birth, she had been very nervous at this stage. But this was the third time, and Rose felt confident enough, though she was certainly not looking forward to it. She just hoped it would be soon over.

The first stage of the labour, which had passed so quickly for Katie's birth, seemed to stretch on and on.

John Henry had stayed home from his work, sorted out his two daughters, and sent Mary off to school. He was downstairs, keeping an eye on wee Katie and seeing that she didn't try to go upstairs and get in the way, when the nurse came down to speak to him.

'You'd best be getting the doctor round, John Henry,' she said briefly. 'I've written him a note. Will you take it round for me now? Take the child with you – I don't want her left here to get under my feet.' She didn't sound her usual cheerful, friendly self.

Suddenly John Henry was worried. 'Aye. I'll go now,' he said, taking the note. He dumped Katie into her push-chair and went.

The doctor had a big house at the other end of the village.

Like Rose John Henry had thought that a third baby would come even more easily than the second. He tried not to panic as he hurried along the wide village street, dodging the hens scratching at the side of the road, praying as he went.

Presently the quick walk turned into a run. He arrived at the doctor's house out of breath and panting. A small, thin-faced maid answered the door. 'Doctor's out on his rounds,' she told John Henry in a superior voice, which he interpreted as meaning that she thought it was no concern of his.

'Can't you get hold of him?' he asked in despair.

'How would I do that, now, and him in his car and me not knowing where he may be?' she asked. But seeing his desperate expression, she softened slightly. 'Come in and you can wait for him in the surgery,' she suggested, holding the door open. 'Bring the wee girl in with you. He'll not be much longer, for he's been away over an hour already.'

'Couldn't I try to find him, if you'd any idea at all which direction he went?'

'What'd be the use of that? And him in the car, don't I tell you, and heading all over the country? Just come in and be at peace for the short time it'll be. I'll make you a cup of tea,' she added, as if, John Henry thought, she expected that tea would solve all his problems.

But in fact the tea, hot and sweet and strong enough to let the spoon stand up in it, calmed him, and as he sipped, and waited for the doctor's return, John Henry went on praying silently while Katie slept beside him.

Meanwhile the midwife was growing more and more worried. For some time now, she had been trying to encourage Rose to push. 'Come on, pet, one more try!'

But however hard Rose tried to push, there was no movement. The head was not engaged, and it wasn't any nearer to moving down than it had been hours ago.

Rose was growing more tired by the minute. Soon she would have no strength left to push any more, and then what? The nurse, who had seen the tragic outcome of other such difficult births, was near to despair although, true to her training, she tried not to let her patient see this.

If only the doctor would come!

But, she wondered silently, what could the doctor do that she couldn't do herself?

If it hadn't been for a lingering belief that all doctors could work miracles when it came to the bit, she would have been more than half inclined to answer her own question: 'Nothing.'

At last – was that someone down below opening the door?

The midwife came out to the head of the stairs, and peered over the banister.

It was very dark inside the cottage, but a burst of sunlight flashed in, making a bright square at the foot of the stairs, as someone pushed the door wide open.

It was John Henry and Katie back and, yes, the doctor with them.

Dr Miller trod up the flight of stairs with no undue haste. 'You stay down there, McClintock, and look after your daughter,' he said. 'You'll only be in the way if you come up.'

Then, pushing the midwife gently out of his way, he went into the bedroom where Rose lay against the pillows, her face white and her eyes closed in exhaustion. For a moment he wondered if she had already gone.

But then the eyelids fluttered, and he knew it was not yet too late.

'Boiling water, Nurse,' he said in the cheerful, brisk voice he kept for times like this. 'I'll need to sterilise this syringe. She'll be the better for an injection. Go and get me some boiling water straightaway.'

And as the midwife faded obediently from the room to fetch the kettle of water she had kept boiling beside the fire in the room below, with a basin to pour it into, Dr Miller made his way over to the bed, and began, with careful hands, to examine Rose, looking for why she could not give birth.

Down below, John Henry could get no more information out of the midwife, except a would-be cheery, 'Don't fret yourself, man, she'll be all right now the doctor's come.' To John Henry, her words held a false note that chilled him to the bone.

If he had not had Katie to look after, John Henry thought he would have gone mad over the next hour. But Katie was there, and in the middle of his prayers he was forced to watch her, keep her from the fire, even sit her on his knee and tell her a story for a while.

When Mary ran in from school, he turned the younger child over to the big sister.

'Go out and get some fresh air, the both of you,' he ordered. 'Play with your ball or your skipping rope.'

But when they had gone outside, he found himself missing the distraction of his children's need for attention. Presently, he sank down on his knees, his head in his arms, resting on the chair where he had been sitting, and stayed there quietly.

Upstairs, the doctor's injection had given Rose some relief from pain. He had examined her thoroughly, and had come to the conclusion that this was a breech presentation. The baby, instead of coming head first, was the other way round. He would need to use forceps to bring it out safely, and even so it would be a chancy business. He was glad to have the help of the sturdy, responsible midwife, with her wide experience of childbirth. She was not likely to panic and let him down.

Gradually things began to improve. He thought he could see his way at last to bringing this baby to safety, without killing the mother. The forceps were doing their job. He hadn't often had to use them before, but he seemed to have managed.

Downstairs, John Henry heard, as if from a great distance, footsteps on the stairs. He sprang to his feet.

The nurse was coming into sight round the twisty bend halfway up. She was carrying some sort of bundle in her arms. 'Aren't you the lucky man, now, John Henry?' she exclaimed, with a broad smile, as she came over to him. 'Here, you can hold him for a moment, if you like. There's another wee John in the family!'

'Thank God!' said John Henry, simply. For a moment he felt unable to move. Then he reached out his hands and took his son in his arms. 'But – Rosie?' he asked. 'How's my wife? I want to see her.'

'You can come up now,' said the nurse. 'But give me that wean first, for I wouldn't trust you to carry him back upstairs without dropping him. Rose is fine, but she'll be needing her rest, mind, so go in and speak to her, just to satisfy yourself she's all right, and then come away again, see?'

John Henry carefully handed over the baby, then went bounding up the stairs, two at a time. But when he came into the bedroom and saw his wife lying there, in the big double bed, looking so faint and pale, his joy dropped from him and he went quietly to bend down beside her. 'Rose, Rose, thank the Lord you're all right,' he managed to say. 'And thank you for my wee son, Rosie. But I'd rather have you, if it had come to that.'

'And so I should hope, Johnny McClintock,' Rose said, in a thread of a voice that yet was laughing at him.

'Now you've to get some sleep, Rosie,' John Henry said. 'Nurse and me'll look after the wee one.'

'Mostly Nurse, I expect,' said Rose. She smiled at him again, then her eyelids drooped shut. In another minute she was deeply asleep.

Rose had come back almost from the brink of the grave, and when she was well enough to hear it, she learnt there would be no more children for her.

It was a blow, but not a serious one, for hadn't they got Mary and Katie, and now wee Johnny, too? He was a beautiful baby, plump and fair and always laughing. John Henry was full of joy every time he came into the house and saw him, and Rose loved him as every mother loves her newest baby. In spite, or perhaps because, of the pains she had endured to have him.

As for Mary and Katie, their noses were not put out of joint, for they were delighted to have a new baby to play with, and were the envy of all their friends.

In the evenings, after his day's work, John Henry would sit with the baby on his knee, teaching him his first words. He was younger in spirit himself than Rose had seen him since he came back from the war to find the troubles raging at home. 'What are you teaching the youngster, Johnny?' she asked him on one occasion. 'Sure, he can say "Mama" and "Dada" as right as rain already, and him only ten months!'

'"Amen!"' John Henry told her. 'I'm teaching my boy to say "Amen", Rosie.'

Rose went back into the kitchen laughing, and ten minutes later came running out in a panic at John Henry's roar. But she need not have worried. It was no calamity. 'He said it, Rosie! He said it!'

And, sure enough, the baby was making a sound that was near enough to 'Amen' to pass muster.

John Henry swung the child up into the air, and danced about the room with him. 'That's the quare, fine boyo!' he exulted. 'You'll never go far wrong, wee Johnny, if you can say, "Amen! So be it!" to the Lord's will.'

Rose couldn't help laughing at the pair of them. Wee Johnny was laughing, too, as his father swung him about.

'Will you give over, for dear sakes, and sit down here to your supper while I put the child to bed?' she exhorted him, and presently peace was restored.

Johnny continued to grow and thrive. Rose nursed him through a bad bout of chicken pox, and John Henry sat up at night with her until the worst was over.

Johnny was flushed and feverish, and nothing would do for him but to have his daddy read to him aloud or, better still, sing.

John Henry sang the old gospel hymns, 'When he cometh, when he cometh, to make up his jewels,' and 'Shall we gather at the river?' and wee Johnny laughed weakly, or fell asleep smiling, his hand held tightly in his father's.

The fever left him after a few days, and soon he was struggling restlessly to get up, and to be allowed outside to play. Rose carefully followed the nurse's instructions, and kept him in bed with great difficulty until she was sure he was fully recovered. 'I'm not letting you out until I know you're well better, Johnny pet,' she told him firmly.

But in no time Johnny was running about again, his cheeks flushed with health instead of fever, and Rose smiled to herself as she worked about the house and garden and listened to him shouting gleefully with the neighbouring children. Both her girls were at school, now. It would be a couple of years before Johnny followed in their footsteps. She would miss him badly, she knew, when he went.

One of his favourite games was to chase the hens Rose reared for their eggs. He would run madly after them across the ground where they pecked and scratched for food, showing no fear of their beaks. But one day when the cockerel descended with dignity from his roosting perch and advanced towards the child, with his bright scarlet wattles hanging beneath his sharp beak, the comb on his head erect, and his voice raised threateningly, it was all too much for the little boy. Johnny balked, stood for a moment, and then backed hastily away. A moment later, he had tripped backwards over a sheet of iron John Henry had brought in to patch up the hen-house and gashed his leg.

Rose was alarmed. Her neighbour, Molly Kelly, a plump, motherly woman who had reared a family of her own, came bustling out to see what the racket was about. Molly had had seven children, mostly now grown and gone. Her greying curly hair was tied back carelessly in a head-scarf, and as she wiped her hands down the sides of the sacking apron she wore around the house, she left wide dirty streaks.

'Now then, boyo, you'll never die of that!' she said bracingly to Johnny, and to Rose she added, 'Give him a sweetie if you have such a thing about you. No? Well, I tell you what, I'll fetch him one from the wee bag I got for our Kevin, for when he comes down next to see me, with his mammy, our Martha, that's my eldest. Stitches? Not at all, Rosie. It's no more than a wee scrape.'

Molly produced the sweetie (Rose was glad to see it had a wrapping to protect it from whatever might be on Molly's fingers) and Johnny cried a bit less once it was in his mouth, but Rose couldn't dismiss the long, deep cut on his leg so blithely.

She put Johnny into his pushchair, and set off to the nurse's cottage.

Nurse was in, and told Rose she had been wise to come. 'Let that get some dirt in it, and it might turn serious,' she said. 'We'll go along to the doctor's and get him to put a stitch or two in it. It's a good time to catch him, for he'll have just finished surgery.'

As they walked through the village street, with Johnny still in his pushchair sucking busily at his sweetie, Nurse told Rose, 'I'd never say a word against that Molly Kelly, for she's a woman with a good heart, but don't you listen to her, Rosie, when she tells you how to bring up your youngsters.

'Molly's own childer mostly survived, but many's the time I was left wondering why, for she was that through-other with them. And it's my belief the two she lost would be with us to this day, if she'd called me or the doctor in sooner.'

Rose shuddered. How dreadful for Molly to lose two of her children. Rose, moving into the village less than ten years ago, on her marriage to John Henry, hadn't known any of this. She was thankful that her own three were so fit and healthy, and resolved there and then never to listen to Molly Kelly's advice, however kindly meant.

Johnny's leg needed seven stitches, and the doctor said she had been very wise in bringing the boy straight to him. If it had been left, the results might have been nasty. He was very pleasant and friendly as he swabbed the jagged cut with disinfectant, making jokes to keep Johnny distracted, for he had a soft spot for the boy whose life he had saved with such difficulty at birth.

'That's the brave boy,' he said, when the last stitch was in, and Johnny had really cried very little, considering. And he gave Johnny another sweetie, from the bottle he kept for such occasions on the high shelf behind his desk. It was a red-letter day for Johnny. Two sweeties! Normally he didn't see such a thing, except on his birthday or at Christmas.

Rose was careful to say little about all this to John Henry, who doted on the child. He had to hear of the accident, of course, but she tried to play it down.

Johnny hobbled round for a few days with a huge bandage, of which he was very proud, but before long his leg healed and he was none the worse for it.

It was just before Johnny's third birthday that scarlet fever broke out in the village. Mary and Katie brought the news home from school. Lizzie Edwards and Jakie Murphy were both off, and said to be very bad. Teacher had said that school would have to be closed because of the risk of infection – 'What's that, Mammy?' – and the Nurse would be coming round to check up on all the children over the next few days.

Rose, while sorry for the Edwards and Murphy families, wasn't unduly concerned about her own three children. She had seen them all safely through various childhood diseases, by now, and didn't expect that this would be any worse. Nurse, when she came to look at the girls, was cheerful and reassuring. 'No trouble there, any road,' she said with a wide beam. 'Two healthy weans as any I've seen the day. Now, just let me have a wee skelly at the child before I go, and that'll be us all set up.'

Johnny was coughing and didn't seem just his usual self. Nurse frowned when she heard him, and looked serious. Then she smiled again, and spoke heartily. 'Well, probably nothing much wrong there either. Still, put him to bed and keep him warm, Rosie, and give him a spoonful of the bottle I'm going to leave you. And I'll mention to the doctor to maybe call by and have a wee look at him.'

Something cold settled on Rose's heart.

Johnny was put to bed, and began to get worse.

Rose battled in vain with her fears, and dreaded telling John Henry when he got home from the linen factory.

To her relief, he took it well, and indeed became a source of strength to her over the next days, as they nursed their son together. He was confident that Johnny would get better. 'The Lord took me safely through a war where men were dying all around me, Rosie, and He gave me a job in these days when two men out of three have to manage without one. And He gave me a son when I had almost despaired of having one, and kept you alive when I had nearly given you up. I won't stop trusting Him now, at the first thing that goes wrong. Johnny'll be all right, you just see.'

But Johnny continued to get worse.

Eventually Rose gathered up her courage to say to her husband, 'John, it may be that we're not to keep him ...'

But she got no further. John Henry turned to her with a look on his face she had not seen since their first quarrel, years ago, when she had tried to persuade him not to enlist. 'Where's your faith, woman?' was all he said. Then he went out of the room, and for some time after she could hear him tramping about overhead.

Then there was silence.

John Henry had been praying as he walked about the room. Now he was sitting beside the big double bed, reading by the faint light of a candle, from the sixth chapter of Matthew.

> *Do not be anxious about your life, what you shall eat or what you shall drink, or about your body, what you shall put on. Is not life more than food, and the body more than raiment? Look at the birds of the air: they sow not, neither do they reap nor gather into barns, and yet your Heavenly Father feeds*

them. Are you not of more value than they? – Consider the lilies of the field, how they grow; they toil not, neither do they spin; yet Solomon in all his glory was not arrayed like one of these ...

It was a passage he had always loved, and come back to time and again. Now it brought him relief, comfort. Johnny would be looked after. He was as sure of that as he was sure of God's love for him, and of his own love for his little son.

But Johnny continued to get worse. The doctor and the nurse came often, and looked grave.

Rose knew that there was little hope.

But John Henry battled on in his stubborn refusal to be defeated. Johnny would recover. He would accept no other possibility.

Johnny lived for another week. The nurse was with him when he died, and she held Rose in her arms.

Rose felt her heart wrenched within her. She could say nothing. It was not until much later that she came to the relief of tears. But John Henry, after one low moan that seemed to force itself from his mouth against his will, ran from the house and kept on running.

Ran until his strength failed.

Ran until his breath came in ragged gasps, and his head was bowed, and his face was white with exhaustion.

He had no idea where he was going. He had left the village road almost at once, striking out across the fields and plunging through the small woods.

Branches whipped his face and arms, almost without his knowledge. He welcomed the pain.

He was torn and bruised and bloody before the first half-hour.

Once he fell on his knees into a wide, deep pool, a hollow recently filled with rain by the thunderstorms of the last weeks; it was surrounded by thorn bushes, with a tangle of reeds and stinging nettles at its brim. He would have stayed there if it had not been for the pain in his heart that drove him on, searching for some further, final pain that was all that could bring him relief. He yearned hopelessly for a sharp knife to cut the lump of agony out of his guts.

He rose to his feet, waded his way across the pool to its edge, and forced his way, regardless of the thorns, and the nettles, up the banks and on further into the wood.

Vague memories of the wood in which he had wandered, lost, during the battle of Passchendaele came to him. There were moments when he thought himself back there, and lived all the misery of that day over again, and the final escape from the wood, only to stumble over the almost dead body of Micky.

He had found relief there, in the end.

But the aching grief of the present returned, and he knew at once there were worse things to suffer than the deaths of his friends and comrades.

There came a time when he found himself walking along a main road. It was dark, his eyes could tell him nothing about his surroundings, but underfoot the hard surface told its own tale. He had already covered many miles, it seemed. He made his way on, along the centre of the road. In the distance he could see the headlights of a car approaching.

John Henry, oblivious to everything around him, continued to walk.

Suddenly there was a screech of brakes, and a car shrieked to a halt a few yards in front of him. Someone hurled open the driver's door and leapt out, cursing angrily. He was a youngish man, about John Henry's own age, but dressed in a flashy linen jacket and white trousers, with a silk scarf tied cravat fashion at the collar of his open-necked shirt. His plump face was red with rage.

'Are you mad, man? Walking along the middle of the road like that! Do you want to get killed? You came as near as you'll ever do to it, you crazy lunatic!'

John Henry shouted back at the driver. He used language he had never used before, even in his early days in the linen factory, scatological words he had heard on the lips of his companions in the army and had never thought would be on his own. He approached the driver, swinging his fists, still shouting, blaspheming. Bringing up out of his pain every curse he could think of. He stood so near that the driver could feel his hot breath, could feel the spittle hitting him on both cheeks as John Henry mouthed obscenities at him.

The man backed away, frightened for his own sake now. He made a dash for the car, got in, and drove quickly away, taking a wide breadth round John Henry that brought him over the verge of the road, and luckily onto nothing worse than rough grass and some low whin bushes.

John Henry strode on. After a while, he turned off the main road and struck out again across the open fields. The ground here was softer, easier to walk on, with grass underfoot. His outburst, which for a few moments had brought him some relief, had left him empty and very tired.

He had little or no idea where he was going. But as he walked on slowly now, he began to smell the first faint hint of the sea, and as he came nearer, the scent grew until it was almost tangible. There was the smell of seaweed, and of salt, and mixed with it an invigorating something he couldn't identify; maybe it was what they called ozone. He had covered more miles than he would have thought possible. He knew now, at least in outline, where he must be – nearly up to the lough, Strangford Lough, he thought. He didn't really care.

He came at last, still in thick, moonless darkness, to the edge of the shore.

The tide was coming in, and water lapped at his feet.

It seemed to him that it might be some relief to wade in until the waters covered him forever.

He sat on an outcrop of rock at the shore's edge, and there were no words in his mind.

The stars came out, the moon appeared, and the night grew cold, and he felt nothing.

He asked no questions, for it seemed to him there was no one to question.

And since his life had been built on the presence of One who occupied the universe, emptiness overwhelmed him. The pain of his loss was swallowed now in that of a yet greater loss.

And so he sat there, and soon he found himself looking upwards, at the stars that now studded the night sky, bright and distant. They danced before his eyes, an eternal dance of beauty. Huge masses of gas, millions of miles distant. Or night lights put there for man's pleasure, to lift heart and thrill him with the mystery and excitement of the created universe.

John Henry had always believed that both these ideas were true. Now, in his returning anger, he hurled away the second.

What beauty could there be in these objects which reflected only an uncaring universe where pain was meaningless to anyone but the sufferer? What did the stars care about him, about what he felt? What relation had the stars to him, except as centres of scientific curiosity, in which he had little interest at the best of times, and tonight, none?

Night wore on, and John Henry sat and looked at the sea.

The moon shone on the water. He had watched it before, and always loved to see it. Now he felt no stirring of pleasure at the sight.

He could smell the fresh tang of the water, the salt and the seaweed, more strongly now. The tide was still creeping gently in. John Henry was immune from its intrusion. He knew that it would not come further than the foot of the rock, for the seaweed clung only to the very low edges, and where he sat was free of any growth. Further out, he watched the swirls and eddies of currents. He could identify depths and shallows, patches of rock, seaweed and sand, by the changing colours. By day these would be light green then dark almost purple and greeny-blue with all the shades between. But now they showed only as different degrees of light and darkness, moving and gleaming. Enticing him to become part of the moving ocean, the immense depths, of which this was only a fraction.

The power of the sea had always spoken to him of mystery. Of strength as yet not experienced. Of depths of love unknown, beautiful and embracing.

On this dark night it spoke only of escape. Of a body floating free, far out. Never again forced to feel such anguish. Never again hurled from the security of years. Never again compelled to realise the built in malevolence of things and events. Life had steamrollered over him, breaking and crushing him, like the huge road-making machines he had watched long ago. The machine had no concern for the stones it destroyed. Only an unthinking, uncaring ability to keep going without ever stopping along its callous route.

To escape from the machine. To hurl himself bodily into the indifferent depths. To feel nothing ever again.

That would be worth doing.

He had made no movement for so long that presently a dark shape heaved itself out of the water, with immense effort, onto the rocks where he sat and flopped down close beside him. It was a seal.

He sat motionless, and the seal rested there quietly.

It was not quite fully grown, a young seal that had yet passed the cub stage. The moonlight gleamed on its silvery grey body, smooth as silk or leather. John Henry, fearing to move in case he frightened it away, watched it with occasional sideways glances out of the corner of his eye. It lay there so unmoving that he almost wondered if it was alive. But the breath from its nostrils touched the back of his hand lightly from time to time and reassured him. Its body was thick and solid. There was a strong animal smell, yet there was something also which was like the smell of fish or of any sea creature. This was no seal woman from the Irish legends of his childhood. Cocooned in the soft heavy warmth of his children he had read the stories to little Mary at bedtime, she leaning on him while Katie, half asleep, pressed in against his other side.

John Henry watched the seal for a long time. He could not remember having been so close to any wild creature before. He wished he could reach out and touch its soft slippery coat but he knew that at the slightest movement of his hand, the seal would be gone. Instead, he remained still, and the seal stayed beside him for what seemed a long time.

Then it slid from the rock back into the deep water.

At last the sky began to change. Streaks of light crept in, pink and pale yellow and white, slowly at first, then spreading ever wider.

John Henry stirred. He was stiff and sore.

All round him came the faint sounds of a new day.

First one, then another, the birds awoke, lifted up their voices, tried out their first cautious notes.

The first he heard was a blackbird, a jet black male with a bright yellow beak, his sweet cry sounding like the clear notes of a flute. Then came a chaffinch, with the two irregular notes that gave him his name – 'chiff-chaff.' Hidden somewhere, perhaps in one of the low bushes set not too far back from the shoreline, a tiny wren, his voice too loud for his size, sang his long, excited verse, interspersed with occasional trills and metallic ringing tones.

Then the dawn chorus broke out on all sides.

The speckled thrush repeated his loud, sweet musical phrases. The robin gave out a rich, cheerful note in keeping with the warmth of the new season. The starling, his black back shot with purple and green light, joined in chattering and whistling.

John Henry knew them all. He lifted his head to listen.

Something pulled at his heart.

He had listened to the birdsong with Rose early one morning when they were first married.

He felt a sharp pressure, as if his heart was about to burst and cried aloud, 'Why? Why?'

Then he buried his face in his hands, and wept as he had not wept since childhood, even in the now far-off days when he had lived through the sufferings of war. And as he cried out, and throughout his weeping, he knew at last that there was someone to question. As he wept, he heard a voice speaking to him, inside his own head; and it seemed that there was help and comfort in the words. 'My son died, too, John. I feel your pain.'

Presently John Henry stood up. It was time, now, for him to set off, to walk the many miles back.

The glow of dawn lit the road and the fields and bushes around him with a numinous light. As he walked, words came to him from a poem read long ago.

> *Earth's crammed with heaven,*
> *And every common bush afire with God.*
> *But only those who see take off their shoes.*

John Henry still had nothing to say. But now it was not because of the numbing pain that had held throughout the night but because there was no longer any need of words.

He walked through fields where the young barley sprouted green and silken around him, keeping, now, to the paths made round the edges by other travellers. He walked beside hedges thick with creamy white haw-thorn blossom, past low banks where purple vetch grew alongside bright yellow dandelions and white puffs of cow parsley. He saw clover, white and mauve, a faint speckling of the pale blue flowers he knew as cats' eyes, and the occasional tall red poppy, so rare in his home county, though so profuse in the Flanders fields that their colour, the colour of blood, had made them an emblem of bloody death. He passed hedges where pink and white columbine, the lesser and the greater, grew in wild profusion, new blossoms every morning replacing those of yesterday, which were dead by nightfall.

Before he had been walking for long, his feet and ankles were damp with the morning dew on the grass, which sprang up on the edges of the paths. Each separate drop reflected brightness, as the sun began to move slowly up the sky.

He smelt the creamy vanilla of the great masses of whin bush, covered in their yellow blossoms. He bent from time to time to sniff a wild rose for its perfect scent. He could still hear birdsong. It was separated now from the joyful chorus of early dawn and dispersed into the individual notes, which he heard from one or other of the birds flying or nesting around him. And as he opened his ears to listen he could pick up the chirp of the cricket and the murmur of the bees visiting flowers. Sometimes he would slow down, to see or smell or touch some element of the world he was walking through. But mostly he walked as quickly as he could, for he had a long journey to complete.

As he came nearer his home he heard a lark soaring into the blue, sweet and growing sweeter as it almost vanished into the heights. He stopped for a moment and his mind went back to the first year of the war, when he had been rescued by the song of a lark from the despair that had weighed on him in the mud and ugliness all round him. Rose had always loved lark song. He wished he had not left her to suffer alone.

He was very tired, but that was not the feeling uppermost in his mind.

He came at last, staggering with exhaustion, to his own village street, and walked slowly along it in the direction of his cottage. As he came within sight of it, a figure emerged, unidentifiable from this distance except for the familiar faded blue dress with the rough white apron.

The sun came up in its full strength, and he could see now, clearly, what he had already been sure of, that the distant figure was Rose, coming in search of the husband who had been gone all night.

As he came nearer, and she in her turn became sure that it was him, she began to run.

John Henry stood where he was, but as she reached his side he stretched his arms out and held her to him.

For many minutes they stood, fastened together by something more than the strength of John Henry's arms.

And as they stood there together, he knew that, although his pain was still heavy, the peace he felt was also real.

John Henry smiled down at his wife. 'Let's go on home, Rosie,' he said. 'I could do with a cup of tea.'

About the author

Gerry McCullough has been writing poems and stories since childhood. Brought up in north Belfast, she graduated in English and Philosophy from Queen's University, Belfast, then went on to gain an MA in English.

She lives just outside Belfast, in Northern Ireland, has four grown up children and is married to author, media producer and broadcaster, Raymond McCullough, with whom she co-edited the Irish magazine, *Bread*, (published by *Kingdom Come Trust*), from 1990-96. In 1995 they published a non-fiction book called, *Ireland – now the good news!*

Over the past few years Gerry has had more than sixty short stories published in UK, Irish and American magazines, anthologies and annuals – as well as broadcast on *BBC Radio Ulster* – plus poems and articles published in several Northern Ireland and UK magazines. She has read from her novels, poems and short stories at several Irish literary events.

Gerry won the *Cúirt International Literary Award* for 2005 (Galway); was shortlisted for the 2008 *Brian Moore Award* (Belfast); shortlisted for the 2009 *Cúirt Award*; and commended in the 2009 *Seán O'Faolain Short Story Competition*, (Cork).

Belfast Girls, her first full-length Irish novel, was first published (by *Night Publishing*, UK) in November 2010 (re-issued July 2012 by *Precious Oil*). *Danger Danger* was published by *Precious Oil Publications* in October 2011; followed by *The Seanachie: Tales of Old Seamus* in January 2012 (a first collection of humorous Irish short stories, previously published in a weekly Irish magazine); *Angel in Flight* (the first Angel Murphy thriller) in June 2012; *Lady Molly and the Snapper* – a young adult novel time travel adventure set in Dublin (August 2012); *Angel in Belfast* (the 2nd Angel Murphy thriller) in June 2013; *Johnny McClintock's War* in August 2014, *The Seanachie 2: Norah on the Beach* in September 2104 and *Hel's Heroes* in June 2015.

More info at:

http://gerrymccullough.com

Belfast Girls

The story of three girls – Sheila, Phil and Mary – growing up into the new emerging post-conflict Belfast of money, drugs, high fashion and crime; and of their lives and loves.

Sheila, a supermodel, is kidnapped.

Phil is sent to prison.

Mary, surviving a drug overdose, has a spiritual awakening.

It is also the story of the men who matter to them –

John Branagh, former candidate for the priesthood, a modern Darcy, someone to love or hate. Will he and Sheila ever get together?

Davy Hagan, drug dealer, 'mad, bad and dangerous to know'. Is Phil also mad to have anything to do with him?

Although from different religious backgrounds, starting off as childhood friends, the girls manage to hold on to that friendship in spite of everything.

A book about contemporary Ireland and modern life. A book which both men and women can enjoy – thriller, romance, comedy, drama – and much more ...

"fascinating ... original ... multilayered ... expertly travels from one genre to the next"
Kellie Chambers, Ulster Tatler (*Book of the Month*)

"romance at the core ... enriched with breathtaking action, mystery, suspense and some tear-jerking moments of tragedy.
Sheila M. Belshaw, author

"What starts out as a crime thriller quickly evolves into a literary festival beyond the boundary of genres"
PD Allen, author

"a masterclass, and a vivid dissection of the human condition in all of its inglorious foibles"
WeeScottishLassie

Belfast
Girls

Gerry McCullough

Published by

Precious Oil
PUBLICATIONS
www.preciousoil.com/publications

Chapter One

Jan 21, 2007

The street lights of Belfast glistened on the dark pavements where, even now, with the troubles officially over, few people cared to walk alone at night. John Branagh drove slowly, carefully, through the icy streets.

In the distance, he could see the lights of the *Magnifico Hotel*, a bright contrasting centre of noise, warmth and colour.

He felt again the excitement of the news he'd heard today.

Hey, he'd actually made the grade at last – full-time reporter for BBC TV, right there on the local news programme, not just a trainee, any longer. Unbelievable.

The back end shifted a little as he turned a corner. He gripped the wheel tighter and slowed down even more. There was black ice on the roads tonight. Gotta be careful.

So, he needed to work hard, show them he was keen. This interview, now, in this hotel? This guy Speers? If it turned out good enough, maybe he could go back to Fat Barney and twist his arm, get him to commission it for local TV, the Hearts and Minds programme maybe? Or even – he let his ambition soar – go national? Or how's about one of those specials everybody seemed to be into right now?

There were other thoughts in his mind but as usual he pushed them down out of sight. Sheila Doherty would be somewhere in the hotel tonight, but he had plenty of other stuff to think about to steer his attention away from past unhappiness. No need to focus on anything right now but his career and its hopeful prospects.

Montgomery Speers, better get the name right, new Member of the Legislative Assembly, wanted to give his personal views on the peace process and how it was working out. Yeah. Wanted some publicity, more like. Anti, of course, or who'd care? But that was just how people were.

John curled his lip. He had to follow it up. It could give his career the kick start it needed.

But he didn't have to like it.

* * *

Inside the *Magnifico Hotel*, in the centre of newly regenerated Belfast, all was bustle and chatter, especially in the crowded space behind the catwalk. The familiar fashion show smell, a mixture of cosmetics and hair dryers, was overwhelming.

Sheila Doherty sat before her mirror, and felt a cold wave of unhappiness surge over her. How ironic it was, that title the papers gave her, today's most super supermodel. She closed her eyes and put her hands to her ears, trying to shut everything out for just one snatched moment of peace and silence.

Every now and then it came again. The pain. The despair. A face hovered before her mind's eye, the white, angry face of John Branagh, dark hair falling forward over his furious grey eyes. She deliberately blocked the thought, opening her eyes again. She needed to slip on the mask, get ready to continue on the surface of things where her life was perfect.

'Comb that curl over more to the side, will you, Chrissie?' she asked, 'so it shows in front of my ear. Yeah, that's right – if you just spray it there – thanks, pet.'

The hairdresser obediently fixed the curl in place. Sheila's long red-gold hair gleamed in the reflection of three mirrors positioned to show every angle. Everything had to be perfect – as perfect as her life was supposed to be. The occasion was too important to allow for mistakes.

Her fine-boned face with its clear translucent skin, like ivory, and crowned with the startling contrast of her hair, looked back at her from the mirror, green eyes shining between thick black lashes – black only because of the mascara.

She examined herself critically, considering her appearance as if it were an artefact which had to be without flaw to pass a test.

She stood up.

'Brilliant, pet,' she said. 'Now the dress.'

The woman held out the dress for Sheila to step into, then carefully

pulled the ivory satin shape up around the slim body and zipped it at the back. The dress flowed round her, taking and emphasising her long fluid lines, her body slight and fragile as a daydream. She walked over to the door, ready to emerge onto the catwalk. She was very aware that this was the most important moment of one of the major fashion shows of her year.

Chapter 1

The lights in the body of the hall were dimmed, those focussed on the catwalk went up, and music cut loudly through the sudden silence. Francis Delmara stepped forward and began to introduce his new spring line.

For Sheila, ready now for some minutes and waiting just out of sight, the tension revealed itself as a creeping feeling along her spine. She felt suddenly cold and her stomach fluttered.

It was time and, dead on cue, she stepped lightly out onto the cat-walk and stood holding the pose for a long five seconds, as instructed, before swirling forward to allow possible buyers a fuller view.

She was greeted by gasps of admiration, then a burst of applause. Ignoring the reaction, she kept her head held high, her face calm and remote, as far above human passion as some elusive, intangible figure of Celtic myth, a Sidhe, a dweller in the hollow hills, distant beyond man's possessing – just as Delmara had taught her.

This was her own individual style, the style which had earned her the nickname 'Ice Maiden' from the American journalist Harrington Smith. She moved forward along the catwalk, turned this way and that, and finally swept a low curtsey to the audience before standing there, poised and motionless.

Delmara was silent at first to allow the sight of Sheila in one of his most beautiful creations its maximum impact. Then he began to draw attention to the various details of the dress.

It was time for Sheila to withdraw. Once out of sight, she began a swift, organised change to her next outfit, while Delmara's other models were in front.

No time yet for her to relax, but the show seemed set for success.

* * *

MLA, Montgomery Speers, sitting in the first row of seats, the celebrity seats, with his latest blonde girlfriend by his side, allowed himself to feel relieved.

Francis Delmara had persuaded him to put money into Delmara Fashions and particularly into financing Delmara's supermodel, Sheila Doherty, and he was present tonight in order to see for himself if his investment was safe. He thought, even so early in the show, that it was.

He was a broad shouldered man in his early forties, medium height, medium build, red-cheeked, and running slightly to fat. There was nothing particularly striking about his appearance except for the piercing dark eyes set beneath heavy, jutting eyebrows. His impressive presence stemmed from his personality, from the aura of power and aggression which surrounded him.

A businessman first and foremost, he had flirted with political involvement for several years. He had stood successfully for election to the local council, feeling the water cautiously with one toe while he made up his mind. Would he take the plunge and throw himself whole- heartedly into politics?

The new Assembly gave him his opportunity, if he wanted to take it. More than one of the constituencies offered him the chance to stand for a seat. He was a financial power in several different towns where his computer hardware companies provided much needed jobs. He was elected to the seat of his choice with no trouble. The next move was to build up his profile, grab an important post once things got going, and progress up the hierarchy.

In an hour or so, when the Fashion Show was over, he would meet this young TV reporter for some preliminary discussion of a possible interview or of an appearance on a discussion panel. He was slightly annoyed that someone so junior had been lined up to talk to him. John Branagh, that was the name, wasn't it? Never heard of him. Should have been someone better known, at least. Still, this was only the preliminary. They would roll out the big guns for him soon enough when he was more firmly established. Meanwhile his thoughts lingered on the beautiful Sheila Doherty.

If he wanted her, he could buy her, he was sure. And more and more as he watched her, he knew that, yes, he wanted her.

* * *

A fifteen minute break, while the audience drank the free wine and ate the free canapés. Behind the scenes again, Sheila checked hair and makeup. A small mascara smear needed to be removed, a touch more blusher applied. In a few minutes she was ready but something held her back.

She stared at herself in the mirror and saw a cool, beautiful woman, the epitome of poise and grace. She knew that famous, rich, important men over two continents would give all their wealth and status to possess her, or so they said. She was an icon according to the papers. That meant, surely, something unreal, something artificial, painted or made of stone.

And what was the good? There was only one man she wanted. John Branagh. And he'd pushed her away. He believed she was a whore – a tart – someone not worth touching. What did she do to deserve that?

It wasn't fair! she told herself passionately. He went by rules that were medieval. No-one nowadays thought the odd kiss mattered that much. Oh, she was wrong. She'd hurt him, she knew she had. But if he'd given her half a chance, she'd have apologised – told him how sorry she was. Instead of that, he'd called her such names – how could she still love him after that? But she knew she did.

How did she get to this place, she wondered, the dream of romantic fiction, the dream of so many girls, a place she hated now, where men thought of her more and more as a thing, an object to be desired, not a person? When did her life go so badly wrong? She thought back to her childhood, to the skinny, ginger-haired girl she once was. Okay, she hated how she looked but otherwise, surely, she was happy. Or was that only a false memory?

'Sheila – where are you?'

The hairdresser poked her head round the door and saw Sheila with every sign of relief.

'Thank goodness! Come on, love, only got a couple of minutes! Delmara says I've to check your hair. Wants it tied back for this one.'

* * *

The evening was almost at its climax. The show began with evening dress, and now it was to end with evening dress – but this time with Delmara's most beautiful and exotic lines. Sheila stood up and shook out her frock, a cloud of short ice-blue chiffon, sewn with glittering silver beads and feathers. She and Chrissie between them swept up her hair, allowing a few loose curls to hang down her back and one side of her face, fixed it swiftly into place with two combs, and clipped on more silver feathers.

She fastened on long white earrings with a pearly sheen and slipped her feet into the stiletto heeled silver shoes left ready and waiting. She moved over to the doorway for her cue. There was no time to think or to feel the usual butterflies. Chloe came off and she counted to three and went on.

There was an immediate burst of applause.

To the loud music of Snow Patrol, Sheila half floated, half danced along the catwalk, her arms raised ballerina fashion. When she had given sufficient time to allow the audience their fill of gasps and appreciation, she moved back and April and Chloe appeared in frocks with a similar effect of chiffon and feathers, but with differences in style and colour. It was Delmara's spring look for evening wear and she could tell at once that the audience loved it.

The three girls danced and circled each other, striking dramatic poses as the music died down sufficiently to allow Delmara to comment on the different features of the frocks.

With one part of her mind Sheila was aware of the audience, warm and relaxed now, full of good food and drink, their minds absorbed in beauty and fashion, ready to spend a lot of money. Dimly in the background she heard the sounds of voices shouting and feet running.

The door to the ballroom burst open.

People began to scream.

It was something Sheila had heard about for years now, the subject of local black humour, but had never before seen.

Three figures, black tights pulled over flattened faces as masks, uniformly terrifying in black leather jackets and jeans, surged into the room.

The three sub-machine guns cradled in their arms sent deafening bursts of gunfire upwards. Falling plaster dust and stifling clouds of gun smoke filled the air.

For one long second they stood just inside the entrance way, crouched over their weapons, looking round. One of them stepped forward and grabbed Montgomery Speers by the arm.

'Move it, mister!' he said. He dragged Speers forcefully to one side, the weapon poking him hard in the chest.

A second man gestured roughly with his gun in the general direction of Sheila.

'You!' he said harshly. 'Yes, you with the red hair! Get over here!'

Chapter Two

1993

There were so many things about her life that Sheila Doherty hated, especially her appearance, her skinniness and her hair, which was a very bright red. She was eight, and just beginning to notice boys. She knew how important it was that other people should think she looked good, and how impossible. How awful it was to be called 'Ginger', to be considered too tall, too thin, too ugly. She hated being called after in the streets, and in the school playground.

When church, Sunday dinner and Sunday school were over, Sheila wandered out into the back garden. Boredom attacked her.

The back garden was not very large and there was nothing much to do there. There was a square of grass, a border bright with flowers in spring and summer, but mostly brown or green on this dull October afternoon, and an empty rabbit hutch against the far wall.

Sheila could vaguely remember the rabbit, a furry, cuddly focus of love a few years ago when she was five or six, and her short but violent grief at his unexplained death from some unidentified rabbit disease.

She mooched over the grass, kicking aimlessly at the few still remaining fallen leaves, and leaned against the wizened old apple tree in the corner near the hutch. Although she was not to leave the garden or go out into the street by herself, it was good for her to be out in the fresh air, her mother said. It might give her a bit more colour.

Sheila's pale skin and red hair, from her father Frank's side of the family, were a source of constant irritation to both Sheila and her mother Kathy. Both would have preferred almost any other combination, but particularly the dark hair and blue eyes for which Kathy had been so widely admired in her youth – as she often told Sheila with some complacency.

Sheila kicked a few more leaves and wished something would happen. If only she had a sister, or even a brother. It would be fun to have someone to play with.

Suddenly a large ball thudded at her feet.

Sheila jumped and said, 'Sugar!' Then she blushed, for she didn't often use what Kathy would call bad language. She picked up the ball and stood with it in her hands, looking cautiously around.

It seemed to have come over the wall which ran between her family's garden and the house next door.

She watched. Two hands were gripping hard on the top of the wall. Then a head rose slowly above the edge.

Black curly hair, blue eyes wide open in inquiry, a mouth which broke into a friendly grin as its owner saw Sheila.

'Hi. Can I come and get my ball?'

Sheila nodded silently.

The girl scrambled over the wall, leaving muddy smears on her light blue jeans as she did so. She advanced on Sheila and took the ball which Sheila held out to her.

'What's your name?'

'Sheila. What's yours?'

'Philomena Mary Maguire, but I get called Phil.'

They looked at each other steadily for a moment. Then Phil again took the initiative.

'We've come to live next door, here. We moved in yesterday. Is this your house?'

'Yes.'

'What's it like, here? Mammy said it would be fun to have a garden. Is it? Do you like it?'

Sheila had never thought about it. She had always had a garden. Didn't everybody?

'Let's play with your football,' she said.

'Okay.' Phil looked back. Another head had risen above the wall. Brown hair, not as dark as Phil's, grey eyes, a round freckled face with a friendly grin.

'This is my brother Gerry,' said Phil. 'Can he come over, too?'

'Yes, g-great!' stammered Sheila.

A moment later, Gerry, who was obviously a year or so older than Phil but still small for his age, had scrambled over the wall and given the football a vigorous kick, only just missing Kathy's favourite rosebush. Sheila giggled. This was going to be fun.

Chapter 2

They played happily together for the rest of the afternoon. Phil and Gerry were inclined to take the lead and to suggest new games.

Sheila didn't mind. It was interesting. Phil was fascinated by the rabbit hutch and the apple tree. She made Sheila see the back garden with new eyes, as an exciting place of endless possibilities.

'We could make a swing from the tree if we had some rope,' Gerry suggested enthusiastically. 'We could use the clothes line.'

'I don't think my mammy would let me –' Sheila began.

But he had already pulled down the line and was starting to tie it to the tree. So Sheila and Phil joined in and helped him. It was great.

The afternoon whizzed by, and there was Sheila's mother, woken up from her Sunday afternoon nap, calling Sheila already for her tea.

'I won't be allowed out after tea,' Sheila said. 'It'll be too dark. Maybe I'll see you at school tomorrow?'

'St Columba's, mine's called,' said Phil. 'I won't know anybody yet, so it'd be nice if you were there.'

Sheila was disappointed. 'I go to Alexander Primary, so I won't see you. But we could play after school?' she suggested hopefully.

'Okay,' said Phil. 'See you, then.'

She and Gerry scrambled back over the wall and Sheila went in. St Columba's was the nearby Catholic primary school, she knew. Alexander Primary was Protestant. She thought maybe she wouldn't mention her new friends to her mother, just yet, though Kathy would have to know sometime that the new neighbours were Catholic.

From then on Sheila and Phil were inseparable.

Gerry was a good friend too, but he had his own mates to hang around with usually and, as they all got older, it was only occasionally that he would join in with Phil and Sheila's games. After all, they were only girls.

It was Phil who stood up for Sheila now when people called her 'Ginger,' or 'Carrots', and made fun of her.

'You leave her alone or I'll twist your elephant ears off!' she ordered Chrissie Murphy when she tried to pull Sheila's hair.

And, 'Leave off my mate or I'll get my big brother to give you such a hidin'!' when Sandy Bell was teasing Sheila more than usual.

Occasionally Sheila would turn to Gerry to help her and the 'big brother' would soon deal with any persistent trouble makers, going so far as to punch big Geordie Patterson in the eye on one memorable occasion.

When they moved on to secondary school, although they were still separated during the school day, their friendship remained strong.

It was against all the rules, they knew, vaguely, for a Catholic and a Protestant to be best friends but, thought Sheila and Phil, who cared?

Danger Danger

Two lives in parallel – twin sisters separated at birth, but their lives take strangely similar and dangerous roads until the final collision which hurls each of them to the edge of disaster.

Katie and her gambling boyfriend Dec find themselves threatened with peril from the people Dec has cheated.

Jo-Anne (Annie), through her boyfriend Steven, finds herself in the hands of much more dangerous crooks.

Can they survive and achieve safety and happiness?

Angel in Flight:
the first Angel Murphy thriller

Is it a bird? Is it a plane? No, it's a low-flying Angel!

You've heard of Lara Croft. You've heard of Modesty Blaise. Well, here comes Angel Murphy!

Angel, a 'feisty wee Belfast girl' on holiday in Greece, sorts out a villain who wants to make millions for his pharmaceutical company by preventing the use of a newly discovered malaria vaccine.

Angel has a broken marriage behind her and is wary of men, but perhaps her meeting with Josh Smith, who tells her he's with Interpol, may change her mind?

Fun, action, thrills, romance in a beautiful setting – so much to enjoy!

"it's a fast-paced read, ... exciting, and you can not put this book down"

Thomas Baker, Santiago, Chile

"I could not stop reading! ... a gripping thriller from beginning to the end"
SanMarie Lamprecht

"a fast-paced, exciting read. From the moment I read the first line, I was hooked"

Cheryl Bradshaw, author, Wyoming, USA

"a sassy bigger then life heroine in an action packed adventure thriller in Greece"

Book Review Buzz

Angel in Belfast:

the 2nd Angel Murphy thriller

Angel Murphy is back, in true kick boxing form!

Alone in his cottage near a remote Irish village, Fitz, lead singer of the popular band *Raving*, hears the cries of the paparazzi outside and likens them in his own mind to wolves in a feeding frenzy.

Next morning Fitz is found unconscious, seeming unlikely to survive, and is rushed to hospital. Has he been driven to OD? Or is someone else behind this?

His friends call in Angeline Murphy, 'Angel to her friends, devil to her enemies,' to find out the truth. But it takes all Angel's courage and skills to survive the many dangers she faces and to discover the real villain and deal with him.

The Seanachie:
Tales of Old Seamus

A humorous series of Irish stories, set in the fictional Donegal village of Ardnakil and featuring that lovable rogue, *'Old Seamus'* – the Séanachie.

All of these stories have previously been published in the popular Irish weekly magazine, *Ireland's Own*, based in Wexford, Ireland.

"heart warming tales ... beautifully told with subtle Irish humour"

Babs Morton (author)

"an irresistible old rogue, but he's the kind people love to sit and listen to for hours on end whenever the opportunity presents itself"

G. Polley (author and blogger – Sapporo, Japan)

"This magnificent storyteller has done it again. Each individual story has it's own Gaelic charm"

Teresa Geering (author – UK)

"evocative characterisation brings these stories to life in a delightful, absorbing way"

Elinor Carlisle (author – Reading, UK)

The Seanachie 2:

Norah on the Beach and other stories

Gerry McCullough

Another humorous series of Irish stories, set
in the fictional Donegal village of Ardnakil
and once again featuring that lovable rogue,
'Old Seamus' – the Séanachie.

All of these stories have previously been published in the popular Irish
weekly magazine, *Ireland's Own*, based in Wexford, Ireland.

"gentle stories laced with Irish humour ...
Like the first collection ... very well written and an effortless read"
Bookworm

"so well written that you find yourself flying through the stories"
Tom Elder

Lady Molly & The Snapper

A young adult time travel adventure, set in Ireland and on the high seas

Gerry McCullough

Brother and sister Jik and Nora are bored and angry. Why does their Dad spend so much time since their mother's death drinking and ignoring them? Why must he come home at all hours and fall downstairs like a fool?

Nora goes to church and lights a candle. The cross-looking sailor saint she particularly likes seems to grow enormous and come to life. Nora is too frightened to stay.

Nora and Jik go down secretly to their father's boat, the *Lady Molly*, at Howth Marina. There they meet The Snapper, the same cross-looking saint in a sailor's cap, who takes them back in time on the yacht, *Lady Molly,* to meet Cuchulain, the legendary Irish warrior, and others.

Jik and Nora plan to use their travels to find some way of stopping their father from drinking – but it's fun, too! Or is it? When they meet the Druid priest who follows them into modern times, teams up with school bully Marty Flanagan, and threatens them, things start getting out of hand.

Meanwhile, Nora is more than interested in Sean, the boy they keep bumping into in the past ...

Books by *Sheila Mary Taylor*:

Pinpoint:
A psychological legal crime thriller

Manchester, UK: a lawyer, a murderer and a policeman – caught in a tangled web of love, loss, terror and intrigue in this driving psychological thriller.

When criminal lawyer Julia Grant interviews Sam Smith who has been charged with a vicious murder, she feels a strange connection to him.

Has she met him before? Does he hold a key to her lost childhood memories?

He feels a connection too. 'Julia, you are the only one who can help me,' he pleads. Is it the same connection? Does he know something she cannot recall?

When he is duly convicted despite her best efforts, he suddenly turns on her in the courtroom and threatens that one day he will make sure to wreak his revenge on her.

But why? What has she ever done to him?

Golden Sapphire:

A love story set in stone

Samantha King has dedicated all her young life to mining sapphires – and at a cost. Her husband is killed in a mining accident trying to get her the biggest sapphire he can find – a golden sapphire she finds clutched in his hand when his body is recovered.

Where there is one such sapphire, there are probably more, and they probably stretch into Old Dan's concession.

When Old Dan dies five years later, his nephew, Mark, comes to the area to wrap up his affairs. He is young, confident, distinguished, and very handsome – and clearly interested in Samantha.

But Samantha is only interested in Old Dan's mining rights. Is there some way she can persuade him to sell them to her?

And is there some way Mark can persuade her life is not just about sapphires?

"an absorbing tale of intrigue, past connections and romance"
ToBeRed. Love it!!!!, Amazon.co.uk

"an excellent story that pulls at the heartstrings from the opening chapter"
NAL, Amazon.co.uk

"Delightful ... written with such flowing detail"
Mrs Loraine K Card, Amazon.co.uk

"Romantic, gritty and gripping, it kept me reading from the first page to the last"
G. Polley, blogger and writer, (Sapporo, Japan)

"delivers with utter credibility ... a veritable jewel of a book!"
Helen S., Amazon.co.uk

Dance to a Tangled Web:

A tale of love, deception and forgiveness

After only one triumphant night of dancing *'Giselle'*, an unexplained injury forces Alana to withdraw temporarily from the dance company and relax her body on the Mediterranean beaches of Menorca.

There she falls madly in love with a married man, whose young daughter is inspired by her, but whose past is inextricably connected to hers in ways that will forever haunt her.

'Dance to a Tangled Web' is a mesmerizing tale built teasingly around the underlying story of the ballet *'Giselle'*. Alana dances towards her fate in the throes of two overwhelming passions – for her lover and for her art – a fate she will re-interpret in a startling way for all those whose lives she has touched.

Non-fiction by *Sheila Mary Taylor*:

Count to Ten:
Fly with a miracle

Few things worse can happen to a mother than for her child to be diagnosed with cancer. It started as a pain, that became a 'hot spot', grew into a tumour, ultimately threatening Andrew's life. At the very least, his leg would have to be amputated, a chilling prospect.

The true story of how Andrew and his family coped with the days, weeks, months and years that followed his diagnosis, of the reliefs, the triumphs, the relapses and the outright screaming panics.

It is a testament to Andrew's passionate determination to pursue his adventurous dreams even in the face of death itself. It is also a testament to a revolutionary new treatment that was applied with care, expertise and wisdom by the dedicated team at the London Bone Tumour Clinic.

It is so easy to love your children. It is so hard to hang onto hope, especially onto their hope – the hope they need to carry on.

"An uplifting and emotionally charged book. Highly recommended."
Sooz Burke, author, Australia

"personal, sensitive, powerful, heart-breaking, uplifting and compelling all at once"
WeeScottishLassie, UK

"a road of many zig-zag turns, bends and bumps, share the journey with them, a wonderful book, I highly recommend it."
Janice Donnelly, UK

<u>Prophetic fiction by **_Raymond McCullough_**</u>:

In Six Hours

... the world changed:

In just six hours the Middle East – and the world – will change forever

A friendship forged in war leads four men on separate journeys to their final destiny in a Middle East heading for meltdown

As bitter enemies race towards nuclear conflict, only a miracle can save Israel from the hostile Islamic forces surrounding her. The USA, Russia and the western world are playing with fire in the Middle East, as Iran rushes towards a nuclear climax.

While fighting the Taliban with the ISAF forces in 2012, four young men from very different backgrounds meet in Kabul, Afghanistan:

Shaul _'Solly'_ Levine, an Orthodox Jew from New York City;

Micky _'Dev'_ Devlin, an Irish Catholic from Boston;

Brandon _'Doubtin'_ Thomas, a black Pentecostal from N. Carolina;

Khan Ali _'Zai'_ Yusufzai, a Muslim Pashtun from Afghanistan.

They discover that they have more in common than they first thought and make a pact that one day they'll meet up again in Jerusalem after the prophesied Six Hour War in the Middle East, taking separate ways to a common destiny.

Meanwhile, they will keep in touch with one another as much as possible and work towards making that meeting a possibility. Will these prophecies come to pass? Will Israel itself survive the coming nuclear holocaust?

This apocalyptic thriller moves from war, to a couple of budding romances in very different locations, to more war and then the ultimate Middle East war. But even in the midst of conflict, new relationships are being formed. Action, friendship, romance ... and yet more action.

"McCullough writes with conviction and clearly knows his subject well ... [his] fluid prose draws you in and his logic and characterisation make for a believable compelling drama. Highly recommended!!!"
Juliet B Madison, author, UK

"So well written and very descriptive, you actually think you're there. Raymond has obvious knowledge of the areas he has written about as that and his passionate way of writing shine throughout. Must read book"
Tom Elder, author, USA

Non-fiction books from

A Wee Taste a' Craic:

All the Irish craic from the popular
Celtic Roots Radio shows, 2-25

Raymond McCullough

*I absolutely loved this! I found it to be very informative
about Irish life culture, language and traditions.*
Elinor Carlisle (author, Reading, UK)

*a unique insight into the Northern Irish people
& their self deprecating sense of humour*
Strawberry

Ireland *– now the good news!*

The best of *'Bread'* Vols. 1 & 2 –

personal testimonies and church/fellowship
profiles from around Ireland

Edited by: *Raymond & Gerry McCullough*

"...fresh Bread – deals with the real issues facing the church in Ireland today"
Ken Newell, minster of Fitzroy Presbyterian Church, Belfast

The Whore and her Mother:

9/11, Babylon and the Return of the King

Raymond McCullough

Could the writings of the ancient Hebrew prophets be relevant to events taking place in the world today?

These Hebrew prophets – Isaiah, Jeremiah, Habbakuk and the apostle John, in *The Revelation* – wrote extensively about a latter day city and empire which would dominate, exploit and corrupt all the nations of the world. They referred to it as Babylon the Great, or Mega-Babylon, and they foretold that its fall – 'in one day' – would devastate the economies of the whole world. Have these prophecies been fulfilled already?

Is Mega-Babylon the Roman Catholic Church?
A world super-church?
Rebuilt ancient Babylon?
Brussels, Jerusalem, or somewhere entirely different?
Should this city/nation have a large Jewish population?
Why all the talk about merchants, cargoes, commodities, trade?

Can we rely on the words of these ancient prophets?
If so, what else did they foretell that is still to be fulfilled?
Do they refer to other major nations – USA, Russia, China, Europe?
What about militant Islam?

"AMAZED when I read this book ... in awe of your extensive knowledge on so many levels: Christian, Jewish, and Muslim culture; the Jewish diaspora ... Greek & Hebrew; ... thought-provoking and troublesome ... many will be offended, but you consistently build your case instead of being sensationalistic."
James Revoir, author of *Priceless Stones*

Oh What Rapture!

Is a *'Secret Rapture'* going to spare believers from the tribulation to come?

Raymond McCullough

Many are convinced that very soon an event referred to as *'The Rapture'* will take place, where bible believers all over the world will suddenly disappear, leaving society at a loss to explain this disappearance of so many. Many non-fiction books, fiction thrillers and movies have capitalised on this theme, earning a fat revenue for their authors/producers.

But is this really what the bible teaches?
Is *'The Rapture'* genuine, or a deceptive false hope?

Are those who trust in it being duped, so that they fail to prepare themselves for what is coming?
And are they being disobedient to the clear command of the Lord?

Written by the author of *Amazon* best-selling book, *The Whore and her Mother*, also on the topic of bible prophecy, this volume focusses on the false teaching of a *'secret and separate Rapture'* – an event which is NOT supported by scripture!

This book investigates the scriptures used to back up the *'secret Rapture'* theory and clearly compares them to the other scriptures concerning the return of the Messiah, Jesus (Yeshua). The evident truth is revealed and the origins of the false *'secret Rapture'* doctrine are exposed.

Believers around the world are taught to expect persecution, some-times even death, for their faith. More have been killed in the past century than in previous centuries combined – in China, Cambodia, Vietnam, Nigeria, Syria, Iran, Iraq, Egypt, Indonesia, etc. Yet many believers in the west confidently expect to avoid any persecution and be *'beamed up'* out of any coming tribulation!

If you thought believers were soon going to be lifted out of a worsening world situation, be prepared to meet the exciting challenge of scripture head on!

"Interesting and gave food for thought ... definitely worth a read"
Kindle customer, UK

www.ingramcontent.com/pod-product-compliance
Lightning Source LLC
Chambersburg PA
CBHW060151130626
46556CB00006B/2598